Also by Mia Sheridan

Travis
Kyland
Stinger
Grayson's Vow
Becoming Calder
Finding Eden

Kyland

MIA SHERIDAN

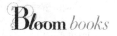 Bloom books

Published by Bloom Books, an imprint of Sourcebooks
P.O. Box 4410, Naperville, Illinois 60567-4410
(630) 961-3900
sourcebooks.com

Originally self-published in 2015 by Mia Sheridan.

Cataloging-in-Publication data is on file with the Library of Congress.

Printed and bound in the United States of America.
KP 10 9 8 7 6 5 4 3 2

To Shirley, my favorite mother-in-law. Thank you for being my number-two fan and for giving birth to my number-one fan.

THE TAURUS LEGEND

The Taurus legend tells of a lonely, wandering bull named Cerus. Though he was not immortal, most people assumed him to be because of his incredible strength.

Cerus was wild and out of control, and belonged to no one. One day, the spring goddess, Persephone, found him trampling through a field of flowers and reached out to him. Her beauty and gentleness calmed him, and he fell in love with her. The goddess tamed Cerus, teaching the bull patience and how to use his strength wisely.

In the fall when Persephone leaves for Hades, Cerus travels to the sky and becomes the Taurus constellation. In the spring when Persephone returns to the land, Cerus returns to join her. She sits upon his back and he runs through the sunlit fields as she brings all of the plants and flowers to bloom.

CHAPTER ONE
Tenleigh

Seventeen Years Old

The first time I really noticed Kyland Barrett, he was swiping someone's discarded breakfast off a cafeteria table. I'd glanced away, attempting to preserve his dignity, a gut reaction on my part. But then I'd looked back as he walked in my direction toward the doors, stuffing the small portion of leftover food in his mouth. Our eyes met, his flaring briefly and then narrowing, as again, I averted my gaze, my cheeks heating as if I'd just intruded on a deeply personal moment. And it was personal. I should know. I'd done it myself. I knew the shame. But I also knew the achy emptiness of a Monday morning after a long, hungry weekend. Evidently, Kyland knew it too.

Of course, I'd seen him before that. I'd bet everyone who was female had let their eyes linger on him, with his strikingly handsome face and his tall, solid build. But that was the first time I really *saw* him, the first time I felt a throb of understanding in my chest for the boy who always seemed to wear an expression of nonchalance, as if he didn't care much for anyone or anything. I was well acquainted with men who couldn't give a rat's ass. That was trouble I didn't want any part of.

But apparently I was the only girl in school who had a problem with trouble because if he *was* in anyone's company, it was always someone female.

It was a large school, serving students from three towns. I'd only had a few classes with Kyland over the three and a half years we'd been in high school, and he'd always sat in the back of the room, rarely uttering a word. I always sat in the front so I could see the blackboard—I guessed I was probably nearsighted, not that we could afford an eye exam, much less glasses. I knew he got good grades. I knew he must be smart despite his seemingly careless attitude. But after that day in the cafeteria, I couldn't help looking at him differently, and my eyes always seemed to find him. I searched for him in the overcrowded hallway—packed with teenagers moving slowly to class like cattle being herded to greener pastures—in the cafeteria, or walking ahead of me up our mountain. Most times I found him with his hands stuffed in his pockets, and if outside, his head down against the wind. I liked to watch the way his body moved, and I liked that he didn't know it. I was curious about him now. And suddenly that look on his face seemed more *wary* than immune or removed. I only knew a little about Kyland. He lived up in the hills like I did. And apparently, he didn't have enough to eat, but there was no shortage of hungry people around these parts.

In the middle of rolling green hills, breathtaking mountain views, waterfalls, and quaint covered bridges lies Dennville, Kentucky, a part of the Appalachian Mountains that would put any urban slum to shame, where hopelessness is as commonplace as the white oak trees and unemployment is the rule more so than the exception.

My older sister, Marlo, said God had created Appalachia and then had promptly left and never come back. Something inside me suspected that more often it was people who disappointed God than the other way around. But what did I really know of God anyway? I didn't even go to church.

What I did understand was that in a place like Dennville, Kentucky, Darwin was the one who had his facts straight: only the strongest survived.

Dennville hadn't always been as bad off, though—there was a time when the Dennville coal mine was open and families in these parts made a decent wage, even if some had to supplement with food stamps. That's when there had been at least a few thriving businesses in town, jobs for people who wanted one, and folks who had a little money to spend. Even those of us who lived on the mountain in a sad collection of small houses, shacks, and mobile homes—the poorest of the poor— seemed to have enough to get by on in those days. But then the mine explosion happened. The papers called it the worst mining tragedy in fifty years. Sixty-two men, most with families relying on them at home, were killed. Kyland's father and older brother both lost their lives that day. He lived in a tiny house a little ways below mine on the mountain with his mother, who was an invalid. What she suffered from, I wasn't sure exactly.

As for me, I lived with my mama and sister in a small trailer nestled in a grove of pine trees. In the winter months, the wind would come howling through and rock our trailer so violently, I was sure we'd tip over. Somehow it had managed to hold its ground so far. Somehow, all of us on that mountain had managed to hold our ground. So far.

One late fall day, as I walked up the road that led to our trailer, pulling my sweater around me as the wind whipped through my hair, I spied Kyland walking a ways ahead. Suddenly, Shelly Galvin went running past me to catch up to him, and he turned and nodded his head at her as she walked beside him, acknowledging something she'd said. They turned at a bend in the road, and I got lost in my own thoughts. A few minutes later when I rounded the curve, they were nowhere in sight, but as I passed a grove of hickories, I heard Shelly giggle and stopped to peer through the brush. Kyland had her pressed up against a tree and was kissing her as if he were some wild, untamed animal. Her back was to me so I could only see his face. I don't know why I stood there, staring at them, blatantly interrupting their privacy rather than moving along. But something about the way Kyland's eyes were closed and the raw, heated look of concentration he wore as he moved his mouth over hers made me clench my legs together as heat flooded my veins. He moved his hand up to her breast, and she made a moaning sound in the back of her throat. My own nipples pebbled as if it were me he was touching. I reached out to grab hold of the tree right next to me, and the small noise of my movement must have caught his attention because his eyes popped open and he stared at me as he continued to kiss her, his cheeks hollowed slightly as he did something with his tongue I could only imagine. And imagining I was. Hot shame moved up my face as our eyes locked, and I was unable to move. His eyes narrowed. As reality came flooding back, I stumbled backward, filled with humiliation.

And jealousy. But I hardly wanted to acknowledge that. No—trouble I did *not* want any part of.

I turned and ran all the way up the mountain to my trailer, flinging the metal door open and rushing inside before falling onto the couch, gasping for breath.

"My goodness, Tenleigh," my mama singsonged, as she stood in the tiny kitchen, stirring a pot of something on the electric hot plate that smelled like potato soup. I glanced over at her as I got hold of my breathing. I groaned internally to see that she was wearing a negligee and her tattered Miss Kentucky Sunburst ribbon across her chest. Today was shaping up to be a very bad day. In more ways than one.

"Hi, Mama," I said. "It was cold outside" was all I offered in explanation. "Need any help?"

"No, no, I've got it covered. I'm thinking of bringing something warm into town for Eddie. He loves my potato soup, and it's going to be such a chilly night."

I grimaced. "Mama, Eddie's at home with his wife and family tonight. You can't bring him potato soup."

A cloud moved over my mama's features, but she smiled brightly at me and shook her head. "No, no, he's leaving her, Tenleigh. She's not right for him. It's me he loves. And he'll be cold tonight. The wind..." She continued stirring the soup, humming some nameless tune and smiling a small smile to herself.

"Mama, did you take your medicine today?"

Her head snapped up, a confused look replacing the small smile. "Medicine? Oh, no, baby, I don't need medicine anymore." She shook her head. "That stuff makes me want to sleep all the time...makes me feel so *funny*." She wrinkled her cute little nose as if it was just the silliest thing. "No, I've gone off that medicine. And I feel *wonderful*!"

"Mama, Marlo and I have told you a hundred times you can't just go off your medicine." I walked over to her and

5

laid my hand on her arm. "Mama, you'll feel good for a little while and then you won't. You know I'm right."

Her face fell just a little as she stood stirring the thick soup. Then she shook her head. "No, this time will be different. You'll see. And this time, Eddie will move all of us up to that nice house of his. He'll see that he needs me with him…he needs *all* of us with him."

My shoulders sagged as defeat made my limbs feel heavy. I was too tired to deal with this.

My mama patted her deep chestnut-brown hair—the same hair she'd given me—and smiled brightly again. "I've still got my looks, Tenleigh. Eddie always says I'm the *most* beautiful woman in Kentucky. And I've got this sash to prove he isn't lying." Her eyes grew dreamy as they always did when she talked about her Miss Sunburst title, the one she'd won when she was my age. She turned toward me with a smile and lifted a strand of my hair. "You're as pretty as I was," she said, but then frowned. "I wish I had the money to enter you in some pageants. I bet you'd win them just like I did." She sighed heavily and went back to stirring the soup.

I startled as the door flew open and Marlo burst inside, her cheeks flushed and breathing heavily. She grinned over at me. "Lordy, that wind is *bitter* today."

I nodded at her, unsmiling and moving my eyes over to our mama, who was spooning soup into a plastic container. The smile vanished from Marlo's face.

"Hey there, Mama, what are you doing?" she asked as she took her jacket off and tossed it aside.

Mama looked up and smiled prettily. "Bringing soup to Eddie," she said as she snapped the lid on the container and walked with it into our very small living/dining area.

"No you're not, Mama," Marlo said, her voice sounding bitter.

Mama blinked at her. "Why yes, Marlo, I *am*."

"Give me the soup, Mama. Tenleigh, go get her medicine."

Mama started shaking her head vigorously as I scooted by her to get her medication, the medication we could barely afford, the medication I bought with the earnings I made sweeping floors and dusting shelves at Rusty's, the town convenience store, owned by one of the biggest dickheads in town. The medicine Marlo and I missed meals for so we'd have the money to buy.

I heard a scuffle behind me and hurried into the bathroom, where I grabbed my mama's pill bottles from the medicine cabinet with shaking hands.

When I ran back into the main area of the trailer, Mama was sobbing and the soup was spilled all over the floor and all over Marlo. Mama sunk down onto her knees in the mess, put her hands over her face, and wailed. Marlo took the medicine from me and I could see her hands were shaking too.

She went down on the floor with our mama and kneeled in the mess and hugged Mama to her, rocking.

"I know he still loves me, Mar. I know he does!" my mama wailed. "I'm pretty. I'm prettier than her!"

"No, Mama, he doesn't love you," Marlo said very gently. "I'm so sorry. But *we* do. Me and Tenleigh, we love you so much. So much. We need you, Mama."

"I just want someone to take care of us. I just need someone to help us. Eddie will help us if I just…"

But that thought was lost in her sobs as Marlo continued to rock her, not saying another word. Words wouldn't work with our mama, not when she was like this. Tomorrow she'd take the sash off. Tomorrow she'd stay in bed all day. Eventually, the medicine would kick in again and she'd be somewhat back to normal. And then she'd decide she didn't need it anymore and secretly go off it and we'd do this all over again. And I had to wonder, should a seventeen-year-old girl be so tired? Just tired down to my bones…weary in my very soul?

I helped Marlo and Mama up, and we gave Mama her medicine with a glass of water, walked her to bed, and then quietly returned to the main room. We cleaned up the potato soup, spooning it from the floor back into Tupperware, preserving as much as we could. We didn't live a life where wasting food was ever acceptable, even food that had been on the floor. Later that night, we spooned it into bowls and ate it for dinner. Dirty or not, it filled our bellies all the same.

CHAPTER TWO
Tenleigh

"Hi, Rusty," I said as I breezed into the convenience store where I worked four days a week after school. I was breathing hard and was damp from the rain. Outside, it was just beginning to clear up.

"You're late. Again." Rusty scowled.

I cringed inwardly at his harsh tone and glanced up at the clock. Walking the six miles from school in Evansly in an hour and fifteen minutes was impossible. I jogged a good part of the way and usually came in the store sweating and breathless. Not that Rusty cared. "Just two minutes, Rusty. I'll stay two minutes after, okay?" I offered him my prettiest smile. Rusty's scowl only deepened.

"You'll stay fifteen on account of that there was a cracked beer bottle in one of the six-packs Jay Crowley brought up to my register this morning."

I pressed my lips together.

The fact that Jay Crowley was buying beer first thing in the morning wasn't surprising, but what a cracked beer bottle had to do with me, I wasn't sure as Rusty was the one who unpacked the liquor. Even so, I just nodded, not saying a word as I went to the back to get my apron and broom.

It was the first of the month so I had to clear and organize the pop shelves quickly because in about an hour, after the food stamp debit cards were credited, Rusty's would be swamped with folks selling carts full of the sugary drinks. It was welfare fraud at its finest—take the five hundred or so dollars a family of four gets to eat for the month, buy pop down the highway at JoJo's gas station and sell it back to Rusty for fifty cents on the dollar, converting the government assistance into two hundred fifty dollars cold hard cash. Cash buys cigarettes, liquor, lottery tickets…meth—food stamps do not. And Rusty was happy to make the profit, never mind that it meant kids would go without dinner. In all fairness, though, if it weren't Rusty buying the pop back, it would have been someone else. That's just the way it worked around here.

A couple hours later, the crowd had dwindled, and I was dusting a back shelf when the door chime sounded. I kept busy, glancing up when I saw someone in my peripheral vision opening the refrigerator door on the back wall. My eyes met Kyland Barrett's as he turned, and I stood up from where I'd been squatting, facing the shelf. My eyes moved down to his hand as he stuffed a sandwich in the front of his jacket. His eyes widened, and he looked shocked for a brief second before his gaze darted behind me where I heard sudden footsteps. My head turned. Rusty was coming up the aisle, a scowl on his face as Kyland stood behind me, his hand and a large lump of sandwich still under the front of his jacket. If I moved, he'd be caught, red-handed.

I made a split-second decision and pretended to trip

ungracefully, knocking several boxes of what surely must be stale Cheerios—the nonsugary cereal never sold—off the shelf and letting out a little scream. I don't know exactly why I did it—maybe the look of shocked fear on Kyland's face touched something inside me, maybe it was the understanding of hunger that existed between us. It certainly wasn't because I knew the quick action would completely alter the course of my entire life.

I stepped ungracefully on the boxes, smashing them and causing cereal to spill out onto the floor.

"What's the matter with you, you stupid girl?" Rusty demanded loudly, stooping to pick up a box at his feet as Kyland rushed by us both. "You're fired. I've had it with you." I heard the door chime and stood up quickly, making eye contact with Kyland again as he turned back, his expression unreadable. He paused very briefly, and then the door swung shut behind him.

"I'm sorry, Rusty. It was just an accident. Please don't fire me." I needed this job. As much as I hated to beg for it, I had people relying on me.

"Gave you enough chances. There'll be a line down the street for this job tomorrow." He pointed at me, his eyes cold and mean. "Should have appreciated what you had and worked harder. Those pretty looks of yours won't get you anywhere in life if your head isn't screwed on straight."

I was well aware of that. *Painfully* aware. All you had to do was look at my mama for that fact to be established.

Blood whooshed in my ears. My neck felt hot. I took off my apron and dropped it on the floor as Rusty continued to mutter about the ungrateful, worthless help.

The sun was just setting over the mountains behind me—the sky awash in pinks and oranges when I stepped out of the store a few minutes later. The cold air held the scent of fresh rain and sharp pine and I took a deep breath, wrapping my arms around myself, feeling lost and defeated. Losing my job was very, very bad news. Marlo was going to kill me. I groaned aloud. "What more?" I whispered to the universe. But the universe hadn't been responsible for my stupid choice. Only I could take credit for that.

Sometimes my life felt so *small*. And I had to wonder why those of us who were given small lives still had to feel pain so big. It hardly seemed fair.

I put my hands in my pockets and started the walk to the base of our mountain, my school backpack slung over my shoulder. In the spring and summer, I'd read as I walked, the route familiar enough to me that I could concentrate on my book. Cars rarely drove this road and I always had plenty of advanced notice if one was coming. But when the fall came, it was too dim once I left Rusty's—not that that would be a problem anymore—and so I walked and busied my mind. And tonight was no different. In fact, I needed the distraction of my dreams. I needed the hope that life wouldn't always be so hard. I pictured myself winning the Tyton Coal Scholarship, the one I'd been working toward since I started high school. Every year, one of the top students was chosen to win the scholarship, which would send him or her to a four-year university, all expenses paid. If I won it, I'd finally be able to get out of Dennville, away from the poverty and the desperation, the welfare fraud, and the drug-pushing "pillbillies." I'd finally be able to provide for Mama and Marlo, move them away from here, get Mama the help she needed from a professional doctor, instead of the hollow-eyed one at the free clinic who I suspected was the center of the pillbilly business. I'd make a stop at Rusty's as I drove out of town, and I'd tell him to shove a stale box of Cheerios up his bony, flea-bitten ass.

As I turned the corner toward the base of the mountain, I saw old Mrs. Lytle sitting on the steps of the now-closed post office eating the last of a packaged sandwich. I squinted at her and smiled slightly when her eyes caught mine. My gaze went to the wrapper in her hand, the one that said "Rusty's Ham and Cheese" with a big red time stamp, dated today. It was the one Kyland Barrett had stolen just ten minutes before. I knew because it'd been the only ham and cheese we had left in the store.

"Evening, Mrs. Lytle," I said. She tipped her chin, her sad eyes blinking as she took the last bite of the sandwich. Mrs. Lytle was almost part of the landscape at this point, an alcoholic who wandered the streets of the tiny town, mumbling to herself and collecting pocket change from the townies to fund her addiction. She'd lost all three of her grown boys and her husband in the mine accident. I suspected she was hoping to follow them sooner rather than later. "You gonna be okay, tonight, Mrs. Lytle?" I asked, stuffing my hands deeper into my pockets. Not that I could offer her anything if she wasn't, but I wanted her to know I cared. Maybe that was something.

She nodded, still chewing. "Oh, I think so," she slurred. "I'll make my way somewhere after I'm done enjoying this fine show." She nodded up to the dwindling sunset.

"Okay, then. Good night."

"Night."

As I turned onto the road that led up the mountain, someone stepped in front of me, and I let out a startled scream, stopping in my tracks and stepping backward right into a mud puddle. Kyland.

I huffed out a breath. "You scared me!" I stepped out of the mud, feeling the wetness seeping into my socks where my soles were cracked or coming loose. *Great. Thanks, Kyland. First my job, now my shoes.*

He studied me for a few beats, his jaw tight. "Why'd you do that? Back at the store? Why'd you help me?" His jaw ticked in anger.

He was angry with *me*? What in the ever-loving hell? "Why'd you give the sandwich to Mrs. Lytle?" I asked. "Why didn't you eat it yourself? I know you need the food." My gaze slipped to the ground at the reference to that private moment in the cafeteria when our eyes had met. But then I quickly looked back up.

He didn't answer me, and we both just stood staring at each other for a few silent moments. Finally he said, "He fired you?"

His face was tense and serious, and I couldn't help but admire his strong jaw, the straight line of his nose, the fullness of his lips. I sighed. No good would come from those observations. "Yeah, he fired me."

Kyland stuffed his hands in his pockets, and when I began to walk, he did too, swearing under his breath. "Shit. You needed that job."

I huffed out a humorless laugh. "You think? No, I just worked sweeping floors because Rusty's charming disposition is so inspiring. Oh, if only there were more Rustys in the world." I brought my hand to my heart as if it were overflowing with love and admiration.

If Kyland noted my sarcasm, he didn't acknowledge it. "That was a really stupid move."

I stopped and turned to him and he halted too. "A thank-you wouldn't be out of line. Rusty would have pressed charges in a New York minute. It would have made his *day* to press charges, maybe even his pathetic life."

Kyland looked behind me, out to the horizon. He sucked on his full bottom lip and furrowed his brow. "Yeah, I know." He paused, his eyes moving over my face slowly. I fidgeted under his scrutiny, wondering what he was thinking. "Thank you."

I took the time to study him too, now that he was up close. He gazed back at me, his gray eyes wary, his eyelashes long and thick. It was hard to really hate someone so good-looking. That was just the unfairness of life. Because I'd have really liked to hate the boy standing in front of me. Instead, I turned away and started walking. He fell in step beside me, and we walked in silence for several minutes.

"You don't have to walk with me."

"A young girl walking in the dark by herself is dangerous. I can make sure nothing bad happens to you."

I snorted. "All evidence to the contrary." I hefted my backpack up on my shoulder. "Anyway, *young* girl? I'm as old as you are. Maybe older. I turn eighteen in May."

"What day?" he challenged, moving ahead of me and walking backward so he could look me in the face.

"May second."

His eyes widened. "No way. That's my birthday too."

I stopped, surprised. "What time were you born?" I asked.

"I don't know exactly...sometime in the morning."

I started walking again and he fell in step beside me. "Afternoon," I said reluctantly. I could see the pleased look on his face out of the corner of my eye and I pressed my lips together.

After a minute, he said, "Seriously, though, you should be careful. There are bobcats on this mountain."

I sighed. "Bobcats are the least of my worries."

"You think so until a hungry one is standing right in front of you. Then it becomes your biggest problem real quickly."

I made an amused, agreeable sound. "And what exactly would you do if a bobcat stepped into our path right now, Kyland Barrett?"

He looked surprised. "You know my name."

"It's a small town. I know everyone's name. Don't you?"

"No. I make it a point not to. I don't need to hear anyone's story, and I don't need to know anyone's name."

I tilted my head as I looked over at him. "Why not?"

"Because when I win the Tyton Coal Scholarship and get out of here, I don't want to carry a bunch of useless information from this useless shithole with me."

My mouth opened, then closed, then opened again. "You're trying to win the scholarship?"

He raised one eyebrow at me. "Yeah, does that surprise you? Don't you see my name on all the top academic lists?"

"I...I mean..." Suddenly, Kyland grinned. I stumbled slightly. I'd never seen him smile like that, not once, and it trans-formed his face into something...utterly beautiful. I gaped at him for a moment before gathering myself and increasing the speed of my steps. He sped up beside me. I shook my head, feeling unsettled and attempting to remember what we'd been talking about. Right—the scholarship. Yes, I *was* surprised. I had seen Kyland's name on academic lists, but I didn't imagine that he had applied for the Tyton Coal Scholarship. He'd never shown up at any study groups or prep courses. It was always me, Ginny Rawlins, and Carrie Cooper. I knew they had applied for the scholarship because we'd discussed it. I thought they were my top competition. Kyland, despite his good grades, always seemed so...disinterested?

"How are *you* going to win the scholarship when I'm going to win the scholarship?" I asked with a lift of my brow.

Kyland looked over at me quickly, amusement on his face as he shook his head. "Not a chance," he said, smirking. "But it does make things more interesting, doesn't it?"

I snorted softly. I didn't need interesting. I needed that scholarship. But I could hardly believe Kyland had much of a chance of winning it if I hadn't heard about him applying until just now. I didn't figure there was much cause to worry.

We walked in silence for a few minutes before I said, "Won't Shelly be mad knowing you're…protecting another girl from bobcats?"

He looked over at me, confused. "Shelly? Why would she—" He chuckled. "Oh, right." He shook his head and ran his hand through his golden-brown hair. I noted that it was thick and glossy and it curled up at his neck. "Me and Shelly, we're just friends."

I let out a small disbelieving chuff which was enough of a comment on that. I had bigger things to worry about than who Kyland Barrett was kissing. "So, where will you go if you win that scholarship?" *Not that you will.*

"Away from here."

"Yeah," I said simply. Kyland looked to the left as we walked past the light blue, wooden house set back from the road, the forest looming large behind it, not a single light on. When he met my eyes again, he was wearing a small frown. "Well," I said when he remained silent, "thank you, Kyland. It was very chivalrous of you to walk me up the mountain, you know, despite the fact that you got me fired from my job, ruined my only pair of shoes, and stole my birthday." When he continued walking beside me, laughing softly at what I'd said, I looked up at him questioningly. "I'm just right up the road. I don't expect there are any bobcats between here and there." I smiled a nervous smile. I didn't know if he'd ever seen my trailer, and I didn't especially want him to.

But he just kept walking next to me silently. "So, Tenleigh…the job, are you going to be okay? I mean…is there something I can do?"

What was he going to do? He had an ill mama at home as well. For all I knew, he was worse off than me. "No. I'll survive."

Kyland nodded, but when I glanced at him, the worried look hadn't vanished from his face.

When we arrived at my trailer, I stopped and gave him a small, tight smile. "Well, good night," I said. Kyland looked at where I lived for long moments as color rose up my cheeks. For some reason, standing there with him, it looked even worse than it usually did. Not only was it tiny and rickety, but the paint was peeling and rusted and there was a dirty film over the windows that I never could clean no matter how much vinegar I used. His home wasn't much better, but I still couldn't help the shame that filled me as I studied my home through Kyland's eyes. He looked back at me, and my embarrassment must have been evident on my face because something that looked like understanding came into his expression. I spun on my heel and walked on shaky legs to my trailer.

"Tenleigh Falyn," Kyland called, letting me know that, in fact, he knew my name too.

I stopped and looked back at him questioningly.

He ran his hand through his hair, looking uncertain for a brief moment. "The reason I gave that sandwich to Joan Lytle…" He looked off into the distance as if he was choosing his words carefully. "Even for people like us, there's always

18

someone who's hungrier. And hunger, well, it comes in different forms. I try not to forget that," he finished quietly.

And then he stuffed his hands back into his pockets and walked away from me, headed back down the road. I leaned against the side of my trailer and watched him until he disappeared.

Kyland Barrett wasn't at all what I had expected. And something about that both confused and thrilled me in a way I wasn't sure I liked.

CHAPTER THREE
Kyland

"Hey, Mama," I said, shutting the door to my house behind me and glancing into the living room where her chair sat in front of the TV.

My mama didn't greet me back, but she never did. I was used to it now.

I went to my bedroom and opened the window as wide as it would go and stood looking out at the early evening sky, my hands braced on the windowsill as I drew in deep breaths of cold air. After a few minutes, I lay down on my bed right next to the window, bringing my arms up and resting my head on my hands behind me.

My mind went immediately to Tenleigh Falyn. I couldn't believe I'd gotten her fired from her job. I grimaced. It was mostly her fault, so why did I feel like such a shit about it? It'd been her own stupid choice to cover for me. But thank God she had. If I'd been arrested for stealing...it would have been bad—very bad.

I hadn't even known exactly why I stole that sandwich

for Mrs. Lytle until I'd attempted to explain it to Tenleigh. And the only reason I'd offered an explanation at all was because I had nothing else to give Tenleigh as thanks for the sacrifice she'd made for me. I'd seen Joan Lytle sitting on the stairs of the old post office and something in the way she was hunched over, as if she was trying to curl up into herself, hit me square in the gut. I'd felt that way too. Only I, at least, had a roof over my head. I, at the very least, was only hungry the last week of every month, when the money ran out. Some force inside me had needed to let her know another person saw that she existed, whether she felt like she did or not. And so I'd swiped the sandwich.

A bad spur-of-the-moment choice that could have ruined everything for me. Still, I wasn't exactly sorry for it, especially when I pictured the way Mrs. Lytle had gotten tears in her eyes when I handed her the food. My regret was for the fact that Tenleigh had been the one to pay the price for what I'd done.

Tenleigh.

My mind moved to the expression that had been on her face as I'd looked at her trailer. She'd felt shame, which was kind of ridiculous. My house was in shambles too. My *life* was in shambles. I was hardly one to judge her situation. But I hadn't really been looking at her pitiful little trailer anyway. I'd been looking at the area *around* her trailer. It was clean and orderly, not a single piece of trash in sight—the same way I made sure to keep my own yard. Up and down this hill, the yards and properties were strewn with garbage—just another way the people in Dennville exhibited their defeat. No one on this mountain could afford a luxury like garbage pickup and most yards were buried under a pile of crap—a good metaphor for most lives in these parts. But

21

each Monday, I gathered my garbage into two garbage bags and carried them down the hill and emptied them in the big dumpster out back of Rusty's. Then I folded the garbage bags up and put them in my backpack. I made them last. When it was a choice between a couple cans of SpaghettiOs and a box of garbage bags, I was going to choose the food. I'd seen Tenleigh carrying a big box down the mountain now and again and wondered what was in it. She must have been doing the same thing. And I knew it was because she had pride. Which, for people like us, could be more a curse than a blessing.

I'd noticed Tenleigh before that too. In fact, I'd watched her in the few classes we had together. She always sat at the front of the classroom and I would position myself in the back so I had the perfect view. I couldn't take my eyes off her. I was amused by the way she reacted unconsciously when she was annoyed by someone who was talking to her, by scratching her bare leg and pursing her lips. I noticed the way she squinted up at the blackboard in serious concentration and nibbled at that pink lower lip, and I liked the way she sometimes stared out the window with that dreamy look on her face. I'd memorized her profile, the line of her neck. A hollow, ill feeling rose in my chest when I noticed the bottoms of her shoes, full of holes and practically falling off. I could see that she had used some kind of magic marker to color in the scuffs on the tops. I could picture her at home, coloring in those spots because she cared what people thought of her old, ruined shoes. It enraged me that she had to do that. Which was completely irrational. And which, of course, meant I had to stay far, far away from Tenleigh Falyn. I couldn't afford to feel the things I felt just watching her. More to the point, I didn't want to.

After the day she'd caught me swiping the leftover food, I'd seen her watching me when she thought I wasn't looking. I was no stranger to the enjoyment of the finer sex. I wasn't one to turn down an offer if I got one—who didn't want the distraction of a willing body to remind you that you hadn't just been made for suffering? But somehow I sensed Tenleigh wasn't watching me with that kind of interest. She looked at me as if she was working out some kind of puzzle—as if she wanted to *know* me. And I couldn't help wanting to know *why*.

She had this quiet about her—something soothing, a strange mix of strength and vulnerability. She was beautiful— I'd definitely noticed that too—but her beauty was obviously something she didn't put much effort into, which made her even more appealing. To me at least. She didn't wear any makeup and her hair was generally held back in a simple ponytail. She obviously didn't consider her looks to be her most valuable asset. And it made me wonder what was. Her smarts? Maybe. Not that she had a chance of winning that scholarship. I'd been working on it since before I even started high school. I had even studied all the past winners' accomplishments and made sure I had every single box checked. I *needed* that scholarship. My whole life depended on it. So as far as what it was about Tenleigh that interested me so much, it didn't matter. I'd be leaving soon and I'd never look back, not at beautiful, green-eyed Tenleigh Falyn or anyone else.

So why couldn't I stop thinking about her?

After a little bit, I dragged my backpack up on my bed and got my textbooks out. I had to stay on track. I only had six months until the school announced the winner of the scholarship that would get me out of this godforsaken shithole, away from the hopelessness, away from the hunger, away from the mine where my father and older brother had lost their lives in the pitch blackness miles under the earth.

———————

I spotted Tenleigh a few days later as she walked ahead of me toward the road leading to our homes. She had a book in her hands and was reading as she walked. One of these days, she was going to trip and break her neck. I lagged behind, watching her as she walked. I figured I owed her a little something for what she'd done for me. I could make sure she got home safe from school. Lord knew she'd never spot danger approaching with her nose plastered to the page of a book. But I'd make sure she didn't see me. I'd make sure I never spoke to Tenleigh again. It was just better that way.

I was taken aback when she suddenly took a turn onto a forest path. What the hell? I stood on the road for a minute, watching her disappear into the woods. That girl would deserve it when a bobcat ate her. I let out a frustrated breath and followed her.

I'd been down this trail before. I'd been down every trail on this mountain either with my brother when he'd still been alive or on my own. But I had no idea what Tenleigh was doing because there was nothing this way except for the abrupt edge of a limestone cliff.

After five minutes or so of trudging along the narrow path, I came out through the trees. Tenleigh's back was mostly to me as she stood staring out at the setting sun, the horizon glowing orange and yellow, white rays emerging from the clouds as if heaven had broken through.

The colorful sky stretched before us magnificent, as if it was trying to make up for the ugliness of our lives, our constant struggles. And for just the briefest, most fleeting of moments, maybe it did. If only I could grasp it and make it stay. If only I could grasp *anything* good and make it stay.

Tenleigh sat down on a rock and looked out at the glowing sunset. I began walking toward her and her head turned to me abruptly as she let out a little shriek, bringing her hand to her chest, her eyes wide. "Good gosh! You scared me! Again. What is it with you?"

"Sorry." I went and sat down next to her.

She rolled her eyes and leaned back, putting her hands behind her on the rock, staring out at the sky once again. She remained quiet for a minute. Finally she looked at me, raising one eyebrow. "I suppose you think if you keep showing up where I am, eventually I'll fall in love with you."

An amused laugh bubbled up my throat, but I remained serious. Tenleigh constantly surprised me. And I loved it. "Very probable."

Or worse, I'll fall in love with you.

She laughed softly. "I'm sorry to tell you, it won't happen. I've sworn off men."

I made a chuffing sound in the back of my throat. "That's what they all say."

She looked at me, amusement dancing in her eyes, lighting up her face. "Hmm, so how long do you figure I have before I succumb to your mesmerizing charms?"

I pretended to consider. "One of my conquests held out for three weeks once."

"Ah. She sounds like a tough cookie." She cocked an eyebrow and looked at me out of the corner of her eye. "How will you know when I've buckled?"

"It's a look, something in the eyes. I've come to know it well." I gave her my most obnoxious smirk.

She shook her head as if in exasperation, but the small smile remained on her lips.

I cleared my throat. This flirting needed to stop. "No, but really, I'm just making sure you don't require my bobcat-fighting skills. It's the least I can do for you after your sacrifice on my behalf."

"You don't *owe* me anything. I got myself fired from my job. It wasn't your fault I did what I did."

"Yeah, but you wouldn't have had to do what you did if I hadn't been stealing sandwiches for old drunks."

"Hmm," she hummed. "So then I expect this will be a regular thing? The bobcat protection service? I mean, until I throw myself at your feet and you cast me aside like all the rest of your victims...er, conquests?" she finally asked, raising an eyebrow teasingly again.

I shook my head. "Regular? No, no, definitely not. This is the last time I put myself in potential bobcat harm for you." I ran my hand through my hair. "It's just that I usually study at school as late as I can. I walk home about this time every night anyway. This was just a coincidence."

She tilted her head. "Oh, I see. Why do you stay at school to study?"

"It's not so lonely." I didn't know what made the words fall from my mouth. I didn't even realize I'd said them until they were out.

Tenleigh looked at me curiously. "Don't you live with your mama?"

"My mama's not much for conversation."

Tenleigh studied me for a moment. She had this way of looking at me like she knew what I was thinking, and it made me feel antsy and overly warm. Regardless, I stood my ground. "Hmm...well, this really is the last time you'll be protecting me from a possible bobcat threat then. I'm only walking home this late because I was asking about a job at Al's."

"Al's? You're too young to work in a bar."

She shrugged. "Al doesn't seem to mind. My sister works there—he said I could pick up extra shifts. So see"—she smiled at me—"you don't have to feel guilty about me getting fired. I've already got a new job. On-call anyway."

I scowled, something strange moving into my chest. Al's was a total dive—and a known pickup place. Still, it was good she'd gotten a job. Around here, that wasn't easy to do. After a minute, she turned to me. "Quite a view, huh?"

I looked out to the sky. "Best seat in the house."

A look of peace came over Tenleigh's face as she gazed at me, her lips parted, and for just a second, I almost couldn't breathe. *Did I think this girl was beautiful? I was wrong. She's stunning.*

Some form of panic rose in my chest.

"So I suppose you want to know my story?" she asked after a moment.

"What?" I asked, snapping back to reality. "No, I don't want to hear your story. I told you..."

"Right. You don't want to carry any useless information with you when you leave, but see, I've got a really interesting one."

I raised one brow at her suspiciously. "There are no interesting stories in these parts, just weary, never-ending tales of tragedy and woe. And toothlessness."

She laughed a short laugh and shook her head, her light green eyes shining. Her skin was aglow in the sunset, glints of gold coming off her brunette hair. When she looked away, I allowed my eyes to roam to her breasts. My dick surged to life in my jeans and I shifted uncomfortably.

"Not my story," she said. "And really, I shouldn't tell you this, but well... In truth, Kyland, my father is a Russian prince." She raised her eyebrows and looked around as if checking to make sure no one was around. "There's a squabble going on regarding my father's title and land ownership." She waved her hand through the air. "It's all very complicated and involves all sorts of Russian aristocracy laws that you wouldn't understand, but in the meantime, my father is hiding us *here* where he believes we're safest until his estate has been settled." She leaned toward me. "I know my trailer looks humble, but it's all a ruse. Inside, although it's small, it's wall-to-wall luxury. And"—her eyes widened—"it's where the royal family jewels are hidden." She winked at me and I burst out laughing. She was being ridiculous. And I loved it. How long had it been since I'd just been...*silly*? Her eyes widened as she took in my expression and then she grinned back.

We stared at each other for a minute, something flowing in the air between us. I looked away first, unsettled again.

"Royal family jewels, huh? You so sure you can trust me with that information? I'm already a known sandwich bandit."

She tilted her head. "Yeah," she said softly, seriously. "I've got a feeling you're mostly trustworthy."

We stared at each other for several beats again, something quickening inside me. Something that felt dangerous— something I didn't exactly recognize but something I wasn't sure I liked at all. I needed to break the damn spell.

"I trust you with my family jewels too," I finally said suggestively, trying to lighten the sudden, strange mood between us. "I'd like to show them to you sometime."

Tenleigh leaned her head back and laughed. I had wondered what her full-out laughter sounded like, and now

I knew. And I suddenly understood that it would have been better if I didn't. So much better. Because I wanted to *lose* myself in the sound of that laughter. It alarmed me and that same feeling came into my chest again, only now increasing. I sat up straighter, something instinctual telling me I needed to run.

Her expression seemed to change as if she could sense my inner turmoil. *Ridiculous.* She stood and I squinted up at her. "Come here," she said, turning her back on me. "I want to show you something."

I stood up and followed behind her to a large rock. I watched as she went to the front of it and ducked down, disappearing somewhere. I leaned over cautiously and saw a tiny, dark cave. Anxiety swept through my body, and I stumbled backward. Tenleigh peeked out, a smile plastered across her face.

"Come in. It's big enough for the both of us. I want to show you something."

"No," I said, a bit more harshly than I meant to. The smile disappeared from her face and she emerged from the small space, nearly squatting as she shuffled along. She stood up and looked at me worriedly. I realized that my hands were fisted by my sides and my body was tensed. I relaxed, shoving my hands in my pockets.

"I'm sorry," she whispered. "Do you not like small spaces? I—"

"It's no big deal," I said dismissively.

She put her hand on my shoulder timidly, and I squeezed my eyes shut for a second before I pulled away.

She watched me acutely for just a moment. "There are some drawings on the wall in there," she finally said and shrugged. "Really, really faint and most likely something

29

someone did recently, but who knows? Maybe a cave family lived in there thousands of years ago."

"Hundreds of thousands."

"What?"

"Cavemen, they lived hundreds of thousands of years ago, not thousands."

She put her hands on her hips. "Okay, *professor*." She arched one delicate eyebrow, and I let out a small laugh on a breath.

"Come on, Princess Tenleigh, we better get back to the road before it's pitch-black." I went for a casual tone to my voice. Tenleigh had obviously noticed my strange behavior when it came to the small cave.

The sun had almost set and it was twilight, the sky a deep blue, the first stars just appearing. A few minutes later, we were back on the road and we walked along in silence.

Tenleigh adjusted her backpack and a book fell out of the tear on the side, the one she had closed up as much as possible with a safety pin. A fucking safety pin. That safety pin filled me with anger. "Oops." She leaned down to pick it up just as I did and we both laughed as our heads collided. She rubbed hers and laughed again. "There's that charm again. I'm a goner for sure."

"Don't say I didn't warn you." I picked up the book and held it up. "*The Weaver of Raveloe*?"

Tenleigh's eyes met mine and she nodded, taking the book from me. "I read a lot," she said, stuffing the book in her backpack and looking embarrassed for some reason. "The Dennville library doesn't have much of a selection so I've read some twice…"

"That one?" I nodded my head toward her backpack as we started walking again.

"Yes, I've read that one before."

"What's it about?"

She was quiet for a minute and I thought she might not answer me. Truthfully, I didn't really care to hear about the weaver of whatever. She could tell me anything. What I wanted was to hear her pretty voice cutting through the cold mountain air—and I liked the things she said. She was different. She kept surprising me with the things that came out of her mouth and even though I didn't want to, I liked it. I liked it far too much.

"It's about Silas Marner who—"

I halted, several emotions suddenly swelling within me. Grief. Longing. Love. "Silas?"

Tenleigh stopped too and looked at me curiously. "Yeah, what's wrong?"

I shook my head, swallowing down the emotions that had suddenly surged without warning. I hadn't been prepared to hear that name. "Nothing," I told her. "That was my brother's name." I shoved the emotions down. I was well practiced at that.

Tenleigh bit her lip and looked up at me, a sympathetic look on her face before we both started walking again. She must have known my brother had been at the mine that day. "Yes, I think I remember that." She smiled. "Maybe your mama read the book and the name stuck with her."

"My mama didn't…doesn't know how to read."

"Oh." She glanced at me and then was silent for a minute. "I know it happened years ago, but…" She touched my arm and when my eyes darted to her hand, she pulled it away. "I'm really sorry about your loss, Kyland."

"Thanks, I appreciate that," I said, clearing my throat.

We walked in a sort of awkward silence for a few

minutes, passing by my dark house. "So what about this Silas Marner?"

"Um…well, he lives in a slum in England and, ah, he's falsely accused of stealing, by his best friend. He's convicted and the woman he's engaged to leaves him and marries his best friend."

"Jesus, sounds like a real feel-good sort of tale. I'm glad you've found a way to escape the harshness of Dennville."

Tenleigh's sweet-sounding laughter made my heart jump in my chest. Somehow making this girl laugh filled me with some sort of pride. *Not good. Very, very bad.*

We arrived in front of Tenleigh's trailer and she leaned back against a tree next to the road. "Well, he leaves the town and settles in a small village near Raveloe. He sort of becomes a hermit, feeling as if he's hidden—even from God." I unconsciously leaned in so I wouldn't miss a word. She tilted her head, looking off into the distance. "But one winter's night, his whole life changes when—"

"Tenleigh!" someone called from the trailer, an older woman with long brown hair the same color as Tenleigh's. "It's cold out there. Come inside."

"Okay, Mama," Tenleigh called before looking back at me, a worried expression on her face. I didn't remember seeing Tenleigh's mama much. She must not have left the trailer very often. "I gotta go. I'll see you around, Kyland." And with that, she turned and left me where I was standing. She ran inside so quickly, her sudden absence jarred me and made me feel lost somehow. I stood staring at her trailer for several moments before I turned and headed for home, the wind cold at my back.

CHAPTER FOUR
Tenleigh

The unfortunate thing about being fired from Rusty's—other than the obvious issues of lost income, humiliation, and possible starvation—was that it was the only place to buy groceries in Dennville. Normally, I'd make the six-mile walk to Evansly just on principle alone, but today it was raining cats and dogs and I just wasn't up for it. So I sucked up my pride and entered the convenience store. Rusty was a dick, but he wasn't going to turn down my money. Thankfully though, his sister, Dusty, was standing at the counter. Yes, Rusty's sister's name was Dusty—the gene pool in that family was clearly something special.

Dusty had an *In Touch* magazine plastered to her face and didn't even look up when I entered. I let out a sigh of relief before moving through the store and throwing things in my basket. Rusty didn't carry any fruits or vegetables, not even the canned variety. Marlo and I had a small garden planted on the far side of our trailer—tomatoes, green beans, watermelon, and potatoes—and in the summertime we sometimes ate from it exclusively for weeks at a time. Several of the families living on the mountain had at least a small garden, and sometimes we traded one homegrown item for another. It was a good way to save money…and a good way to avoid the scurvy you were likely to get if you ate food solely from Rusty's.

In the winter months, I'd usually make it a point to walk through the snow to Evansly at least once a week to stock up on canned fruits and veggies. When we were heating our trailer, we couldn't afford the fresh variety, so for three or four months we made do with canned. And then when the spring came, Marlo and I watched the ground with something close to glee as the first shoots unfurled.

You had to appreciate the small things in life when the big things made you want to curl up in the corner in the fetal position and give up.

"Hey, Dusty," I said by way of greeting when I was ready to check out.

She didn't acknowledge me and still didn't look up, blindly grabbing at my items until she felt something, glanced at it, and typed the price into the cash register.

"So how's life?" I asked, leaning my hip on the counter.

Dusty finally tore her eyes from the magazine, a blank expression on her plain face. "Life sucks," she said.

I nodded to the magazine in her hand. "Not for those celebrities."

She narrowed her eyes, smacking the gum in her mouth before glancing quickly at the magazine and then back at me. "There was a big wedding in the Hamptons last weekend. All the stars were there. They ate thousand-dollar steak, and sipped champagne," she offered.

I nodded slowly, running my tongue over my front teeth. "Must be nice."

"Yeah," she said. "Must be real nice." She grinned, showing me a mouthful of rot—commonly referred to in these parts as "Mountain Dew Mouth." Then, as if to make my point, she picked up a half-full bottle of Mountain Dew and took a big swig. I struggled not to flinch. She finished ringing up my items, and I paid, took my bags, bid her farewell, and headed toward the door. As I was walking through, Dusty called my name and I turned around and looked at her questioningly.

"Rusty is a rat-faced motherfucker," she said.

Well that was one way to put it. A really good way to put it, actually. "Yeah," I agreed. "He really is."

She gifted me another brown-and-yellow grin, stuck her hand up, and gave me a thumbs-up sign, and then plastered the magazine back to her face.

I started walking back toward home, lost in my own world, trying to decide what I'd do on this chilly Saturday. Marlo was working and then she had plans with some guy she'd met at Al's. I really wished she wouldn't have anything to do with the guys she met there—most of them were far from worthy of her. I thought Marlo and I had good reason for distrusting men, but while I had sworn them off, Marlo had decided that dating lots of guys she didn't care about meant she was the one in control.

Marlo had opened her heart once, and things hadn't gone well.

A few years before, she had met *Ronald*, a young, handsome executive in town for some big corporate meeting at the mine. He'd come into Al's every night for a week just to sit in my sister's section and watch her work, talking about fate and destiny, which swept her right off her feet just like he was her prince charming come to rescue her from her dreary existence. As if any prince was ever named *Ronald*—that should have been her first clue right there.

She kissed him up against his shiny, red BMW and he made all sorts of promises to her about moving her out to his condo in Chicago. Then three minutes after she'd given him her virginity, he drove her to the base of our mountain and dropped her off at the side of the road. When she asked him what happened to the condo in Chicago, he laughed at her and told her he'd never bring an ugly, bucktoothed hick home with him. And then he'd sped off, splashing mud up on her new, white sweater, the one we'd walked six miles into the Evansly Walmart to buy, the one I could tell made her feel pretty. At least up until then. After that, Marlo never seemed to feel pretty, and she'd started laughing with her hand over her mouth to hide her teeth. Truth be told, they *were* sort of bucked—not in a way that was ugly, but in a way that showed off those full movie-star lips of hers, in a way that was sweet and endearing. In a way that was Marlo.

Whenever I thought back to the day we excitedly walked through the aisles of Walmart, talking about how her night would go, spraying testers of perfume on our wrists and spending the last of our money on a sweater for her date, it made me so angry. Angry that we'd allowed ourselves to include Ronald in our dreams, that we'd spent even one second giving him the power to dash our hopes. And most of all, that Marlo had given something precious to a loser who didn't deserve it.

Marlo had told me the story of Ronald that night when she'd come into our trailer, muddy, shivering, and defeated. She'd cried in my arms and I'd cried too, for her, for me, for dashed dreams, for the pain of loneliness and the deep hope that someone would come along and save us. And the fact that no one ever did. Of course, we both should have known better after what happened to our mama, but I supposed the promise of love is about the strongest pull there is. I didn't blame Marlo. Our father had been the first one to teach us that men were ultimately selfish and uncaring and would put themselves before anyone else, regardless of who depended on them. And even still, for me, it was so hard not to dream that somewhere out there, there was someone strong and gallant who would dance with me under a starlit sky and call me his beloved—and mean it.

"Hey."

I let out a small scream, startled abruptly from my memories and musings, dropping one of my bags, and watching as groceries rolled out onto the ground. When I looked up, it was Kyland. "This is funny to you, isn't it?" I asked.

He held his hands up in a surrender gesture. "Sorry, sorry. I swear, this really is a coincidence. I was walking back from Evansly. I saw you come out of Rusty's." He bent down, picked up my bag of groceries, and then gestured for me to give him the other one. I almost resisted, but then I decided he should at the very least carry my bags after giving me a mini heart attack for the third time in a week.

"Hmm, likely story," I muttered.

He grinned when I handed the bag over and some sort of strange tickling feeling moved through my rib cage. I gave a dramatic eye roll in response.

"Still holding strong, huh?"

"It's been quite the effort, let me tell you," I said.

He laughed and my stupid heart flipped. Evidently I was kind of bad at this swearing-off-men thing—a few smiles and I had a full-blown crush. Truthfully, he hadn't even worked that hard to get me to this point. How completely annoying.

"How's the ever-charming Rusty?" he asked after a minute, moving his head backward to indicate the store.

"Rusty wasn't there. Dusty was."

"Oh, well how's Dusty? In-bred as usual?"

I laughed but sucked it back in. "That's mean." I paused. "Dusty, she's all right."

"I know. I'm just kidding. I mean…mostly." We walked in silence for a few minutes.

I looked to my left when I heard a car engine approach and watched as a black Mercedes drove slowly by. I could hear the way my mama would have called his name. Eddie! I averted my eyes quickly, turning my head away and toward Kyland who furrowed his brow, obviously having noted my response to the luxury car. "Do you know Edward Kearney?" he asked.

I kept looking at him until I heard the car drive past us and then shook my head. "No. Not really," I said, blushing slightly as I watched the back of his car move away—the car that cost more than the yearly salary of three miners. Kyland didn't need to know my family's dirty laundry. I wondered what Edward Kearney, the vice president of drilling operations at the Tyton coal mine and the administrator of the yearly Tyton Coal Scholarship, not to mention my mom's once-upon-a-time affair, was doing driving through this town, though. There was nothing here that would interest him. I should know.

"They found all kinds of safety infractions at the old mine," Kyland said, his eyes still on the back of the disappearing car. "After the collapse, Tyton Coal paid a fine. A *fine*," he repeated bitterly.

"I know," I said. "I heard that." I couldn't blame him for being bitter about that. He'd lost so much. We walked without speaking for a while, the birdsong in the trees ringing out around us, filling our silence. After a few minutes, the mood seemed to lift, Kyland's shoulders relaxing.

As we were about to approach the trail that led to the cliff where Kyland had followed me a few days before, he said, "The sun's about to set. Should we catch the show, princess?" He winked and my hormones went a little wonky.

Damn. And yet, despite the fact that I didn't necessarily want to experience all these hormonal reactions to a boy, it was also exciting and different and gave the moment a certain sparkle that I couldn't even explain. I shifted my weight from one foot to the other. "Well…I was going home to soak in our multi-jet hot tub, maybe eat some bonbons, but…oh, sure."

Kyland smiled and steered me onto the damp trail. "By the way," he said, "if this is your way of luring me into the woods so that you can take advantage of me, I want you to know, I'm not that kind of boy."

I snorted. "Oh, you're exactly that kind of boy."

He looked behind him, pretending to be offended.

I laughed. "And you're the one luring *me* by the way. This was *your* idea."

His glance was quick this time, his cocky smile just a shade darker. "You can trust me."

I laughed. I'd already told him I thought he was trust-worthy, so I couldn't really deny it. Even so, I shot one word over at him, "Doubtful." As we walked, I wondered, though—he'd never seemed wanting of female company, so what was he doing with me? Why *did* he keep showing up where I was?

We came out on the other side and settled ourselves on the same rock we'd sat on before, Kyland placing my grocery bags next to him.

We sat for a minute, looking out at the sunset that rose red and orange above the line of fog as if the whole top of the sky had lit on fire. Our thighs touched, his warm against mine. The smell of the rain was still in the air and raindrops glistened in the trees around us.

We had been joking and laughing a few minutes before, but suddenly, the mood between us had shifted once again. I glanced over at Kyland and his face was tense. What was he thinking when he suddenly started brooding like that?

"So you never told me what that Silas dude found that changed his life," he finally said.

I squinted over at him. He was staring straight ahead as if he didn't care what my answer was.

"Why don't you read the book?" I offered.

"Pfft. Just what I need. To waste my time reading about someone else's sucky life."

"Then why are you asking about it?"

"Just making conversation."

Then why would I waste my breath recounting an entire plot? There were other things to make conversation about. "So," I said, "what colleges have you applied to?" I knew that, like me, he must have if he was hoping to apply the scholarship to one.

"All schools on the East Coast," he said, still looking out to the sky. After a second, he turned to me and said, "Mostly schools in or near New York City. All my life, I've just felt like…" He paused as if searching for the right wording. "I was meant to *do* something, you know? *Something.*" His voice had become animated as he was talking and he suddenly looked embarrassed. "What about you?"

"I applied to a couple around here and a couple in California."

"California?"

I shrugged. "I've always wanted to see the ocean."

Kyland watched me for a moment before giving a nod. "Yeah," he said simply. I stared back at him, my eyes darting down to his lips and suddenly, something ignited in the air—something unseen but real all the same. I felt it and I knew Kyland felt it too by the way he moved his head back very slightly. He adjusted himself where he sat. I felt my cheeks flush and was surprised at how hard it was to breathe properly. There was something intense and almost pained in Kyland's expression. He moved toward me, and up close like this, I could see a light sprinkling of freckles on his nose, under his tan—as if his childhood sat just beneath his skin. And the outer rim of his stormy gray eyes was a soft blue, like sunny days were there too, but off in the distance.

"Kyland—"

"Tenleigh." He leaned toward me, his breath just a whisper away, his voice strained. I breathed in his scent, a thrill racing down my spine. He smelled like a mixture of clean, pine-scented mountain air and something that must just be him—something that whispered to me in an intimate, secret way. Something I didn't need to analyze to understand. My eyelashes fluttered. I glanced down at his lips again. God, his lips were nice. And they looked so soft. Would they be soft on mine? My heart beat wildly in my chest as I waited for him to kiss me. He moved a centimeter closer and I held my breath.

"Have you been kissed before, Tenleigh?" he rasped as his hand went to the side of my head, his fingers weaving into my hair.

"No," I whispered, my body swaying toward him. No, but I wanted to be. Oh God, I wanted to be. I felt practically drunk with expectation. Would he touch me while he kissed me? Would his hands move over my body, under my clothes? A jolt of electricity raced up my thighs and ended between my legs.

I liked him so much. He was a boy who was sweet but would take charge. My blood was buzzing, racing through my veins.

His eyes gazed into mine for several frozen seconds until he squeezed his eyes shut and pulled away from me. I let out a huge breath as I tipped toward him and caught myself, pulling back suddenly too.

Kyland stood up and spun away from me, breathing hard. "You shouldn't give your first kiss to me."

What the…?

I blinked, feeling stunned, almost as if he'd just slapped my face. Humiliation engulfed me. I made a chuffing sound in the back of my throat and wrapped my arms around myself.

He turned toward me as suddenly as he'd turned away. "Why haven't you ever kissed anyone?"

I shrugged, feeling hot, my skin prickly. I lifted my chin. "I've never found anyone I wanted to kiss before," I said, going for nonchalance. But in actuality, it was pretty true.

"And you want to kiss me?"

I snorted.

Conceited asshole.

So not only was Kyland not going to kiss me, he was going to make me feel embarrassed and inexperienced? This was the *exact* reason I had sworn off men. "Not anymore." I stood up, grabbing my grocery bags and moving past him. But I was caught up short when he grabbed my hand and tugged. I whirled back around. "Let go of me," I hissed. "You're right. I don't want to kiss you. I'm going to go

42

away to college, and I'm going to let a real man kiss me, not some stupid hillbilly who thinks his lips are God's gift to Kentucky girls."

Kyland let go of my hand, looking truly insulted. "That's not what I think."

I made a sound of disgust and kept walking. I felt flushed all over and I was shaking, trying in vain to dismiss my deep sense of hurt and disappointment. "Well good, you shouldn't. You don't have anything every other man doesn't have too, Kyland Barrett," I called, and raced back toward the road and fast-walked all the way home. I had no idea if Kyland followed me or not and I told myself I didn't care.

CHAPTER FIVE
Tenleigh

The following week, on a blustery Sunday, I walked with Marlo down the hill. She was headed to work and I was headed to the Dennville Library.

"Don't stay long, okay?" Marlo said as we prepared to part ways.

"I won't. I just need a few new books." We tried our very best not to ever leave our mama alone for long in the trailer. Not that she would do something rash if she was taking her medication properly. But it was difficult to know if she was—we couldn't exactly force it down her throat, and counting pills hadn't worked. She knew well enough to hide the ones she wasn't taking if she decided to go off her medication. But either way, our mama was what I guess you would call *delicate*. If she wasn't sleeping, she didn't care for being alone. Frankly, it was exhausting, but it was the hand we'd been dealt, and we did what we had to because we had no other choice.

I often wondered what it was like to have parents that cared for *you*, rather than the other way around.

As we stepped onto Main Street's sidewalk, a man looking down at his phone was walking toward us. "Oh God, turn away!" Marlo hissed.

"Huh?"

Suddenly the man looked up. "I'm so sorry," he said, brushing my shoulder and taking a big step to the left. "Oh, hey. Tenleigh, right?"

I swore I heard Marlo let out a small exasperated groan. "Yeah. Hi, Dr. Nolan?" I glanced at Marlo and she had a small, phony smile on her face. I hadn't met Dr. Nolan before, but I had seen him and I knew he was a dentist who had set up a practice in Evansly. Apparently, he was here to save the Mountain Dew mouths of Appalachia—a valiant intention. Maybe he could brighten a few smiles. I couldn't help but cringe every time I saw a baby sucking down a bottle full of pop. Needless to say, I cringed a lot. And evidently, most of his clients, if they could pay at all, paid in things like homemade moonshine. And yet, he was still here. And surprisingly sober.

The other thing I knew about Dr. Nolan was that Marlo had had a one-night stand with him a few months back when he'd come into Al's for a Sunday afternoon beer.

And that she'd ignored him since. She was obviously how he knew my name.

"Call me Sam," he said, glancing around me at Marlo. "Hi, Marlo. How are you?" he asked, pushing his glasses up on his nose. Frankly, he was adorable in a Clark Kent sort of way. His hair was parted too severely; he wore black-framed glasses and a shirt buttoned all the way up to his throat. But he was handsome despite all that, and he looked fit. I glanced at Marlo, raising my eyebrows.

"Hi, Sam. I'm good. How are you?" she said, giving him a big, bright smile that was completely fake.

If a man was capable of swooning, he did. "Uh, I'm good. I came by Al's a couple times, but you weren't working," he said, his cheekbones flushing with color. Adorable.

I grinned over at Marlo.

"Oh. Sorry to hear I missed you, Sam. You must be busy with your practice." Marlo was speaking slowly with exaggerated formality. I squinted my eyes, trying to get a better read on her face.

"Oh, uh, yeah. I'm swamped." There was an awkward pause that he jumped in to fill. "You know tooth decay in Appalachia is a real epidemic." He glanced back and forth between Marlo and me. "Of course, your teeth are beautiful. You must take good care of them. Oral health is so... You must floss well, which is great. It's mostly the soda that's the problem, though. Or pop as you call it here. And a bad diet, of course..." He grimaced as if he was pained by the conversation.

I held back a grin. "We've observed the problem. What you're doing is very admirable."

"Oh, no, I get more out of it than anyone. To see a twelve-year-old come into my office with a mouth full of rot and then send him walking out with a beautiful smile, well, it's hard to explain that feeling. I have the ability to change someone's life, you know?" His eyes brightened and his voice was filled with enthusiasm. "There's nothing that compares to that." Clearly he was passionate about his endeavor. Adorable.

"Where are you from, Sam? You have an accent."

He chuckled. "I'm from Florida. To me, you have accents." He glanced at Marlo. "I love it."

Oh geez.

Marlo seemed unmoved. "Well," she said, "I need to get to work, so you have a good day, Sam. Tenleigh, I'll see you at home."

"Oh. You're going to work?" Sam asked. "Well, let me

46

drive you. I'm headed back to Evansly anyway. I was just dropping off my card to some homes in this area, trying to get to know all the folks in the community and letting people know I'd see them free of charge if they were interested."

Marlo hesitated and I jumped in. "Great! What a stroke of luck, Mar. I'll see you at home."

She stared daggers at me for a moment but then smiled over at Sam. "Okay, great. Thanks, Sam."

They turned to walk to his car, Sam waving at me and Marlo widening her eyes in a "we'll talk later" way. I turned around and headed toward the library, chuckling to myself. Either Marlo was trying *really* hard not to like Sam, or well, she really didn't like him. If I had to guess, I'd go with the former. I'd seen Marlo with guys I knew for a fact she wasn't interested in, and she didn't act like that. She also didn't cover her smile in front of Sam. I liked that most of all—he made her feel pretty.

I pulled the door to the library open—really nothing more than a small one-room shed with several bookshelves inside, holding as many books as could fit, and operating on the honor system. I had helped one of the teachers at my high school take up a fund to set it up several years ago and folks had donated what they could. The budget had been small and didn't buy many books, but it was better than nothing. And it was usually empty. So I was surprised to see someone standing at the shelf on the back wall leafing through a book.

I walked in quietly and as I got closer, I saw it was Kyland. *Stupid Kyland.* I couldn't mistake that broad back and the caramel-brown hair curling up at his neck. It looked like he was returning a book to the shelf. I cleared my throat and he whirled around, the book still in his hands. My eyes moved from his surprised expression down to the title he was holding, *The Weaver of Raveloe.*

Well, well. I leaned my hip against one of the shelves and crossed my arms over my layered sweaters, a feeling of satisfaction moving through my body as I took him in.

Kyland leaned back against the shelf behind him, sucking at his bottom lip. We stood there staring at each other for a minute in some kind of strange standoff, despite the fact that *I* was the only one who should be bitter here. "A little girl. That's what he found that winter night. Abandoned in the snow," he finally said.

I nodded slowly, my eyes moving over his face and hair, so carelessly handsome. "She gave his life meaning. She made him feel alive in a way he never had before."

"Then he lost all the gold he'd earned after he exiled himself."

I shrugged. "Yes, and it didn't matter. He didn't care about it once he found Eppie. She ended up being his greatest fortune because she gave purpose to his lonely life."

Something shifted behind Kyland's eyes. He turned around slowly and returned the book to its place. He must have checked it out the week before—after we'd talked and after I'd returned it. Just making conversation, my ass. He'd wanted to know how it ended.

"Are you going to check out another one?" I asked.

"No." It came out clipped and certain.

I walked toward him to return the one I'd finished reading, *The Bluest Eye.* I leaned toward Kyland to put the book back in its place. He didn't move to accommodate my closeness. "Well," I said, "if you were setting out to prove to me you're not the illiterate hillbilly I pegged you for, you—"

"Tenleigh." My eyes flew to his at the raspy sound of his voice.

There was something hard and resolute in Kyland's

expression. The air was thick with tension. We both stood silently, his jaw clenching. He moved even closer to me and my heart started beating wildly, my breath coming out raggedly, the anger I'd held on to since he'd rejected me, turning to confusion…and attraction. Dear God, he was beautiful and I could smell his skin, clean and masculine with the slight hint of salt. I wanted to open my mouth and breathe in the air around us so I could taste him on my tongue. My tummy flipped and my eyes fluttered. He continued to stare, seeming to note my body language and he looked…*mad*? Intense. I stood taller and lifted my chin. I didn't understand what was happening, but I wasn't backing down from this, whatever *this* was.

Kyland moved in close to my body until his face was right above mine. I looked up at him, blood whooshing through my body. "I'm going to leave here, Tenleigh. Nothing is going to stop me. Not you, not anything. Not anyone. Do you hear me?" His voice sounded strained, and his eyes were heated and yes… angry.

My breath quickened as I attempted to get hold of my racing heart, and scattered thoughts. I didn't need him to stay here. I didn't need him to feel indebted to me for any reason. But I did need him to kiss me. Right that very second. I moved my eyes to his lips and Kyland made a strangled, groaning sound in his throat and moved his face close to mine. "I'm leaving this place behind when I go. Everything about it. Even you."

Well, why wouldn't he? I was nothing to him.

"Okay," I gasped. He paused for one brief second, his eyes flaring, and then his lips met mine. He took my face in his hands, his fingers weaving through my hair and his tongue pushing into my mouth. My whole body felt like it would combust as I brought my arms around his neck and pressed myself into his hard form, melting into him. He groaned, a tortured sound, and tilted my head with his hands as his tongue plunged more deeply into my mouth. I moaned back, my tongue dancing with his, playing, tasting. I broke from his mouth, gasping in air as he nipped and kissed up my throat. "Yes, oh God, Kyland, don't stop," I begged. And if he would have laid me down on the floor right there and made love to me, I would have let him. I was very close to begging him to do just that. Blood pumped furiously between my legs causing a pounding drumbeat of need. My breasts felt heavy and achy.

His lips returned to mine and he plunged his tongue in and out of my mouth as if he were starving for me. *And I loved it.* I wanted the kiss to go on and on. I never ever wanted it to end.

Suddenly, Kyland pulled away from me and stepped back, breathing harshly, looking dazed and somehow still angry, the evidence of his own arousal tenting his jeans. "Holy *fuck*, Tenleigh. What are you doing?"

My blood ran cold as suddenly as it had heated only moments ago, my eyes widening as I stared incredulously at him. "What...what am *I* doing?"

And just like that, Kyland turned and walked out of the Dennville Public Library, leaving me alone and confused, my lips and my heart bruised.

I had let him do it to me again! What was wrong with *me?* I leaned against the bookshelf behind me and vowed never again to let Kyland Barrett humiliate me. He wasn't the only one with plans to leave here. *Why did he even have to register on my radar?* God, I *hated* him.

I had a sneaking suspicion you probably weren't supposed to think about someone you hated all day and all night.

50

Damn.

But I did make it a point to avoid Kyland Barrett the entire next week. Once I saw him at the end of a hallway in school and I made a sudden turn so I didn't have to pass him, and another time I glanced out the window of one of my classrooms and saw him outside walking with Shelly Galvin. I quickly looked away, jealousy filling my chest, making me feel angry and brittle. He hadn't seemed to have a problem kissing *her.*

Again, this was why it was my plan to avoid men around these parts—they were either entitled users or backwoods losers. For a brief moment, I had thought Kyland was different, but he wasn't. He had purposely humiliated me, knowing I was attracted to him. Well, never again. There were plenty of other girls happy to have him play with them around here. He wouldn't die of loneliness anytime soon. I had seen proof of that.

I sat chewing on my pencil, unable to get him off my mind, though. I had liked him. I had allowed myself to think about him as I lay on the small couch in our trailer, drifting off to sleep. I had dreamed of him staring into my eyes with the same wondrous expression he'd worn as he looked at the sunset. I had dreamed of him touching me, kissing me, even loving me. I had dreamed of seeing him with his shirt off, my fingers trailing down his warm, suntanned skin... Even though my mind had warned me to stop dreaming, the very thought of it had sent a current of electricity straight to my heart. *Stop, Tenleigh. Just stop.*

Plan Swear Off Men: officially reinstated.

After school, I went to the library so I wouldn't encounter Kyland walking up the hill to his home. I knew he wouldn't be checking out any more books. I was safe—and I liked it there. It was like my own personal office. I could sit at the small table in the back, spread my homework out, and have all the privacy I needed. No one in this town was too interested in reading except for me. And it was a lot more comfortable than the small pullout table in our trailer, the one that squeaked every time I pressed down on it to write.

My breath plumed in the early December air as I made my way quickly to the small building. I rushed inside, closing the door behind me, breathing in the slightly musty air. There wasn't any heat in here, but it was warmer than outside, and it'd certainly be a lot warmer than our drafty trailer. I spread my stuff out on the table in the back and got started on my homework. I lingered over my assignments, not wanting to leave, happy in my solitude.

A little while later, when I closed my binder and stood up to choose a new book, I noticed a small white piece of paper sticking out of *The Bluest Eye*, the novel I'd returned right before Kyland kissed me. Recalling his kiss, I childishly made a disgusted sound aloud in the quiet room—just because it felt good—and then reached for the book. I pulled out the slip of paper, my heart skipping a beat when I saw tiny, slanted script:

One of the bleakest books I've ever read, offering no hope whatsoever. Made me want to throw myself off the nearest cliff.—KB

I paused, reading the line over again. KB. Kyland Barrett. Was he trying to be funny? My anger rose as I sat to write my reply:

Only an ignorant hick would fail to see the true point of this novel, which is that we all have an internal dialogue that either keeps us trapped or sets us free. As far as a cliff, I'd suggest Dead Man's Bluff—the name alone is optimistic as far as your cause. In addition, it's the highest one in the area and offers lots of jagged rocks in the basin, practically guaranteeing your demise.—TF

I smiled and stuck the paper between the pages, leaving it sticking out the top. Then I perused the books I'd read, looking for the most depressing, disturbing one I could, finally pulling *Brighton Rock* off the shelf, leaving an obvious gap where it had sat.

Two days later, I brought it back and three days after that, when I returned to the library, a note was sticking out of the top:

An enjoyable read. I was especially impressed by the character Pinkie.—KB

I made a disgusted sound in my throat, quickly scrawling out:

Only a truly disturbed person would be impressed by a villainous, sociopathic gang leader, who cruelly destroyed the beautiful, decent girl who loved him. What happened to Dead Man's Bluff?—TF

Then I looked over the shelf, choosing a book that was not only depressing, but disgusting as well.

Five days later, *The Road*:

An exciting tale of the Apocalypse...survival...cannibalism... underground bunkers. A book every guy will devour!—KB

I frowned.

I see what you did there with the word "devour." You really are a sicko.—TF

I went for gusto, choosing arguably the most depressing book ever written.
Four days later, *The Bell Jar.*

Nice try. I'm onto you.—KB

I laughed out loud despite myself. And damn him, I had tried to hang on to my anger and now here I was smiling at his damn note. The smile faded slowly. I perused the shelf for another book, some kind of melancholy gripping my stupid, lonely heart. I leaned back against the bookshelf, biting my lip. I liked him. Still. Even after he'd hurt me. And what was the point? And why he was bothering to amuse himself with me, I didn't know. But I had seen what happened when a woman got hung up on a man who wasn't interested in her, and I wasn't going there. I was not. Better to leave things as they were. I wasn't going to encourage this game. It would only create hope, and when it came to Kyland, hope was not something I would entertain. I sighed and gathered up my stuff, leaving the library and lowering my head against the cold as I trudged up the mountain.

CHAPTER SIX
Kyland

I went to the small library every morning for the next week, but there was never a note waiting for me. I tried to convince myself it didn't matter—it'd just been a fun distraction, and I'd actually enjoyed the books. They'd helped me pass several lonely nights. But the truth was, I was disappointed that Tenleigh, apparently, was done with our exchange. And I gathered she might still be mad at me. Who could blame her? I'd acted like an idiot, kissing her after I'd vowed not to, and then acting as if it was her fault. I just felt so damn helpless around her and it pissed me off.

I brought my fingers to my lips as if some small part of her still remained there. God, she'd tasted so good, even better than I'd imagined. It had taken everything in me to pull away and I'd dreamed about that damn kiss every night since. I wasn't going to do it again, though. As much as I wanted to. I wasn't going to take something from her I could never give back—her heart, her purity. Tenleigh had had enough taken from her in this life. I wasn't going to be responsible for giving her false hope and then leaving her high and dry when I left. She deserved better.

And as for me, I didn't want any connection to Dennville, Kentucky. I wanted to leave and never ever look back—in every sense. There would be no forming connections with dreamy-eyed girls who'd expect me to write them love letters from my college dorm. I planned to be kissing *plenty* of girls, now and after I left, but none of them would be Tenleigh Falyn. That's just the way it needed to be.

I walked out of the library and shut the door tightly behind me.

It was a bitterly cold morning, snow still on the ground from several recent snowfalls, and I'd stupidly forgotten my gloves. I stuffed my hands in my pockets and headed toward the road home. "Hey, Ky," I heard from behind me.

I looked over my shoulder and saw Shelly. "Hey."

She smiled and increased her speed to catch up, meeting me and looping her arm through mine. She squeezed me to her and said, "Brr! It's cold."

I nodded, wanting to shrug her off but resisting. Shelly and I messed around when one or the other of us wanted to. It'd been going on since we were fifteen. I considered it casual, and I was mostly sure she did too. Although she didn't seem to like it when she found out I'd been with someone else. Secretly, I hoped she'd find a boyfriend and move on even from our casual encounters. They were starting to bore me. Shelly never said unexpected things that caught me off guard. Shelly never got faraway dreamy looks on her face. But Shelly, like me, seemed to prefer casual. And Shelly met my other requirement too: she didn't live up on the mountain—she was poor, but not the desperate kind of poor. Not poor like Tenleigh was poor. I felt an odd clunk in my chest and gritted my teeth. I didn't need to worry about the survival of anyone other than myself.

"Where are you headed?" I asked.

"Well, I was headed to Rusty's for an ingredient my grandma forgot to buy for dinner. But..."—she looked up at me flirtatiously—"no one will notice I'm gone if I don't get back for a little while."

"I'm headed home, Shelly. My mama needs me," I lied.

Her expression fell. "Well, all right, then. Hey, wanna come with me to the play at school later? They're performing *A Christmas Carol*." She grinned. I knew Shelly liked to get out of her house whenever she could. She was stuffed in there with her dad and four brothers. Her mama had died when she was little. She described her home like it was a zoo, but truthfully, it didn't sound half-bad to me—at least no one was ever lonely.

"Is it Christmastime already?" I asked. I knew very well it was Christmastime. And I hated it. I had successfully avoided the major funk I usually found myself in this time of year with the little book club Tenleigh and I had going on, but now I'd have to deal with it.

Tenleigh. *Stop, Kyland. Stop thinking about Tenleigh.*

I put my arm around Shelly and pulled her closer and she smiled up at me. "It's the twenty-fourth, Ky," she said. "Winter break started two days ago. Did you not notice?" she asked on a laugh.

"No. I noticed. I was just kidding." And truthfully, getting out of my house later didn't sound half-bad, and they always offered food at intermission. Some of it might even be more than cookies or cupcakes. Last year, they'd had these little pigs in a blanket...

57

"Yeah, all right, let's go see the play tonight. Sounds festive." We stopped in front of Rusty's.

"Good! My brothers are going too, so I'll meet you there." She squeezed me tighter. "And if you're free afterward…" She let that idea linger, letting go of me and blowing me a kiss as she walked away.

I met Shelly outside the school, my boots soaked from walking through the snow. I stomped them off and brushed the snowflakes off my hair as Shelly grinned at me and pretended to shiver as she pulled her red wool coat around her. "I'm freezing. Warm me up." She latched on to my arm and pressed herself into my body. Her strong vanilla fragrance filled my nostrils.

We went inside the warm lobby, a large decorated tree in the middle of the open space. The school went all out for the Christmas play. Most likely, I thought, because many of the parents from Evansly, the ones who worked in the executive offices of the mine, would be there. As I looked around, I saw several of them, their thick winter coats and fur-trimmed boots and hats giving them away. Shelly took my hand and led me inside to some empty seats near the middle of the auditorium. There was a low buzz of voices—chatter and laughter—and the room was dim and warm. I was suddenly glad I'd trudged through the weather to come here. I looked forward to the refreshments that would be served during intermission—it'd been a rough month. Heating my house, at least enough to survive, became as much of a priority as eating. When I was younger, I used to chip coal off the highway embankment. But it was illegal, and a very *public* illegal act at that, and I didn't think it was worth the risk. I was so close to everything I'd worked for... *so close*. I followed Shelly, scooting past the people already seated in the row she'd chosen.

We sat down, and Shelly removed her jacket and leaned back, letting out a sigh of comfort as she grabbed my hand. I looked over at her...and met Tenleigh's eyes sitting right next to Shelly. I jolted and couldn't help the smile that immediately took over my face. "Tenleigh, hey," I said, leaning forward, and there was almost a feeling of relief that moved through my chest as if I'd been waiting to see her for far too long. *Had I?*

Tenleigh looked slightly stricken but didn't say anything as her eyes moved from mine down to my lap, where Shelly's and my hands were linked. I let go quickly, as if I'd been caught doing something wrong, and Shelly frowned. Then she looked next to her at Tenleigh and back to me, her frown growing. She grabbed my hand again just as the lights dimmed. I sat back, feeling uncomfortable, jittery, and telling myself I shouldn't. Tenleigh and I didn't have anything more than a friendship...if even that. And neither did Shelly and I, as a matter of fact. Although I'd certainly been more intimate with Shelly. So why did I feel as if I'd done something wrong to *Tenleigh*? Why did I suddenly feel guilty and distracted by her presence right next to us? Why did I suddenly feel the need to *explain* this to her?

The show started and I didn't hear a word of it. I tried to see Tenleigh in my peripheral vision, but she had leaned all the way back and Shelly was now blocking her. I glanced at her quickly when a kid started crying in the aisle down from us and saw that she was staring straight ahead, rigid.

Suddenly, Shelly took her jacket from behind her and spread it on her lap as if she were cold, moving it so it covered half of me as well. I felt her hand moving over my crotch and jumped slightly. She ran her palm over my dick and then squeezed it through my jeans, still looking straight ahead, a small smile on her lips. I reached under the jacket and removed her hand from my body and put it on top of her coat. I felt her questioning gaze on me but didn't look her way.

I sat through the first half of the play tense and uncomfortable, trying my best to get into the performance, but to no avail. I was painfully aware of Tenleigh, as if she were some sort of magnet, not allowing me to feel anything other than the pull of her mere presence.

Relief swept through me when the lights came on and flashed for intermission. In the few seconds it took me to stand, Tenleigh had already turned and headed out the other side of the row we were in, moving with the crowd toward the lobby.

I followed the people in front of me out the other side of the aisle, Shelly right behind me, and looked around in every direction, peering over the heads of those in front of me when we flowed out into the lobby.

Shelly was saying something behind me, but I wasn't paying attention.

The smell of coffee and sweets filled the open space and Shelly pulled me over to a line at a table. "Are you hungry?" she asked.

Always. But not for food right now. For...something. For someone.

"Yeah, sure." I walked with Shelly to one of the tables laden with food and stood in line, continuing to look around.

All of a sudden, the outside door opened and a woman stood there, hair blanketed in snow, wearing only a wet evening gown, and what looked like a dingy-looking pageant sash. I blinked and focused in on her. *Oh shit.* It was Tenleigh's mama. And she looked like a crazy, drowned rat. The dress clung tightly to her body, clearly showing her puckered, pink nipples and a dark triangle of pubic hair. Oh no.

She was shivering violently, but at the sight of the crowd, she seemed to instantly warm as a bright smile took over her face and she pulled her shoulders back, gliding forward into the lobby where everyone was now growing silent as they all stared, confused expressions on their faces, some younger kids snickering.

I looked around desperately for Tenleigh, a need to protect her from what I sensed was coming, gripping me, making me feel desperate, hot, itchy.

"Eddie," Tenleigh's mama singsonged, moving more quickly toward someone standing at the back of the lobby. "Eddie, darling. I'm sorry I'm late." My head swiveled and my eyes first fastened on Tenleigh, standing frozen, a look of horrified shock on her face, and then followed her gaze to Edward Kearney.

Shit. Fuck.

He was staring at Tenleigh's mama as she came toward him, his eyes wide, his expression one of pure and open horror. His wife, standing next to him said quietly, "Oh my God," as she gathered a girl who looked to be about ten years old to her. Her tone was full of disgust.

Suddenly the door swung open again and everyone's head swiveled as a woman I recognized as Tenleigh's sister burst through, wet and shivering like her mother, without the proper snow attire on. I started making my way over to Tenleigh as quickly as I could, as Tenleigh's sister called out,

"Mama! Come here." I looked back at her as she let out an embarrassed laugh, looking around, obviously trying to act as casual as she could in this awful, embarrassing, very public situation.

I felt someone grab my hand and tug, and when I looked backward, it was Shelly. I shook her free and turned back to Tenleigh.

Tenleigh's mama looked behind her, a confused smile on her face, and when she saw her daughter, she stopped and said, "My goodness, Marlo, what are you doing?"

"Mama, we're not supposed to be *here*," she said, reaching her, and grabbing her hand. I moved closer to Tenleigh and I heard Shelly call after me once, but ignored her.

"Of course we're supposed to be here," she said. "This is where Eddie is. Eddie!" she called again, trying to move toward him. "Eddie, baby, I knew you'd be here, I walked all this way..."

"Mama," Marlo hissed, pulling on her harder. Tenleigh was moving toward them now too, away from me. I wanted to call out to her, but I didn't want to call attention *to* her.

"Jesus Christ, she's a nut," I heard Edward Kearney say to my right. "Let's get out of here, Diane. There's a side door."

Tenleigh reached her mother, took her other arm, and tried to help Marlo guide her to the front door, but when her mother saw Eddie and his family leaving, she tried to race forward. Marlo lurched to grab her, and Tenleigh tripped over Marlo's feet and went sprawling onto the floor, letting out a pained cry. *Shit! Shit! Shit!* I ran toward her.

Marlo grabbed her mama as her mama started screeching, "Eddie! Eddie!" turning around to flail out at Marlo, connecting with her face as Marlo cried out too.

I reached Tenleigh and grabbed her under the arms,

lifting her up and pulling her into me and to the side, as her mother continued to screech and wail and punch out at Marlo. I started to step forward to help Marlo when a couple men I recognized as local police officers who must have had kids in the play rushed forward and grabbed hold of Tenleigh's mama. She clawed at them and screamed Eddie's name.

As she fought, her dress fell off her shoulder and exposed one of her breasts. I looked away.

"Get her in your car, Bill," one of the men said. "She practically has hypothermia." The man named Bill took off his sports coat and wrapped it around Tenleigh's mama's shoulders, although she continued to struggle weakly.

"Will you drive us to the hospital?" I heard Marlo say to the officers as I looked back to Tenleigh.

"Of course we will," one of the men answered.

Marlo looked behind her as the men held her mother up and began walking her out of the building. The look on Marlo's face was panicked as she looked between their mama and Tenleigh, clearly unsure about leaving her sister. I clasped Tenleigh's hand in mine. "I'll walk her home. I'll make sure she's safe," I said.

Marlo's eyes darted to Tenleigh's and Tenleigh nodded her consent. Marlo's face relaxed very slightly and she mouthed, *Okay. My turn. Meet you at home.*

As her mother was practically dragged from the building, I looked at Tenleigh. She seemed to be in shock, her cheeks bright pink, her neck covered in red splotches as she stared straight ahead. "Tenleigh," I said gently as she took her hand away.

Her eyes moved to mine and the heartbreak I saw there made my chest squeeze so tightly, I almost brought my hand up to massage the pain away. She looked shell-shocked as her eyes moved slowly around the room, people still gawking at her and talking in whispers that weren't soft enough not to float above the crowd.

...crazy...affair years back...never right...gotten worse... shameful...disgusting.

I wished they'd all shut the fuck up. *Tenleigh doesn't deserve this.*

"Tenleigh, I need to go tell someone I'm leaving and then I'm going to take you home, all right?" As she looked at me, some sort of understanding seemed to come into her eyes. But she remained quiet, the same look of devastation on her face. "Okay," I confirmed. "I'll be right back. Stay right here. I'll be right back," I repeated.

I started making my way back to Shelly—it wasn't like I was her ride, but I figured it was the decent thing to do, and I heard the door slam behind me. I glanced back and Tenleigh was gone. *Shit.* I looked over to where Shelly was standing watching me expectantly, pausing only briefly before I turned and ran after Tenleigh.

CHAPTER SEVEN
Tenleigh

The tears started before I'd even taken three steps out of the school. The sudden blast of cold was like a slap to my face. It felt like the physical version of what I'd just experienced emotionally, in front of most of the student body and a good number of parents too—humiliation and deep, deep shame. I ran faster, the wind hitting my skin like razor blades, my feet slipping on the icy road.

"Tenleigh!" I heard called behind me. Kyland. Stupid Kyland who had sat two seats away from me in the dark theater as a girl fondled him under her jacket. And I had no right to be filled with hot, painful jealousy. And yet I had been. He hadn't even wanted to kiss me. He'd made that blatantly clear by pushing me away, and yet seeing him with another girl sent hurt ratcheting down my spine. I'd wanted to cry and throttle her...or him, or both, I wasn't even sure. And I had no right—I was no one to him. All my *life* I was just a nothing, a nobody. And it hurt so badly.

"Go away, Kyland!" I screamed back at him, hiccupping and picking up speed.

"Tenleigh, stop! You're going to hurt yourself. Stop!"

"What do you care?" I yelled, still running, slipping and jutting my arms to the side, righting myself before I went down.

"Tenleigh!" I heard him gaining on me and so I picked up some snow and turned around and threw it at him, letting out a small sob. I was being an immature child—I knew it. And yet it didn't seem that I had anything to lose. The snowball hit him in the shoulder and I turned and kept running, my steps clunky and ungraceful in the snow.

"Jesus, Tenleigh!" Kyland yelled. I turned around and picked up more snow and started hurling it at him over and over as he ducked and swore but kept coming toward me. I turned around again and ran. I got about three steps and my feet went out from under me, sending me sprawling into a snowbank to my right where I lay sobbing, staring up at the clear winter sky as fat snowflakes fell on my face. I felt utterly desolate and utterly alone.

I registered Kyland's footsteps quickly approaching and then I was scooped up, his warm arms around me, lifting me out of the snow as I continued to cry, the fight in me gone. "Shh, I've got you," I heard in Kyland's smooth, masculine voice. "You're okay. You're okay, Tenleigh. I've got you."

"I don't want you to have me."

He sighed. "Well. I do. I do. I've got you."

I wrapped my arms around his neck, shivering, trying to press myself closer into his warmth, his soothing words.

He carried me a little ways and then sat down and held me to him as I cried more tears from a seemingly never-ending reservoir of pain. He was murmuring something against the top of my head that I didn't compute, words of comfort. And although I didn't process them, they soothed me all the same. And I needed that so badly, just to be soothed. To be held. To matter to someone. Even for a moment.

I thought back to the looks on the faces around me as my mama was dragged down to the ground in her dingy, see-through dress. I squeezed my eyes shut. It had to be one of the worst hurts in the entire world—being embarrassed by someone who was meant to protect you, not humiliate you. And yet I still loved her so much.

After a little bit, my tears stopped, but I didn't lift my head. Kyland kept gripping me tightly, and when I finally looked around, I saw that we were sitting in the doorway of a closed hairdressing shop—protected from the weather by the small overhang above the door. We sat together, breathing, still shivering slightly, Kyland's arms around me as I gripped his coat in my fists and took comfort in his closeness.

"Kyland," I finally murmured.

"Yes, Tenleigh?"

"I'm sorry I threw snow at you," I whispered.

"It's okay. I deserved it... Tenleigh, I'm sorry for tonight. With Shelly...it..." He sounded unsure of what to say.

I released a defeated sigh. "You don't have anything to apologize for. You made it clear that we're not anything to each other." I glanced up at him and he was running his tongue thoughtfully over his bottom lip, a small frown creasing his brow. I didn't blame him for not wanting to kiss me. Who would want to kiss the daughter of the town crazy? Who would want to attach himself to a girl like me? The thing I heard kids sometimes whispering at school was true—I was nothing but trailer trash. He might be poor too, but his parents didn't humiliate him in public. In fact, his father and his brother died heroically, working hard to provide for their family. My own father had taken one look at me and hit the road. A tremor ran through me as much from the cold as from thoughts of *him*. I pushed them away. I desperately needed to lighten the mood, or I'd break.

I lifted my head and met Kyland's eyes—dark and in shadow in the dim light of the covered doorway. "I have to tell you something," I said.

He used his thumb to wipe away a tear still on my cheek. "What do you have to tell me?" he asked softly.

"I'm not really the daughter of a Russian prince."

He blinked at me and then laughed, sudden and deep and warm.

I let out a small laugh too, and started to remove myself from his arms. But he held me tighter, so I sunk back into him, knowing I was all over the place and suddenly not caring. I needed to smile. I needed some tenderness. God knew I did. And right that second, I was going to take what Kyland was offering me. It may be temporary, but it would be enough for now.

"No family jewels?" he asked.

"Not a family *pebble*. Not even a family grain of sand."

I heard his lips move into a smile.

"That was just a stupid pretend game my sister and I used to play."

"It wasn't stupid," he murmured.

"It was," I said, my voice breaking again. Kyland didn't answer, but his arms tightened around me. I wished I had known that it was dangerous for girls like us to pretend to be princesses. In that moment, dreaming of anything felt dangerous. Dreams failed, and when they did, reality hurt that much more.

"I have to tell you something too," he said.

"What?" I sniffled.

"There aren't really any bobcats on our mountain. I mean, there are, but they're no danger to us. The Bobcat Protection Service was all a ruse."

"I know," I said softly. I had enjoyed his company too. I figured that's why he had made it up.

We held on to each other in the doorway for a little while until the wind changed directions and found us again and we both started shivering.

"Let's get you home," Kyland said, helping me to a standing position.

"I'm okay now. I know you left Shelly behind—"

"Shelly got a ride with her brothers. I went for the food and the heat." He stuffed his hands in his pockets.

Oh.

"Yeah, me too," I admitted. We each let out an embarrassed laugh.

"Tenleigh...I'm sorry I kissed you." He grimaced. "I mean, shit...I'm not sorry I kissed you. What I'm sorry about is that I'm not going to do it again." He laughed a small, uncomfortable laugh. "I mean, I'm sorry for me, not for you. I know I'm missing out. I'm missing... The truth is, Tenleigh, you might have noticed, I'm not exactly a catch anyway."

Sympathy filled me, and understanding. Forgiveness. Maybe the truth was that neither of us was exactly a catch—somehow, though, that didn't make me feel better. And somehow, Kyland telling me he wasn't a catch felt like a lie he didn't even know he was telling.

"I don't have anything to offer. In six months, I won't even be here," he said.

"Kyland," I interrupted, "how about this? Let's just be friends. I could use a friend, I guess." I paused, thinking. "And when we both leave here, under whatever circumstances we do, when we both *are* catches, we'll remember fondly the friend we once had back home and that'll be that. Okay? Simple." My eyes welled up with tears again and I wasn't even sure why. It didn't feel simple. I wished it did. "Do you have any friends?" I asked. So often, I'd seen him alone.

He shook his head, staring at me, the wheels turning behind his eyes. I couldn't read the expression on his face. "I haven't had a real friend since my brother died."

It felt like a balloon was inflating in my chest, pain for him replacing my own and making it difficult to take a full breath. "Seems like we could both use one then."

"Yeah," he finally said. His voice sounded sad. "Yeah."

CHAPTER EIGHT
Tenleigh

I put my head down against the sting of the wind and cold as we started to walk. After trudging along for a little bit, my feet were wet and I started shivering again. Kyland put his arm around me and pulled me close and I let him. By the time we made it to Dennville, the snow had stopped. My feet were still wet, but I was a little warmer from walking and from Kyland's warmth.

"I should call the hospital to make sure Marlo and my mama made it there," I said. There was a pay phone outside the old post office—a rarity nowadays from what I knew. But up on our mountain, cell phone reception was sketchy and many people didn't have landlines. As for us, we couldn't afford either. Kyland nodded and guided me to the small booth, where I used the phone book to look up the number to the hospital where we always took Mama—the hospital that accepted Medicaid. I fished fifty cents out of my pocket. A few minutes later they had patched me through to the floor my mama was on and were able to put Marlo on the phone.

"Hey, Ten. I'm so sorry. I was watching her. I just took a damn shower. Are you almost home?"

"Yes, and don't be sorry, Marlo. You and I both know it wasn't your fault. I'm okay. I promise. Do you need me? I could probably figure out a way to get there."

"No. It's my turn. You stayed here last time. You even missed school. And I don't have to work until Tuesday. I'm just sorry you'll spend the holiday alone. We might be here for a few days. I didn't even think about Christmas until I got here and saw the tree in the hospital lobby."

"I'm good. Don't worry about me. I love you." We both knew Christmas didn't mean much in our trailer anyway. It was just another day.

"I love you too, baby sis. Oh hey, they need me to fill something out. Call me here if you need anything, okay? I'll be curled up in the waiting room, but I'll check for messages at the nurses' station."

Well, at least she'd be warm in the waiting room. "Okay. Bye, Mar."

"Bye, Ten."

I paused for a second, staring at the phone and when Kyland looked at me questioningly, breathing into his hands to warm them up, I said, "They're okay. Settled in. They'll be there through Christmas, which...well." I took a deep breath. "That's just the way it is." I was silent again, considering something before I picked up the phone book again and looked up a number in Evansly. After a couple rings, a man's voice answered.

"Hi, Dr. Nolan? Sam?"

"Yes? How can I help you?"

I cleared my throat. "This is Tenleigh Falyn...I, shoot I..." I suddenly had doubts. Marlo would kill me. What was I doing?

"Tenleigh, what's wrong?" he asked.

"I...well, our mama, uh...had an incident and well, Marlo's at the hospital with her and I just thought, I mean, I wondered if you'd want to..."

"I'm putting my jacket on, Tenleigh. Which floor is she on?"

"The twelfth." I knew because we'd been there so much.

He was quiet for a second. "The mental ward?"

"Yes," I whispered, closing my eyes, shame making me doubt what I was doing again. "I know you're a dentist, not a doctor, but I thought...God, I don't even know. I'm sorry. It's Christmas Eve." I glanced at Kyland, who was watching me closely as I fumbled my way through the phone call.

"You did the right thing. At the very least I can go and keep Marlo company. Are you okay?"

I released a breath. "Yes, I'm fine. And that's really nice of you," I said, gratitude making my voice squeaky.

"I'm really glad you called me. Thank you."

"No, thank you. Truly, thank you. Bye, Sam."

I hung up and took a deep, calming breath. Marlo would likely murder me, but I felt good about what I'd done. Maybe Marlo didn't want to date him, but he was a nice guy. I had a good feeling about him. And everyone could use a nice friend or two, right?

"That was a friend of Marlo's," I said to Kyland. "I just called him to see if he would go sit with Marlo. The floor my mama's on, it's not the most pleasant of places, and there's absolutely nothing to do except read the same brochures again and again."

He nodded sadly, and we set off up the hill. I was glad Kyland didn't ask me any questions at that moment—I wasn't quite ready to say any more. Half an hour later, we were at my trailer, where I threw the door open and we hurried in. At least Marlo had closed the door before running after Mama or it'd be

73

freezing inside. Our breath still plumed in the air. I turned on the two small portable heaters we had, although I knew it'd be a while before our drafty old trailer felt even remotely comfortable. I started stripping my wet boots off, and when I looked up at Kyland, he was standing by the doorway uncomfortably.

"You should get dry," I said. "I mean…unless you need to get home. Oh!" I slapped my forehead. "You need to get home. Your mama—"

He shook his head. "No. My mama's fine. She's not waiting up for me. I just…I wish I could offer you a ride to the hospital. Will your sister need you there?"

I threw my boots aside and started peeling off my wet socks, still shivering. "No. We…take turns. It's what we do," I said. I didn't offer more than that, but Kyland nodded as if he understood, removing his shoes and socks too. We took off our coats and I tossed him a blanket folded up on the couch where I slept. I pulled one around me as well and settled back, nodding to the spot next to me.

He hesitated for a second but then sat down and pulled a blanket around himself too.

"I like your tree," he said, nodding at our miniature Christmas tree.

I smiled. "Thanks." We'd cut it down ourselves. It was a little lopsided and we didn't have a lot of decorations, but we had a string of white lights and I loved them. Somehow, even our small, dingy trailer looked pretty in the glow of those twinkle lights.

We were quiet for a minute before he spoke. "Tenleigh, I'll understand if you don't want to talk about it, but if you do…"

"My mama? You mean what's wrong with her?"

He nodded.

I pulled the blanket more tightly around me, finally

feeling warm. The wind whistled mournfully through the trees outside.

"My daddy brought her here when she was pregnant with Marlo. He left when I was three days old. Walked right out the front door of this trailer and never looked back."

"Shit, I'm sorry."

"Don't be. Not for me at least. I never knew him, and after what he did to my mama, I'm glad I didn't."

"Is that what…" Kyland paused, seeming to be searching for the right words.

"Made her the way she is?" I shook my head. "No. I mean… maybe it made her worse, I don't know, but my mama, she's always been up and down…delusional sometimes. The doctor in town who prescribes her medication says she has a depressive disorder, but I'm not sure. It seems like a little more than that and he doesn't seem to know what he's talking about anyway." It was weird to talk about this with anyone except Marlo. But I found that the words flowed more freely than I would have thought and part of that was because of the way Kyland was listening so attentively, empathy in his eyes, but no pity.

"My mama met my daddy at one of her pageants," I went on. "She used to be a beauty queen—her big claim to fame was the Miss Kentucky Sunburst win." I gave a short, humorless laugh. That damn pageant that was the highlight of Mama's life. "Anyway, my daddy was working as part of the lighting crew and they fell madly in love. Or at least that's what my mama says. She came from a good family, but when she told them she was pregnant and running off with a tattooed boy from a small mining town, they disowned her. She's tried to contact them over the years, but they won't even take her calls." I shook my head. "He moved her here, worked at the mine for a couple years, decided a wife and family didn't work out so well for him, and hit the road. That was that." I brushed my hands together indicating what my daddy had done with us: brushed off, brushed aside.

"What happened with your mama and Edward Kearney?" he asked.

Oh. This subject was harder. I sighed. "They started having an affair when I was eight and Marlo was eleven. He told her he was going to leave his wife, take care of us, move us into his big house in town. My mama, she thought he was some sort of savior."

"Are you sure that's true? I mean, if your mama sort of has a skewed—"

I shook my head. "That's what he told her. This trailer is small, the walls are thin." I looked at him pointedly.

His eyes widened. "He came here?"

"Yup. All the time."

He ran his hand through his hair, his lips pressed together. "Jesus. What a fucking pig." He looked like he wanted to say more, but he didn't.

"He liked it, I think. Coming here. I could see it in his eyes. It gave him some sort of weird thrill. He'd leave money on the table before he left."

Kyland made another disgusted sound in his throat.

"Anyway, this went on for a couple years. He used my mama like she was a whore. She thought he was in love with her." I shook my head again. "One year, my mama dragged us into town to confront him and his wife. The three of us walked eight miles to his house, knocked right on his front door. She refused to be talked out of it. I was so humiliated." I looked to the side, running my index finger along my lower lip, the despair of that moment coming back to me. I didn't want to meet Kyland's eyes.

76

Kyland remained quiet, waiting for me to continue.

"Edward, he came to the door, and when my mama told him why she was there, he spit on her." I turned my eyes to Kyland's. "He *spit* on her," I repeated. "And then he slammed the door in her face. His son Jamie... you know Jamie from school, right?" Kyland gave a nod. "I saw him watching from an upstairs window." It'd made the shame that much worse. It was why I avoided him at school. I refused to even make eye contact.

"Tenleigh," he whispered. "I'm so sorry he did that to you all."

I looked off behind Kyland, picturing the way the sky was a deep, twilight blue, picturing the look of devastation on my mama's face, picturing the dust our shoes kicked up as we walked silently home, looking down the whole way. But I acknowledged his understanding words with a nod and a sigh. "It's just the way it is, I guess."

"No wonder you swore off men," he said, tilting his head and giving me a teasing smile.

I smiled back. It was just what I'd needed to drag me out of those awful memories. "That's why it's a good thing we're just friends."

He chuckled. After a second he asked, "Do you feel weird about applying for the scholarship with Edward Kearney being the administrator and all?"

"Not really. Tyton Coal awards it. He's just the face for it. And if it helps me get out of here, I'm willing to set aside any pride I might have about that."

He nodded, looking thoughtful, his eyes focused downward.

After a few beats, he brought his eyes to mine. God, he was so handsome. Our gazes met and held. I blinked, warmth unfurling in my belly. "Do you want some hot chocolate?"

"Uh, yeah, sure."

I got up, the blanket still around me, and went to the small kitchen at the front of the trailer. Kyland followed me, his blanket around him as well. As I went about boiling water, Kyland watched me, leaning his hip against the small doorway. I looked away, concentrating on my task. His masculinity suddenly seemed to fill the trailer. Maybe it was because I wasn't used to having a male share my space, or maybe it was just because I was hyperaware of him in general. And I hated that. I hated it because we *were* friends. I'd declared it myself. After he'd told me he'd never kiss me again, true. But if we weren't going to kiss, then it was either friends or nothing. And I found... well, I didn't want nothing.

I poured the hot water into the two mugs I'd already dumped the hot chocolate mix into, turned off the hotplate, and then handed one of the mugs to Kyland. Our hands brushed when he took the handle from me and our eyes both darted upward. "Sorry," I whispered.

"For what?"

"Um..." *For not being able to stop wanting you to kiss me until I'm breathless. For not being able to stop thinking about the way you tasted. For wondering if I'll ever feel the same thrill again that I felt when your lips first touched mine. For lying and pretending I'm happy just being your friend.* "For making it so hot." My eyes moved down to the mug in his hand.

"Hot is good. It'll warm us up."

I scooted past him. I needed some space. What I really needed was a blast of frigid winter air in my face, but I wasn't willing to freeze myself again now that I was finally getting warm.

What do friends do?

"So...do you want to play Scrabble or something? I have a few old board games. They were my dad's."

"Sure. What do you have?"

"Uh, let me look." I went over to a small closet and peered inside at the top shelf. It'd been forever since Marlo and I had played a board game. Suddenly, it sounded like a really fun idea. "Scrabble...Uno...Monopoly..."

"Monopoly!" Kyland said enthusiastically. I laughed and reached for the game.

I sat on the couch and Kyland sat down next to me as I pulled the coffee table closer to us and started setting it up.

"What's this?" he asked, unfolding the small piece of paper that had fallen from the box that I could see had Marlo's handwriting on it. "Don't ever play this game with Ten—"

I grabbed the note from him, crumpled it up, and threw it across the room. "That's nothing," I said. *Really, Marlo? Leaving instructions for my future monopoly opponents?* I loved my sister, but the girl had no competitive spirit.

I placed the money tray in front of me so I could be the banker and handing him the real estate cards.

"I'd rather be the banker," he said.

I frowned. I was always the banker. But he was my guest after all. I handed him the tray of money.

"And I'm always the shoe," he continued.

Well, that is unacceptable. "I'm always the shoe," I informed him.

"Oh, no, uh-uh. I'm *always* the shoe."

"Why would you want to be the old, grungy-looking shoe anyhow? Don't you want to be the luxury car?" I raised an eyebrow at him, trying to fake him out as I held the car up and swept my hand toward it in a lofty presentation.

"No. The shoe represents hard work. And hard work leads to riches. I'm always the shoe."

I raised my eyebrows.

"Why do *you* want to be the shoe?"

"Because the shoe looks unassuming. No one expects the shoe to come from behind and win it all. Everyone keeps a watchful eye on the luxury car...but not the shoe. That guy, he flies right under the radar or *walks* as the case may be."

Kyland laughed, looking pleased. "I like that answer. I say we roll for it."

"Deal."

I rolled first. Four.

Kyland rolled second. Three. He laughed. "All right. You're the shoe. Fair and square."

An hour later we had survived a stock market crash, were deeply involved in several land deals, and had passed Go more times than I had kept track of. Kyland was winning and I was not happy. I landed on another of his damn railroads.

He laughed and my eyes snapped up to his. "What's so funny?"

"I never would have guessed you to be so competitive, Tenleigh Falyn." He grinned, quite pleased with himself.

"Hrrmph," I grunted, counting out money for the railroads and practically throwing it at him.

"Monopoly tip: always buy the railroads first."

I narrowed my eyes. "You're not winning so much that you get to give me winning strategy advice just yet, mister." I paused. "I never buy the railroads. Railroads are boring."

"Well, you should. Compared to the other properties, the flow of revenue from the railroads is more constant over time. Owning all four of them is a cash cow. You can use them to fund your other monopolies."

I glanced up at him. I knew he was working toward the scholarship, but I hadn't realized just how smart Kyland really was. And suddenly it hit me—he couldn't stay here.

He had to get out if he was going to utilize those smarts of his. Something that felt like deep sadness filled me, but I was confused. Being smart was not a sad thing, especially with the lack of it going on in Dennville, Kentucky.

"I shouldn't be giving you all these tips, but obviously"—he swept his hand over the board indicating the fact that he was winning—"you could use them."

"Asshole," I muttered.

An hour after that, I was utterly bankrupt and practically seething. Kyland couldn't keep the amusement off his face. It was maddening.

Really, though, I hadn't had that much fun in forever.

"All right, I concede. You've officially wiped me out and hung me up to dry. Congratulations." I picked up the board and dumped the pieces into the box as Kyland laughed.

"If you're lucky, I'll give you a rematch."

"Hmmph."

There was a knock on my trailer door and I looked up, confused.

"Who is it?" I called.

"It's Buster."

"Buster…" I rushed to the door and opened it, a blast of icy air making me step back. "Get in here." Buster West was my neighbor, one of the oldest on the hill, a strange but kindhearted guy who would bring us rhubarb by the basketful in summer.

"Hi there, missy," he said, smiling and pulling his hood down.

"What are you doing out in this weather, Buster?"

"Just came to drop off a Christmas gift." He looked over at Kyland.

"Buster, do you know Kyland Barrett? He lives down the hill."

"I surely do. Hi, son. How's your mama?"

"Hi, sir. Uh, she's okay. Doesn't get out much, you know."

"No, don't reckon she does." He looked at Kyland for just a beat too long. What was that about? I looked over to Kyland and he had his hands in his pockets and was looking down at the floor.

"Ah, so, here you go." Buster held out something wrapped in white tissue paper.

"You didn't have to do this," I said, smiling uncomfortably as I took his gift. I knew exactly what it was and I didn't want to open it in front of Kyland. But Buster was standing there looking so pleased and expectant, so I unwrapped the tissue and held up the piece of whittled wood, trying my best not to cringe. I couldn't help the heat I felt making its way up my neck, though. Buster was a pornographic whittler. As far as I knew, he was making his way through the *Kama Sutra*. This one featured a woman kneeling in front of a man, giving him a blow job as he yanked on her hair, his head thrown back in ecstasy.

Well.

"Wow, Buster. This is...very...romantic."

Kyland made a strange choking sound in the back of his throat and began coughing.

Buster smiled dreamily. "That it is," he said. But then his face grew concerned. "How's Annabelle?" he asked, referring to my mama.

"She's in the hospital again."

"I figured. Saw her ripping out of here in that sash. I came straight across to get Marlo," he said, putting the *t* on the end of the word across as mountain folks did. "Poor girl was in the shower." He shook his head. "Glad they're gettin' her patched up."

Well, that was one way to put it. "Thanks, Buster. Oh

hey, I have something for you too," I said, reaching for a small tin under the Christmas tree.

I handed it to him, and he grinned. "Lavender tea. My favorite. You're a gem, Miss Tenleigh."

"You're welcome." Truthfully, I made lavender tea for him whenever I could, not just at Christmas, because I knew he loved it. So it wasn't anything too exciting. But he was very sweet to act as if it were.

"Well, you two have a merry Christmas." He pulled his hood up, smiled over at Kyland, and then kissed me on the cheek, his lips cold and dry.

"You too," I said.

I let Buster out and then turned to Kyland, the smutty whittled art in my hand. "I've got a whole collection of them," I said. Kyland laughed and I joined him. "I swear, that old man has a screw loose. But I love him."

Kyland shook his head, still chuckling. "Can I see that?"

I handed him the figures and he looked closely at them, turning them this way and that. "Damn, Buster has mad whittling skills." He kept looking for a minute, seeming to remember suddenly that I was watching him. His face sobered as our eyes met. Something seemed to shift between us.

I turned away and put the gift under my small tree and when I faced Kyland again, his expression was intense and heated. My skin prickled and I suddenly felt flushed in an... unfriendly sort of way. I picked at the hem of my sweater. I didn't know how to address this tension between us.

"I better get home, you know, in case my mama needs me."

"Yes," I said quickly. "Right. Of course." I glanced at the clock, noting that it was almost ten o'clock.

Kyland looked uncertain. "You sure you're okay?"

he asked as he quickly put on his socks and stepped into his shoes.

"Yeah." I smiled. "I am now. Thank you." I looked down, feeling shy again for some reason. "Thank you so much."

He nodded, his eyes straying to my lips before he jerked them back up to my eyes again. We both moved at once, me toward the door to let him out and him to his jacket that was now dry. He pulled it on.

"You be safe walking home," I said softly as I opened the door. "It's slippery, and—"

"Bobcats," we both said at once and then laughed.

Kyland sobered. "I'll be safe, I promise," he said, his eyes lingering on me again.

"All right."

"All right."

He took the two steps down until he was standing in the snow. "Lock the door behind me. When I hear it click, I'll go."

I nodded. "Good night, Kyland."

"Good night, Tenleigh."

I shut the door and clicked the lock into place. I walked slowly back to the couch, bringing the blanket around me as I sat staring blankly at our small Christmas tree. The trailer suddenly seemed too quiet and lonely. And something was bothering me—something was niggling at my mind about Kyland but I couldn't figure out exactly what right then. I tried to focus, but I was so tired. My eyes grew heavy. I lay back and in minutes, I was fast asleep.

I didn't wake up again until the light of Christmas morning was shining through the windows of our trailer, a chorus of winter wrens singing their greeting.

CHAPTER NINE
Kyland

It was snowing. I stood at the window looking out at what might have made another person sigh in wonder at the clean, white landscape. It didn't always snow on Christmas. Some would say this one was special. Not me. *Christmas.* Melancholy rolled through me and I did my best to tamp it down. It was just another day on the calendar. If I didn't pay any attention, it would have just rolled by. Today was really no different than any other day except in my own mind. "Get it together, Kyland," I muttered to myself, taking another sip of hot coffee.

A knock sounded at the door and I looked up in surprise. What the hell? Who went to someone's house on Christmas morning? I frowned as I walked to the front door. "Who is it?" I demanded, on guard.

"Tenleigh." I blinked. Tenleigh? *Shit.* I paused for just a second before opening the door a crack.

She was standing there, her small Christmas tree in her hands, a paper bag with handles on her arm, a timid smile on her face, cheeks pink with the cold, and snowflakes adorning her dark hair. She was stunning. I opened the door just a little wider so I could see her better.

"What are you doing here?" I asked. Damn, that sounded cold. But she needed to leave. She couldn't come in.

The smile disappeared from her face and she looked down for just a beat before raising her eyes to mine, and whispering, "How long has she been gone?"

My brows furrowed. "She? She who?"

"Your mama."

My eyes widened as we stood there staring at each other across the threshold. Snow continued to gather in her hair and on her dark jacket.

"What... Why would you..." I started. But then I let out a big breath and ran my hand through my hair. "How'd you know?"

Her expression grew gentle. "There are never any lights on in your house, the way Buster acted last night when he brought her up...a few other things..." She shook her head. "I just guessed really." She bit her lip and my heart did something crazy in my chest that I tried my best to ignore. "I'm sorry I was right." She paused. "I just figured if you were alone, you probably didn't have any Christmas here. And so I"—she thrust the small tree out in front of her—"brought Christmas to you." She smiled hopefully.

I opened the door all the way and waved my hand for her to come in. Her smile grew bigger, relief filling her eyes as she entered my house. For a minute she just stood looking around and I shoved my hands in my pockets as I tried to see the place through her eyes. It was small and the furniture was old—the same stuff my mama had gotten from my grandma as hand-me-downs after my grandma died, stuff that wasn't nice then and definitely wasn't now—but I kept the place clean and uncluttered.

Tenleigh's eyes lingered on the armchair with the table next to it that held a photo of my mama, the one I'd put there initially because I hoped so hard she'd come back... the one I'd gotten in the habit of greeting. I really needed to take that down.

Tenleigh turned toward me, smiling. "It's nice," she said. And damn it, my heart flipped over in my damn stupid chest again because I could see that she really, truly meant it and that was not acceptable. A girl like Tenleigh should see this place for the dump that it was. And she didn't. And something about that pissed me off as much as it filled me with some strange happiness.

"Can I take your jacket? Your Christmas tree? Your paper bag?"

She laughed and set the tree down on my coffee table as she shrugged off her coat. She flicked a switch on the tree. "Battery-operated lights," she said. "We can put it anywhere." She arranged it on the coffee table to her liking and then stood up, looking down at it, that same unsure look on her face again. An awkward silence ensued.

"I'm sorry, Kyland," she finally whispered, shaking her head slightly. "I'm barging in on you here. I just..." She bit her lip again. "What were you going to do today?"

"Watch some TV...study...wallow in loneliness."

She didn't laugh. She probably realized I hadn't been joking, although it was only her reaction that made me see that too.

"You have TV?" she asked.

"Sometimes. When I have electricity."

She nodded and we were both silent for a second.

"What happened to her?" she asked very quietly.

I paused. I had never told anyone about this. I *couldn't* tell anyone. I hadn't planned on *ever* telling anyone. But right then, for some very strange reason, I desperately wanted to tell Tenleigh about it.

"She left us. A week before the mine accident."

Her eyes filled with sympathy, but she didn't say anything.

"My dad was so *embarrassed*." I shook my head and scratched the back of my neck, pushing those memories away, even as I revealed them. "So ashamed about it. He was such a prideful man. He made us swear not to tell anyone until he was ready. I think…I think maybe he was trying to come up with a story that sounded better than, 'she just didn't want us anymore.'" I paused. "Or maybe he was hoping she'd come back. My mama, though, she was never happy with our life. My dad, he didn't even have a high school education, didn't make much at the mine. They fought all the time." I ran my hand through my hair and grimaced. "See, Tenleigh, your dad left you when you were three days old, and that hurts because he didn't want to get to know who you are. But my mama, she knew me—she knew I loved her. And she left anyway."

"Kyland," she whispered.

I shook my head, unable to stop the words that seemed to be flowing out of my mouth of their own accord. "Then the mine accident happened and—" I took a deep, shaky breath, surprised I could still get emotional about this. It felt like I'd lived with it for so long. But speaking of it was bringing it to life somehow… "They died and it seemed like every family up and down this mountain was grieving for someone. No one noticed that my mama didn't show up to any of the memorial services—or they figured she was sick with grief. Other people were too. I waited for her to come back. I figured she had to have heard. She *had* to have. She must have known I was alone. I waited and waited for her to come back for me, but she never did." I took a deep breath. "I didn't want to be sent to foster care. I wanted the chance at that scholarship. I wanted a chance at…*life*. And the only way I was going to get it was if I kept working toward it. And so when people asked, I said she was laid up."

"No wonder," she said sadly.

"No wonder what?"

"No wonder you hate it here so much."

I stared into her eyes.

"You don't have to be lonely anymore." She reached her hand out and grabbed mine, a look of sorrow in her eyes. Her hand was cold and soft. It felt small within my own.

"Tenleigh…you don't understand. Whether I win that scholarship or whether I don't, I'm leaving here. In a few short months, I'm leaving. If by some small chance I don't win that scholarship, I'll sell everything of any value in this house and I'll hitchhike out of here. I'll get a job somewhere and work my way across the country. I can't work in that mine. And I can't be hungry anymore. I'll leave here, and I won't look back. I'll never think about Dennville, Kentucky, again."

Her eyes wandered over my face for several beats before she nodded, releasing my hand. "You already said that. And I told you that's okay."

Jesus. This girl.

"Yeah, I guess I did."

"I really, truly mean it. You have a friend." She smiled at me hopefully.

Friends. Yeah. That's what we'd decided. It hadn't made me happy last night and it didn't make me happy now.

The molecules in the air surrounding us seemed to speed up and heat the space around our bodies. "So," she said brightly, "I brought you a Christmas present."

I slowly raised an eyebrow, trying to shake off the heat that had started buzzing through my system. I wanted her. I wanted to strip her naked. I wanted to thrust into her, hard and fast, and watch her face as I did it. I wanted to know what she was thinking as my body filled hers. I wanted to hear her talk, hear the way the Kentucky twang she tried to hide became more pronounced when she was emotional in some way. I wanted to see that fiery side of her that only came out every once in a while, like a sudden and stunning bolt of lightning racing through a clear, cloudless sky. I wanted to take her virginity— and not gently. I wanted to hurt her like she was hurting me each time I looked at her. I wanted to mark her, claim her, let everyone know that she belonged to me and *only* me.

Fuck!

No.

No.

No.

I couldn't let myself think *any* of that. I was leaving here and I was leaving Tenleigh behind. That was that. I wasn't such a jackass that I would de-virginize her and then split town, never to contact her again. I wouldn't do it—not to her or to myself. I wanted a fresh start. I didn't want to leave any part of myself in Dennville. I had worked four fucking years for that. And it was right within my grasp. A beautiful girl with a spirit so bright I wanted to squint when I looked at her was not going to derail me now.

She took something out of the paper bag she'd set on the floor and looked at me quizzically. "That's a really intense look on your face."

I snapped to the present. "Sorry. Just thinking."

Tenleigh cocked her head. "Can we try not thinking today? Just for today? Can it be like last night when we just enjoyed each other? That wasn't so bad, was it?"

"No, that's the problem. I'm going to want more."

She blinked at me.

"Shit, Tenleigh." I ran my hand through my hair and turned away from her. "This isn't..." I sighed loudly. "What do you have for me there?"

She suddenly looked uncertain. "Uh...well." She stared down at the small object wrapped in tissue in her hands briefly and chuckled uncomfortably. "This suddenly seems weird."

I raised an eyebrow. "Now I really want it." I reached out and she hesitated but then put the object in my hand. It looked similar to the one Buster had given her the night before. I paused. It couldn't be... I unwrapped it quickly and sure enough, one of Buster's erotic whittles was sitting in my palm: a woman on all fours as the man fucked her from behind, his hands gripping her hips, her back arched. And damn if it wasn't outrageous, but damn if it didn't turn me the hell on. And damn if I didn't want to do that very thing to the girl standing in front of me. Here. Right now.

I looked up at Tenleigh, who suddenly looked mortified. "I have a whole collection," she said. "I thought you might get a laugh out of it." Her words faded as we stared at each other. She couldn't know how much this would turn me on. She wouldn't have given it to me had she known how much I wanted to carry out exactly what had been whittled by Buster. *With* her. *To* her. I glanced back down at the figures.

And then I couldn't help it. I burst out laughing, the ridiculous object just sitting in my hand. Tenleigh laughed too, tentatively at first and then harder as we both stood there cracking up. Finally I gathered myself enough to walk over to the kitchen window and place it there. Perfect.

I returned to Tenleigh, smiling. "Thank you. Seriously." And I meant it. She hadn't set out to give me a homemade piece of whittled wood. She'd set out to make me laugh. And she had. And for me, that was the best gift of all.

"I brought a ham too," she said, nodding to the paper bag. "Al gave one to all the full-time employees. My sister got one. Maybe we can heat it up later?"

"Sure, that—"

Before I even had time to fully answer, she clapped her hands together and I startled, my words cutting short.

"Sledding!"

"What?"

"Sledding. That's what we could do today. Marlo and I used to find a couple tire inner tubes in someone's front yard and go up the hill a ways. I know some of the best spots."

I stared at her. "I bet I know some better ones. My brother and I used to do that too."

She grinned. "Really? I'm surprised we never ran into each other."

I laughed softly and shook my head. Only Tenleigh had the ability to turn my mood from one extreme to the other. How had it been that I was just telling her about one of the most traumatic things I'd ever experienced and now I was laughing?

"I guess it's as good an idea as any. What else are we gonna do?"

The question hung there for a few heavy beats. "Right," she said. We stood looking at each other for a minute until she shrugged and said, "So...let's go."

"Okay." But I stood frowning for a minute. "I'm gonna

have to get you some of my brother's snow stuff. You'll have to roll it up and we'll have to improvise on a few things, but...I only have one set for myself."

She nodded, but her eyes looked wary as if she was trying to read whether I was okay with that or not. Truthfully, I didn't even know. I'd spent so long trying not to even think about my family because it hurt too much, and now I was openly talking about them with Tenleigh. *Remembering.* And somehow...wanting to for reasons I couldn't even explain to myself. I sighed and went and got the clothes. In the span of fifteen minutes, this day had turned into something completely unexpected, and although I was filled with uncertainty, I was also filled with happiness.

This girl.

CHAPTER TEN
Tenleigh

Fifteen minutes later, we were bundled up as much as possible, hiding behind some trees next to Dell Walker's trailer. Trash lay strewn around his yard, half covered in snow.

You'd think we could just stride onto his property and take what we wanted, with it being trash and all. But mountain folk were strange about their stuff, and Dell was likely to come out with his shotgun if he saw us rooting through his garbage. And if we asked him if we could have it, he'd likely realize it had some value and try to charge us. Plus, Dell was a mean old bastard. A mean old bastard with a shotgun. And a penchant for consuming copious amounts of liquor.

Kyland pointed to an inner tube lying half-submersed in snow a hundred feet from where we hid. He put his finger up to his lips and shot me a wink. Butterflies started flapping their tiny wings in my belly and I gave him a nod. Then I watched as he ran quickly to a small shed to the right of us and ducked behind that. A few seconds later, I saw him emerge from there and sprint through the snow to the inner tube, swooping it up and hanging it on his shoulder as he ran back. He ducked behind the shed again. I laughed softly into my hand, covered in a thick sock with a plastic bag over it, tied around my wrist—makeshift waterproof gloves.

As I waited for him, my mind moved to what he'd told me back at his house. I'd been horrified, stunned, when I'd considered it back at my trailer. But somewhere inside, I'd known it was true. When he'd confirmed it, though, it shocked me all over again. Poor Kyland…living alone for all that time…grieving his whole family—all by himself. No one at all to help him through it. And then, the loneliness. How had he survived it? I suddenly understood his need to get out of Dennville. I understood his need to make a life for himself somewhere that didn't remind him of the deep pain he must have lived with all these years. And it made me want to love him. Which wasn't good. *At all.* Because he wouldn't love me back. He wouldn't *allow* himself to love me back even if he wanted to, which he might not. And that had to be okay. I couldn't even really blame him considering what he'd told me about his family. He avoided commitment but not girls, while I avoided boys completely—both of us tarnished by abandonment.

He ran back to the grove of trees, breathing hard, his cheeks flushed and a smile on his lips. And he looked as beautiful as I'd ever seen him.

Ugh. Double ugh.

"Ready?" I whispered.

"Yeah," he said, still smiling.

We headed up the hill after snagging a second inner tube from Cletus Rucker in the same fashion as the one we'd taken from Dell Walker. Kyland led me up the hill to a spot he promised was the best sledding hill on the mountain. He wasn't wrong.

When we stepped through a forest of pines, we were standing at the top of a hill that dropped off in a perfect slope, one that was steep but long, and ended with plenty of time to come to a stop on the flat surface at the bottom before a new forest started.

"Oh my God!" I exclaimed, looking down at it. "Marlo will die when she sees that we missed this one all these years."

Kyland shook his head. "Uh-uh. You're not allowed to disclose the location of this sledding hill. It's top secret. Classified."

I laughed. "Okay. But how'd you find it?"

He set his inner tube down at the top of the hill and I followed suit, setting mine next to his. "My brother found it. He loved these hills. We explored every inch of them, I swear." He didn't smile, but something in his expression looked tender. I took his hand and his eyes rose to meet mine, almost shyly, as if he was remembering being a little boy.

"Let's hold hands as we go down."

"Okay." We both sat down on the inner tubes and positioned our bodies.

Kyland looked over at me, a look that I loved on his face—and one I'd never seen before—one of breathless anticipation, like something really good was about to happen. His expression made my breath catch in my throat. There was something so *pure* about it, so completely unexpected. Time seemed to melt like the snow eventually would under the warmth of the sun. I'd thought I saw him for the first time when I witnessed him swiping food that day. But no. That was just something he had to do to survive. This, this was me seeing *him* for the very first time. No pretense, just unabashed delight. And I was part of it. I didn't want the moment to pass before I'd committed it to memory.

"Ready?" he asked softly.

No. "Ready."

I looked out over that hill, the trees below us and the town of Dennville even farther below those, smoke rising lazily out of the chimneys, the tobacco farms just dots on the horizon. From up here, there was only peace, only freedom and beauty. I sucked in a huge breath as if I could capture the feeling of that moment in my lungs and hold it there forever.

We both leaned forward and grasped hands, our inner tubes gliding faster and faster down the hill, gaining speed so quickly that I threw my head back and screamed and then laughed uncontrollably. The wind whipped through my hair and Kyland's hand held mine tightly, even through the thick socks and plastic bags. Normally, the inner tubes would spin in circles, but with our hands grasped together, we went down straight. Next to me, I could hear him laughing too.

We came to a slow stop right before the grove of trees below, our feet dragging in the snow.

Kyland looked over at me, his cheeks flushed and a huge grin on his face. "Again?" he asked.

I laughed and nodded, and we made the slow trek back up the side of the hill.

All that afternoon, we played like kids, spinning down the hill as I shrieked and Kyland's deep laugh echoed through the quiet hills. We made snow angels, pointed out three bright red cardinals, and saw a couple of deer nibbling on some twigs at the edge of the forest. It was the best Christmas of my whole life.

When it was lunchtime, we sat at the top of the hill on our inner tubes, eating the smashed bologna sandwiches

Kyland had wrapped up in wax paper and stuck in his pocket before we left.

As the sun started to fade just a little, Kyland suggested we should get going. I was wet and cold, but I'd been willing to ignore it for the fun we were having.

"One more time down?" I asked.

"Okay." He laughed.

"Let's make it a good one."

"All right. I'll give you a push and then I'll be right behind you."

I nodded, grinning. I positioned myself on the inner tube and looked back at him to let him know I was ready.

"This is going to be fast."

"Good!" I said, laughing.

Kyland put both hands on my inner tube, and with one giant shove, he sent me flying down the hill, spinning in immediate circles, the cold air whipping at my face and causing me to shriek again and again.

Suddenly, my inner tube hit something under the snow that must have been uncovered in all the tracks we'd made down the hill. I went airborne, screaming, my inner tube shooting out ahead of me. *Oh no, this is gonna hurt.*

I landed facedown in the snow, the air whooshing out of my lungs. Somewhere above me, I heard Kyland yell my name. I lay there for a minute, unhurt but surprised, with cold, wet snow pressed into my nose and mouth.

All of a sudden, I was flipped over and Kyland's panicked face was staring down at me. "Tenleigh, oh my God," he choked out. "Tell me you're okay."

He looked so scared, his eyes moving all over my face. I felt dazed but not hurt. "I'm fine," I breathed out. "I'm fine, Kyland."

His shoulders relaxed and he released a big breath. He kept staring down at my face, something intense coming into his expression, as if he'd made some kind of decision. The moment seemed to slow, to still. I quietly watched him, waiting for him to do something. He opened his mouth as if he was going to say something but then snapped it shut.

And then he leaned in and his mouth was on mine, soft and warm on my frozen lips. He used his tongue to trace them, his breath mixing with my own before he pressed his lips to mine again and allowed the kiss to go deeper. He tasted like the remnants of salt from our sandwiches and something deeper and more masculine: *need*.

My heart rate accelerated and warmth raced through my veins, ending in a rush of wetness between my legs. But still, I held back. He had done this before and then he'd pushed me away. *Please don't push me away this time.*

"Kiss me back, Tenleigh," he whispered, his voice strained. "God, please kiss me back." He brushed his lips softly over mine again.

And that was all I needed.

I wrapped my arms around his neck and tilted my head, our eyes meeting once before he pressed his body into mine and gripped my face in his hands. His tongue ran along the crease of my lips and I opened immediately, a moan coming up my throat at the taste of him. He was all *boy* and mountain air and my body pressed upward into his, wanting to accept anything and everything he was offering.

Our tongues met and tangled and then he was moaning too, sweeping his tongue as deeply into my mouth as he could. My body was tingly and alive and I felt his kiss all the way down to my toes.

The world faded out around me, the cold disappeared. It

was only him and his hot, wet mouth on mine—*in* mine—and the taste of him, the weight of his hard body pressed into my own.

"Kyland, Kyland," I moaned out shamelessly when his mouth came off mine and his hot breath was suddenly at my throat. Maybe I should hold back, but I didn't even know how. I was drowning in sensation overload. I arched my head backward into the snow as his lips feathered up the tender skin of my neck. And that shot more sparks between my legs, my nipples pebbling almost painfully under the layers of my clothes. "I need…oh God…" *Everything. I needed everything.* My body felt achy and empty and desperate.

"I want to take you home," he whispered against my skin.

I froze. "What?" Was he rejecting me *again*? I swear I'd claw his eyes out.

"To *my* home." His gaze moved down to my mouth. He looked back into my eyes, something like fear in his as if he was waiting for me to hurt him.

Or as if he was hurting himself.

"I won't take your virginity, but God help me, I need to touch you. I need to taste you."

Oh yes, yes, I want that too. I nodded, swallowing heavily.

"But I thought…" I whispered.

He shook his head. "I can't resist you. I tried. I really did." He brushed his lips against mine again, and I opened my mouth and drank in his air.

"You don't have to. I don't want you to resist me."

He leaned his forehead against mine, my face still cupped in his warm hands. "I don't want to hurt you. I don't want to hurt *me*."

I shook my head. "I understand that you're leaving, Kyland. I already know."

And I want you anyway. Maybe I shouldn't. But I do.

"This won't change anything. I have to know you understand that." He frowned, shaking his head. "I know that makes me an asshole. I know. I do. I just—"

"It doesn't make you an asshole. It's okay. I promise, it's okay."

His eyes moved over my face as if trying to ascertain if I was telling the truth. Finally he leaned forward and took my mouth in another warm kiss. He kissed me until we were both panting again, and my heartbeat was pounding so furiously between my legs it was almost painful.

Kyland suddenly broke free from my lips and kneeled up, pulling me with him. "Let's go," he said, his voice hoarse and clipped as if he was in pain too.

We stood up and started walking up the hill for the hundredth time that day. But now suddenly the air all around us seemed to be dancing with static electricity.

We walked in silence along the trail through the woods, our inner tubes on our shoulders. I had been cold and a little hungry before, but now all I could focus on was the wetness between my thighs as I took each step, my breath coming out in sharp exhales. I could feel Kyland behind me as if his very presence made the air all around me heavier somehow.

Finally, his house came into sight and he grabbed my hand and we ran the last couple hundred feet, laughter bursting from my chest. I didn't know if I was nervous or just filled with anticipation or what, but my whole body was buzzing.

"Stay here for a sec," Kyland said as he took my inner tube and walked to the back of his house, putting them somewhere I couldn't see. Then he was back, taking my hand again, pulling me into his house, shutting and locking the door behind us.

CHAPTER ELEVEN
Kyland

I was quite possibly about to make the biggest mistake of my life, and I just couldn't care anymore. It was too much damn work trying not to be attracted to Tenleigh. I couldn't do it anymore. The hormones had won out. Only I knew very well it was more than hormones that attracted me to her—and that's the part that scared me so damn much. I needed to touch her naked skin more than anything I'd ever needed in my life before. It was like those Monday mornings at school when someone had left food on one of the cafeteria tables, and I was so hungry after not eating all weekend that reaching out to take it was a primal response, one I could barely control—a survival instinct. That's how Tenleigh affected me. I wanted her so desperately I felt like some part of me was starving for her.

Was this normal? It couldn't be. I'd never felt this way for another girl before. Maybe I just needed to get my fill of her so that this feeling would begin to fade, so that I could gather some control over it. Half of it had to be the anticipation alone.

Right?

Tenleigh walked into my house first and then turned around to face me. "You have that really intense look on your face again," she whispered, her light green eyes wide, her lips red from the cold and my kisses.

Goddamn, I was so hard I was almost in pain.

"We need to take off these wet clothes," I said, ignoring her comment and starting to strip off my coat.

She nodded, color moving up her cheeks, her eyes cast downward as she removed her own jacket.

She looked so innocent, so beautiful. I hesitated.

Her eyes snapped up to mine and some kind of resolve filled them. She took the five steps or so to me and then her lips were on mine and I was gripping her face in my hands and sweet little moans were coming from her chest. Any control I had had a few seconds before was gone.

Long gone.

Somewhere in Eastern Asia.

I walked her backward as we kissed, licking and sucking at each other's lips and tongues. She tasted like something I couldn't even identify, something so delicious that it drove me to the next level of crazy. Kissing her was like tipping over the edge of sanity. Like being drunk. The feeling was so intense I could hardly describe it. My kisses weren't gentle— they were ravaging and wild. Desire, molten and powerful, pumped through my veins.

Somehow we made it to my room, and when the backs of her legs hit my small twin bed, she sat down and lay back. I immediately followed her down and continued to kiss her, pressing my throbbing erection down into her and moaning at the sensation. How was I going to resist fucking her? My need to press into her warm, wet body was so intense, I was practically shaking with it. But I *would* resist. I had to. I broke from her lips and looked down into her face, filled with arousal but still that same beautiful innocence.

"Make love to me," she whispered.

Yes! No.

I closed my eyes tightly for a second and then looked back into her face. She was going to drive me out of my mind. "I can't, Tenleigh. I won't," I said. "But I'll give you what you need, okay?"

An expression of hurt crossed her features, but she nodded.

I kissed her once again quickly, then sat back and removed her boots, her damp socks, and then her layered pants. No girl had ever been more desirable in a more ridiculous, unbecoming outfit.

Underneath her pants, she had on a simple pair of pink cotton underwear. My dick pulsed again and I almost groaned.

God, you make me weak, Tenleigh.

She sat up and removed her layered tops, and when she finally took off the long john shirt under it all, she sat before me in a white bra, her breasts spilling out of it as if it was a couple sizes too small. It probably was.

For a second, I just stared at her. She looked like a dream come to life. White creamy skin and dark hair spilling all around her shoulders and down her back. Her breasts were round and full, her waist slim, and her legs long and shapely. I'd never seen anything more beautiful in my life than Tenleigh Falyn sitting on my bed in her plain cotton underwear. My stomach muscles clenched.

"Tenleigh," I whispered, "you're so beautiful."

She blinked at me and then smiled shyly. I noticed there were goose bumps on her skin. "Get under the covers," I said.

She looked over her shoulder and then scooted her body

so she could pull the quilt, blankets, and top sheet back. She lay on my pillow, gazing up at me.

I stripped my clothes off so fast I didn't even remember doing it, but the cold hit my naked skin and I climbed beneath the blankets with her. I took her lips again, our cool, bare skin finally making contact as we both sighed. I pulled the covers all the way up, almost over our faces, and it only took a few minutes until we were in our own little warm cocoon.

I brought my hand up to her breast and rubbed the nipple lightly with my thumb. Tenleigh gasped out my name and my cock jumped. I wasn't going to be able to take much more of this before I came on myself without even being touched. God, this girl. I needed to make her come and then I needed to take care of myself in the shower.

"Tenleigh, have you ever had an orgasm?" I asked softly, trailing my lips up her neck.

She shook her head.

"Not even one you gave yourself?" I asked.

"Our trailer's really small."

I nodded, my eyes taking in her beautiful features. Something warm filled my chest when I considered that I'd be the first one to make her come. I wouldn't be the first one to make love to her, but I had this. This was mine and mine alone. And maybe that wasn't right either but I couldn't convince myself to care.

I reached behind her and she arched her back as I unhooked her bra and took it off her, tossing it on the floor. Her eyes watched my face, looking full of both desire and nervousness.

I leaned down under the covers and put my mouth on her nipple, sucking it gently into my mouth. The taste of her was heaven on my tongue.

"Oh, Kyland," she moaned. Her hands came up to my head and she raked her fingers through my hair. I licked and sucked one nipple for a minute, laving it with my tongue, going around and around, until she was bucking her hips up into me. I adjusted my own hips to the side to avoid the sweet torture of her pressing right into my erection and moved my mouth over to the other nipple.

"You taste so good," I said between sucks.

"Ahhh," she moaned out. I could hear her moving her head from side to side on the pillow. I trailed my hand down over her silky, flat stomach, my mouth still on her breast, and when I slipped my fingers into her underwear and between her legs, it was me who moaned out.

She was slick with arousal. I dipped my finger inside her and brought it in and out slowly, mimicking the movement I wanted to be making with another part of my body. Her breathing grew ragged. I brought my now-wet finger to her clit, circling it gently as she cried out.

I wanted to put my face between her legs and taste her there, but we had all night—I hoped. If she'd agree to stay, I would make her feel good in every single way I knew how.

I continued to stroke her clit with my thumb as I dipped my finger into her wet opening. She sighed out and pressed upward into my hand.

"Tell me what you're thinking," I begged. "Tell me what's in your mind right now?" I wanted her. And I couldn't have all of her, but the parts I could have…her sweet responsiveness, her pleasure, and the things swirling through her mind, I *could* have those. For now, at least.

"I can't…I can't make sense of any of it." She moaned deeply as I changed tempo with my fingers. "I think I used to have problems and…concerns, but I can't remember one of them. All I feel is good, oh God, Kyland, that's so good."

I smiled down at her, tenderness filling my chest. She was silky and soft and warm, and she smelled so damn good. And God, I hoped she wouldn't regret this. I circled my finger faster and closed my lips around her nipple again.

Seconds later, she cried out. Her body tensed and shuddered and I felt satisfaction unlike any I'd known before.

"Oh God, oh God…" she groaned. I leaned up and watched her face as she came down, her eyes opening. She gazed at me with some kind of wonder and then she smiled, so brightly I startled very slightly. Tenleigh was a beautiful girl, there was no doubt about that, but every once in a while she did something or made an expression that *dazzled* me and rendered me speechless. This was one of those moments.

"Wow." The word was mostly breath.

I chuckled softly and then fell to the side, my head on the pillow next to her, my erection throbbing with the need for release.

"I'm going to go take a quick shower," I said, starting to sit up.

"No," she said, sitting up too and pushing me back down. "I get to enjoy you too. Fair is fair."

"Tenleigh," I groaned. "You truly are going to kill me."

She laughed and then moved until her body covered mine.

Somehow, she was well versed in torture techniques. She was applying each and every one to me in this bed. She wiggled on top of me. *Case in point.*

"I'll tell you whatever you want to know," I groaned. "Anything."

She laughed. "What?" But then her hand moved down over my rib cage and I couldn't talk at all. She scooted to the side and her hand ran down my thigh.

"Touch me, please." Now I was begging. And I didn't care.

Her hand ran tentatively back up my thigh and then finally, finally, she gripped my cock, wrapping her warm fingers around it and squeezing lightly. Goose bumps broke out on my body and I groaned again, pleasure bursting within me. I brought my hand around hers and showed her how to slide it up and down the way I liked. She leaned in and kissed me, her taste filling my mouth again as her smooth body rubbed against mine, her hand moving up and down on my cock. She kissed down my jaw, to the side of my neck, her breath tickling my ear as her hand stroked me. Tenleigh was so innocent and yet every movement, every touch, every gust of her breath on my body was so perfect, so thrilling. I barely made it two minutes before an orgasm exploded, so intense I gasped out and shuddered. The waves of ecstasy slowly diminished, Tenleigh's hand slowing as her now wet, sticky fingers loosened their grip.

She smiled down at me. I was in a daze. I barely knew where I was. "Holy shit," I finally mumbled.

Tenleigh laughed and leaned in, wrapping her arms around my waist. "No wonder people lose their minds over sex," she said. "I liked that very much."

I laughed. God, I wished I could teach her everything there was to know about how great sex could be. I wished I could let *her* teach *me* everything about how great sex could be. Because I was somehow sure it *would* be great with her. I sobered. Unfortunately, that couldn't happen and I needed to keep reminding myself of that.

I rolled to my side and so did Tenleigh until we were

facing each other. I ran my finger down the side of her face, tracing her delicate cheekbone. "Are you warm enough?"

"Yes," she whispered.

"Hungry?"

She nodded.

"How about I put that ham in the oven? I have some potatoes. And some canned green beans."

"That sounds like a fine Christmas dinner, Mr. Barrett."

"Well good, Miss Falyn. Come on. Bring that quilt with you."

We got up and I went to the bathroom to clean myself off and returned to the bedroom to put my jeans on. The house was cold but not frigid. Still, thankfully, I had some coal for the cast iron stove in the living room. I'd get the house nice and warm for tonight, even if it meant I'd be cold for the rest of the week.

I went about the business of getting a fire going while Tenleigh put her clothes back on and then settled herself on the couch, the quilt wrapped around her and the glow of the lights from the small Christmas tree on her face.

I put the ham and potatoes in the oven and went to sit next to her as dinner cooked. Just for tonight, I was going to allow myself to enjoy the gifts of Dennville, Kentucky. After all, it was Christmas.

CHAPTER TWELVE
Tenleigh

We ate dinner sitting on the floor in front of the wood stove in Kyland's living room, our plates on his coffee table. Food had never tasted so delicious to me in my entire life. His house was warm, my belly was full, and I felt genuinely happy. Maybe I shouldn't have let myself be so joyful, but I couldn't help it. I could accept that Kyland was leaving soon. I could accept that he wouldn't look back. But was I going to be okay if I got any closer to him? Probably not. Even so, something pulled me toward him, something I had trouble resisting, something that felt so good, I didn't *want* to resist it. I finally understood the pull. I finally had an inkling of what my mama and my sister had felt—and I finally understood why Marlo didn't want to experience the pain of having it end. And in my situation, I was assured—over and over as a matter of fact—that it *was* going to end. And maybe that was better. At least I wouldn't be blindsided when he packed his bag and left. I'd have time to prepare. But if *I* won that scholarship, we'd *both* be packing our bags…but still for separate lives. And yet I still wanted to be here with him. Was I wrong to feel like it was worth the pain *later* for some happiness *now*, no matter how temporary it may be?

"Now who's the one with the intense expression?"

I startled and looked over at Kyland and then started laughing.

"I'm breaking my own rule." I breathed out another small laugh.

Kyland chuckled. "I'm really glad you're here. In case you're wondering. This day has been…incredible. You're incredible. I want you to know that."

"Why does it sound like you're kicking me out?"

Kyland shook his head. "On the contrary. I'd really love it if you'd stay with me tonight."

"I'd like that too," I whispered. Kyland let out a breath and smiled as if my response was a relief.

There was a knock on his door, and we both looked at each other, confused. Kyland paused as if considering whether he'd answer or not. But then we heard the unmistakable sound of a banjo outside his door. I started laughing. "Oh God, the moonshine is flowing."

"Oh shit," Kyland said, laughing too. He walked to the door and I got up, pulling the quilt around me. I wasn't properly dressed, but if I knew the group of hillbillies outside his door right now and their love of moonshine, they wouldn't notice.

Kyland swung the door open and we stood there laughing and listening to a band of drunk hillbillies perform their own version of "Jingle Bells," playing banjos and homemade instruments and singing in loud, cackling voices. They were awful and ridiculous. Mostly because they were rip-roaring drunk. I couldn't stop smiling. They were mine. *Ours.* They were home.

Old Sally Mae, who had all of three teeth left in her mouth, took Kyland by the arm and executed a rowdy two-step with him, whipping him around and causing him to laugh out loudly. My heart clenched at the look of open happiness on his face. And for a moment, the world around dissolved until it was only him, laughing and linking arms with Sally, the expression of joy on his face increasing as he spun her, finally offering a gentlemanly bow at the end as she curtsied and flirted. I leaned on the doorframe for support.

They offered us a swig of moonshine from their jug and I took a couple burning sips of what tasted to me like battery acid and coughed as Kyland did the same, grimacing and wiping the back of his hand across his mouth. Then they danced off down the snowy road, their clanging music disappearing into the clear, cold night.

Kyland closed the door and reached his hand out to me and I gripped it, still holding the quilt around me with the other. He twirled me around once like he'd done to Sally Mae and I giggled and fell into his chest. He had the most beautiful body. It was muscled but lean, his shoulders broad and his waist narrow. It wouldn't be mine forever, but I was going to enjoy it while I could.

"They're pretty ridiculous," Kyland said, offering me a crooked smile.

"Yeah," I agreed, laughing. "But awesome."

Kyland pulled me with him back to his bedroom, where we fell onto his bed, laughing. He kissed me and we both sobered as the kiss went deeper. I sighed and wrapped my arms around his neck, running my nails over his scalp.

He groaned and that groan sent tingles between my legs.

Was this how sex was for everyone? How did couples who were really into each other ever leave their houses? If Kyland was mine—if he was promised to me, if we lived in this house together—I'd want to keep him here all day. I giggled against his mouth and he pulled away.

"What's funny?"

"Nothing's funny. I just like sex."

"You haven't had sex yet," he said, running his nose along mine.

"You could remedy that," I suggested. "My sister's had me on the pill as long as she's been on it. She gets packs of them at the free clinic. I take it regularly." I felt unsure, shy, giving him that information, but if birth control was part of the reason he was hesitating, I wanted him to know he didn't need to.

"Tenleigh," he groaned.

"I want you, Kyland. I want you to be my first. I don't care if you'll leave afterward."

"No. No, don't say that. Don't feel that way. *I* care. *I* can't do that." He shook his head for emphasis. He smoothed a piece of hair behind my ear. "Tenleigh, someday you're going to meet a man who wants to give you a life, a man who wants to give you everything he has to offer. And I'm not going to take the thing that's yours to give to him as a gift."

I pushed at him, feeling unreasonably hurt and angry. "You really know how to ruin the moment, you know that?" I stood up, pulling the quilt with me. "What girl wants to hear about some other guy when the guy she *wants* right then is kissing her? I suppose next you're going to tell me about the woman who you'll deem worthy to give all of yourself to someday once you make it out of here? Do I have to hear about her too? I guess she'll be sophisticated and worldly. Maybe a New York socialite? She'll talk like a proper lady, not like a Kentucky hick? She'll wear pearls and drink tea with her pinky—"

"Tenleigh. Stop. I didn't mean that. Will you just listen for a minute? Jesus, moonshine makes you angry." He swore softly, sitting up and running his hand through his hair. "Do you see why this is a mistake? God, woman."

"Now I'm a mistake?" I seethed, filled with hurt. I reached for the nearest object and hurled it at him. Unfortunately it was a pillow and he barely flinched. I looked around, but the only other thing that was within arm's reach was another pillow. So I chucked that at him too.

Kyland stood up and wrapped his arms around my waist, tackling me on the bed where he held me down and then sat on top of me. I struggled and beat at him, but he didn't budge. He wasn't putting his whole weight on me, but he was as strong as a bull, and he wasn't going anywhere unless he was the one who decided to.

"Are you done?" he asked softly as I glared up at him.

"Will you listen to me for a second? What I said...it didn't come out exactly right." He looked away as if searching his own mind. "What I meant is, sex between us would change things in a way we couldn't change back. I feel it, and I think you feel it too."

I stopped struggling. "I can handle it."

"I don't want you to have to."

"It's just sex, Kyland."

"That's not how it'd be with us. Hell, just kissing isn't just kissing with us." He looked pained as if that was very bad news.

"You've had sex with other girls."

He shook his head. "You're not like them. And I've never

been anyone's first. I've...been with girls, yes, but never in a way I thought was unfair to them. If you and I had sex, it'd be unfair to both of us."

Maybe I should have been happy he apparently held me in such high regard. But the only thing I could manage to feel was hurt and jealous that he wouldn't do the things with me he'd done with plenty of other girls. "Fine. Let me up," I huffed.

"Tenleigh," he groaned, looking up at the ceiling as if he was completely frustrated. "Stubborn spitfire," he muttered, but there was a smile in his voice.

I made a scoffing sound and started struggling again, but Kyland leaned down and planted his mouth on mine. I made a sound of resistance, but it might have been overruled by me pressing my body up into his and the fact that I wove my fingers through his hair to pull him more firmly into my mouth. He kissed me hard and with intensity and I ground my body into his to get the relief I needed.

Suddenly Kyland was off me and the quilt was ripped from my body as he hurriedly removed my clothes and then his own. He was quickly back over me, and when I saw his erection jutting out stiffly in front of him, I thought maybe he'd changed his mind. He came down on top of me and I opened my legs to him.

He groaned as if in pain and slid down my body. My eyes sprung open wide when I felt his warm, wet tongue make contact with my most sensitive area. I reached my arms out and gripped the bedding in my fists as I threw my head back and moaned deeply. "Good God, Kyland," I gasped as he lapped at me, circling my swollen tissue. I felt like I might scream with the pleasure.

I gripped his head in my hands and pressed shamelessly

into his face until I couldn't hold back the ecstasy that tore through me, causing me to arch my back and gasp out Kyland's name again and again.

When I opened my bleary eyes, he was over me. "Are we friends again?" he asked, grinning.

I put my hand on his cheek and said very seriously. "We were never just friends."

His smile faded. "I know."

"But you are good at that."

He nuzzled his head into my neck. "I know." I pushed at him and he chuckled. "I'm just kidding."

"No, you're not."

"Okay, I'm not."

I went serious. I didn't like to think about how he'd gotten so good at that. A ball of red-hot jealousy was burning in my chest and I felt like throwing things again, or flipping tables the way I'd done to make Marlo put that note in the Monopoly box.

"Come here," he said, pulling the blankets over himself and holding them open for me to slide inside next to him. I did. He spooned into me as he pulled the blankets up over us. I could feel his arousal pressing against my ass. I wiggled into him and he hissed. I reached behind me to stroke him, but he held my hand against my hip. "Let me just hold you," he said into my ear.

"But you—"

"Let me hold you," he repeated.

I paused but relaxed back into his hard chest. "Have you"—I bit my lip—"held other girls like this?" I dared to ask. I held my breath, waiting for his answer. I so desperately wanted just one part of him that he hadn't shared with another girl.

"No," he said quietly. "Just you." I relaxed again in happy satisfaction. He brought his arm around me and pulled me even closer. He was warm and big, and I melted into him, feeling safe and protected and so very, very comfortable. I sighed and he kissed my shoulder. "Sleep, little spitfire," he whispered.

We were both quiet for a few minutes and I wondered if he'd fallen asleep.

"I won't regret this when you leave," I whispered.

For a minute there was only the sound of the wind outside the window. And then he said very softly, "Neither will I."

I fell into a peaceful sleep, and when I woke to Kyland's hand running lazily between my legs in the middle of the night, I sighed and opened my eyes, watching the gently falling snow through the window next to his bed. He brought me to orgasm and then I returned the favor, stroking him until he panted and groaned out his own release, calling my name into the darkness of the room.

In the deep of the night, I heard what sounded like choking sounds and I woke up tangled with Kyland, his skin clammy and his muscles tense. "Kyland," I whispered, shaking him slightly. He startled awake.

"You were dreaming."

He sucked in a big breath. "Yes."

"What was it about?" I ran my fingers gently through his hair.

He paused for several moments. "Them. Down there, buried alive under the earth. I dream of them sometimes. And it feels like I'm choking."

I pressed myself closer to his body and wrapped my arms around him, holding him tightly. Just like when he'd told me about his mama, I was surprised he was letting me in again, and making himself vulnerable in front of me. Surprised, but grateful. "I'm so sorry."

He exhaled a loud breath. "They lived for three days underground before the oxygen was gone. Three days."

I hadn't known that. I knew there was a rescue effort, and I knew when they found the men, they were all dead, but I hadn't known they'd been able to tell they had lived for three days. I shivered, imagining what that must have been like.

"Is that why you have—"

"Claustrophobia?" He paused. "Partly. When I was about seven, my brother and I were playing hide-and-seek in the woods next to the Privens' house. We were always outside..." He cleared his throat and continued. "Anyway, there was this old refrigerator on the ground at the edge of their property and I climbed inside to hide. It latched behind me and I couldn't get out." His voice sounded strangled with the memory alone and I kissed his chest and squeezed him tighter. "They finally found me, but it'd been hours and I thought I would die in there. It was like being buried alive. And then when my father and my brother died the way they did, I felt that feeling all over again and imagined the anguish and terror they must have experienced. Suddenly, small spaces made me feel like I'd lose my mind. Even being in the shower sometimes...I have to keep the shower curtain open." He chuckled self-consciously. "It's irrational, but..."

"Not it's not. Not at all."

He brought his arms around me and stroked my arm as he held me and I thought about how he'd been so alone... for so long.

"Kyland?"

"Hmm?"

"How do you…that is, how *have* you…survived all this time? How do you have money for food? Heat?"

He was quiet for a second. "I don't like talking about that, Tenleigh."

"You don't have to. It's okay." My words came out in a whispery rush. *Oh, Kyland. What do you do? How do you take care of yourself?* I kissed his bare skin, letting my lips linger there.

We were both silent for a few minutes. Finally, he said very quietly, "I do whatever I have to do. I collect scrap metal on the weekends. I set traps for muskrats and rabbits and sell them or eat them if I have to. I've collected bottle caps…whatever I have to do, that's what I do. Mostly I'm fine. Sometimes I even have a little money for electricity. Sometimes I don't. The end of the month is always the hardest, when I've paid the bills I can and don't have anything left."

I won't cry. I won't cry.

He'd said he didn't like to talk about this, but even so, he'd just shared a such personal part of his heart with me. Maybe it was that I had shared my pain with him. Maybe it was because the dark made it easier to tell secrets. I wasn't sure.

What I did know, was that the things you did to survive were the most personal of all—the fight to live would humble you in ways you didn't ever want anyone else to know about. Because sometimes it was unspeakable. Sometimes it was ugly and shameful and beautiful and courageous all at once. And he'd just given me some of that. I felt sad, horrified, anguished for him, but I felt deeply honored too. I squeezed him tighter. "I think you're amazing," I said, "and so very brave."

"I'm not brave, Tenleigh. I get up and live my sucky life. What else can I do?"

I was quiet, thinking about that, thinking there were a

119

thousand different ways a person could give up, and Kyland hadn't chosen any of them. He had no idea how strong and courageous he really was.

"Hey, Tenleigh," he whispered after a while.

"Yes?"

"That book *The Road*?"

"Hmm hmm?" I murmured, remembering his bad joke, using the word "devour" in reference to a book about cannibals. I smiled sleepily.

"There's this line in it that talks about keeping a little fire burning inside, 'however small, however hidden.'"

"Yes," I said softly.

"I think about that line sometimes. I think about how that little fire is *hope*. I think about how you have to keep it burning to get you through the hard times, the times that seem so painful you don't want to continue on."

I opened my eyes, looking around at the shifting shadows in his bedroom. "What keeps your fire burning?"

"The hope that life won't always hurt so badly. The belief that I'll get out of here someday—that I won't be cold or hungry forever. It keeps me going. It's my fire. It helps me do the things I need to do to survive, and it helps me hate myself less for doing them."

Oh, Kyland.

I turned my face into his chest and kissed his skin again. He brought his arms around me and held me tightly to him.

After a few minutes, his breathing grew even and I knew he'd fallen back to sleep. I lay there in the dark for a long time thinking about the amazing boy Kyland had to become to be able to survive against such odds. Until that moment, I didn't know my heart could be filled with awe and grief, joy and sorrow, all at the exact same time.

CHAPTER THIRTEEN
Tenleigh

I left early the next day, pulling on my clothes in the frigid morning air and kissing Kyland goodbye as he slept. He hadn't had any more bad dreams, but I didn't want to wake him. We'd been up most of the night. A warm flush covered my skin as I relived what we'd experienced together in his bed. I wanted to dive back under those warm covers and experience every bit of it again. But I didn't know what time Marlo would be home and I wanted to be there when she arrived with our mama. And so I snuck out of his room quietly, leaving my Christmas tree glowing in the corner, and closing his front door behind me.

Something about the whole world seemed different to me this morning as I trudged through the snow to our trailer. The cold seemed colder, the air fresher, the pine trees more fragrant, the blue sky even brighter. I felt *alive*.

I rushed through our trailer door and turned up the heaters just enough to make it comfortable inside. I took a quick shower and changed into clean clothes, layering two sweaters and two pairs of worn wool socks. I towel-dried my hair and then piled it up into a messy bun on top of my head.

There was some oatmeal in our cabinet, so I made that and added some cinnamon, eating it sitting on the couch, wrapped in a blanket.

My mind went immediately to Kyland. I thought about everything I'd learned about him since yesterday. I thought about the loneliness he must have faced. I thought about all it had taken for him to survive and my heart pinched. I wondered if he was still sleeping. Hopefully. What would happen between us now? I didn't know if I should expect anything at all. Perhaps last night was a one-time experience. The thought alone was deeply disappointing.

Oh, Tenleigh, don't be stupid. This won't end well for you if you hope for anything.

I sighed, and spooned more oatmeal into my mouth. He had spelled it out for me. I could never say that he'd promised me anything more than what we'd had last night. From what I gathered, he had resisted even that for as long as he could. *He hadn't wanted any entanglements.* Which meant me. And kissing me—sharing our bodies—didn't change that. He'd offered what he could honestly, and I'd accepted.

Maybe I was making this way too complicated based on my mama's and my sister's experiences with men. Couldn't I enjoy Kyland temporarily and then part ways when it was time for that? I'd probably be sad—maybe I'd even shed a few tears over it—but then I'd move on and so would he. The memories would fade as life continued forward.

And he was probably right to limit our sexual interaction. Maybe he was thinking more clearly than I was on that matter. After all, he had more experience. I tapped my spoon on the plastic bowl. Would he still be seeing other girls?

Could I ask him not to? No, I had no right. I let my head fall back against the wall behind me, grimacing as I pictured him with another girl in his bed, doing the things we had done.

I put my empty bowl on the coffee table and wrapped my arms around myself. Clearly, I was already doing badly at separating my body from my heart.

An engine sounded outside my trailer, followed by doors slamming and then footsteps. I bolted up, flinging the door open.

Marlo and Sam and my mama, supported by both of them, were almost at the door.

"Mama," I breathed when I saw her, reaching my hand outside the door to take hers as she walked up the steps. She gave me a small, tired smile and stepped into the trailer. Marlo and Sam followed her. I quickly moved the blanket I'd been using aside on the couch and made a place for her.

"Sweetheart, I'd like to lie down," Mama said weakly.

"Of course, Mama," I whispered, shooting a questioning look at Marlo, who looked tired. She smiled, though, and gave me a reassuring nod, indicating Mama was okay.

I led Mama to the small bedroom she and Marlo shared in the back of the trailer and she lay down on the bed. I removed her shoes and brought her quilt up over her. "Thank you, Tenleigh." She reached her hand out for me and I took it, sitting beside her on the bed.

Her expression was filled with sadness. "I'm so sorry, baby. So sorry."

My eyes filled with tears. "I just want you to get better, Mama."

"Me too. I just can't quite figure out how. It's all such a mess. I'm such a mess. I try to stop it, baby, I really do. But when the darkness comes…" Her words faded as she squeezed her eyes shut.

"I love you, Mama. No matter what, I love you."

Tears slipped from her eyes. "I know you do, baby. And that makes it better. It does." She turned on her side, seeming to be done talking for now, looking sleepy; she was probably medicated. I smoothed her dark hair back out of her face and watched as her pretty features relaxed into sleep.

I sat there for a few more minutes, gathering myself, and then I left her alone to rest, closing her bedroom door behind me.

"She seems better," I said to Marlo quietly. Marlo and Sam were sitting on the couch, Sam's elbows resting on his knees as he looked around our trailer. If he was shocked by the size and condition of our living situation, he didn't show it. He'd probably seen worse if he'd made any house calls.

"She is. For now," Marlo said and sighed. We knew the drill. How long she'd be better was the mystery.

"Well, Sam, thank you for your help this weekend," Marlo said, standing, clearly dismissing him.

He raised his eyebrows as if he hadn't been expecting the instant dismissal yet got up to leave. "Of course. Are you sure you don't need me to…?" he trailed off, seeming to be unsure of what to offer exactly.

"No. We're good now. Thank you."

Well, this is uncomfortable.

"Thank you so much, Sam," I said, reaching my hand out to him and offering a warm smile. "It was so kind of you—"

"My pleasure." He glanced shyly at Marlo who was biting her nail. "If you can think of anything at all that you need, please don't hesitate to call me."

I nodded and Marlo started walking him toward the door. "Oh," he said, turning back around and almost colliding with her. They both laughed uncomfortably, color staining his cheekbones. He really was a handsome man—sort of nerdy with his glasses and parted hair, but he had definite potential. He seemed to really like her, if his awkward, bumbling behavior around her was any indication.

He took what looked like a pharmacy bag out of his pocket. "Make sure your mother takes this just as instructed. The doctor seemed like he was optimistic that this cocktail would really work well for her."

We'd been optimistic before.

Marlo nodded. "I will. Thank you again."

He hesitated for just a second, but then he smiled and nodded at both of us and walked out the door of our trailer, shutting it firmly behind him. A few seconds later, we heard his car start up.

Marlo dropped down on the couch and let out a loud sigh.

I sat down next to her and turned my body toward her. She looked at me sideways. "I should be very upset with you, little sister."

"But you're not?" I asked.

She took a deep breath, looking thoughtful. "I guess not. Sam, he's…a nice guy, mostly harmless, I think." She tilted her head and bit her lip. "And he was very helpful with Mama."

"She seemed tired but better than she has coming home from the hospital in the past."

"Yeah. Just Sam's 'doctor' title, or maybe just the fact that he's a man, got him a lot further with the doctors on Mama's floor than you or I ever did. They put her on a new cocktail they thought would help her."

"Cocktail…meaning a mixture of medications… meaning more than one…meaning—"

"We won't be able to afford it, I know." She let out a sigh. "And maybe it won't even work any better. But Dr. Nolan, *Sam*, he paid for the second medication even though

125

I told him not to." She looked at me almost guiltily. "It was for Mama, though, so I let him."

"It was the right thing to do, Mar," I said. I knew she wouldn't do it again, though. And like she'd said, maybe the new combination of medication wouldn't make a difference anyway. Lord knew we'd been through enough medications that did nothing at all for Mama—some that even made her worse. Some that had terrible side effects.

I eyed Marlo. "So, Sam...I think he really likes you."

She made a scoffing sound. "Sure, for now."

"Marlo—"

"No, listen. He's a nice guy and good-looking...but he's a successful man. He doesn't even *belong* here. Not really." She paused. "But he did help make the time there go by more quickly, so for that, I'm grateful."

"Thanks for taking this turn,"I said. "Missing Christmas..."

She looked over at me sadly. "I had company at least, though. You, you were all alone in this trailer." She grabbed my hand. "I figured you spent it reading. Were you okay?"

I looked down, my cheeks heating.

"What's that look?"

I opened my mouth to speak, but hesitated.

"Tenleigh." Marlo's voice held a warning note as if I better start speaking and fast.

"Well... I wasn't exactly alone. And I wasn't exactly here."

"What? Where the hell were you?"

She already knew Kyland had walked me home from the Christmas show that had gone so horribly wrong. I hesitantly told her everything that had happened before that, how I'd first met him just recently even though we were in school together and lived so close, what had happened at the library, the play... She was my sister, my best friend. I told her everything.

When I was finished, she studied me for a moment. "Wow, Tenleigh. I certainly missed a lot when I was lying around in that waiting room." She paused, seeming to consider all I'd told her. "And at least he's been honest with you about where you stand. At least you know he's leaving. He's not trying to trick you into something and then take off like most of them do."

I nodded. I couldn't deny that had been our collective experience thus far, but something inside of me still wanted to argue against it. Something inside of me still wanted to believe some men were good and honorable. And sometimes they stayed.

Only Kyland wouldn't stay. He'd made that exceedingly clear.

"Can you handle it, Ten?" Marlo asked softly.

"I don't know," I answered honestly. "But there might be nothing more to handle. You know, Christmas is lonely, and we have this attraction..." I ran a finger over my lips remembering the feel of his mouth on mine. "It might have just been the timing of everything, you know? That might be the extent of my nonrelationship with Kyland Barrett. We didn't make any promises and we didn't make any plans." I sat up straighter. I'd be fine, though. I always was. I'd be fine because I had no other choice.

Marlo smiled and squeezed my hand. "I'm going to take a shower and then I'm going to go lie down with Mama," she said, standing up, yawning. "I barely got any sleep at all in that hospital waiting room. Although it sounds like you didn't get much either."

After she'd shut the bathroom door behind her, I sat on the couch alone again. After a few minutes, I grabbed my book and lay back. I had trouble concentrating, thoughts of Kyland swirling through my mind, a feeling of melancholy overwhelming my heart, and the words I'd said to Marlo condensing and repeating in my mind: *No promises, no plans.*

CHAPTER FOURTEEN
Tenleigh

Something roused me from sleep. I blinked and sat up, registering a soft tap on the door. It was utterly dark. What the heck?

The tapping came again. I pulled the quilt around my body and said very quietly against the door, "Who is it?"

"Kyland."

My heart flipped. I pulled the door open. There Kyland stood in his coat and hat, his hands shoved in his pockets, and a look I couldn't read on his face.

"Hi." I smiled sleepily. "What are you doing here?" I asked, glancing back at the bedroom where my mama and sister were sleeping.

"I, uh, I just wanted to make sure you were okay."

I furrowed my brow, pulling the quilt more tightly around myself as the cold air from outside chilled me. "Why wouldn't I be okay?"

"Uh, I figured your mama was home. You know, I just wanted to check on you…her…"

"In the middle of the night? You could have come by earlier today."

Kyland looked up at the dark, starlit sky as if this was the first time he'd realized it was nighttime. When his eyes met mine again, the expression on his face embarrassed and unsure. I studied him standing there under the winter sky, the vapor of his breath rising in the cold air.

"Are you lonely, Ky?" I asked softly.

"What? No, I mean, that's not why I'm here. I'm not here for me. I'm here for you."

I tilted my head and licked my bottom lip. His eyes darted to it and he swallowed.

"It's okay to want something for yourself sometimes."

It's okay to want me. I hope you do. God, I hope you do.

"I know, I just thought you'd probably be getting your mama settled. How is she?"

"She's okay. Better. She got up and helped make dinner tonight. So that was a good sign."

He nodded and we were both silent for a second as he shifted on his feet. "You should tell me to go, Tenleigh. And say it like you mean it. Tell me to leave because I can't seem to do it on my own."

"I don't want you to leave," I said softly.

A loud whoosh of air escaped his throat and he shifted on his feet some more.

"Do you want me to come back to your place?"

"Could you? I mean, you can? You would?"

"Yeah. Hold on." I stepped back inside and quietly closed the door. I quickly wrote a note to Marlo, letting her know I'd gone to Kyland's and that I'd be home in the morning. She'd make an excuse for me to Mama. We didn't talk to Mama about that kind of thing. We just simply never had. It'd be weird to start now.

I was already wearing sweatpants and a long-sleeved shirt, so I just pulled my boots and jacket on quietly and left the trailer.

The look on Kyland's face when I stepped outside was pure relief. "You sure this is okay?" he asked.

"Yes, it's fine. I *figured* you hadn't gotten your fill of my body yet, so I wasn't surprised to see you at my door."

He stopped, looking stricken. "Tenleigh, no, that's not why I'm here. I'm not here to use you. I just…sleeping with you last night was so…and I couldn't, and I thought, maybe you couldn't…" He laughed a humorless laugh, frowning up at the sky. "I'm really fumbling this. And I woke you up in the middle of the night—"

"Kyland, It's okay. I was teasing. I liked sleeping with you too. Just the sleeping part." I smiled. "I mean, I especially liked the other parts, but the sleeping part was good too. So can we get to that? It's late. If you've done enough tortured brooding, I mean."

He paused, rubbing at the back of his neck and then chuckling softly. "I don't brood."

I snorted. "Oh, you brood. You could give lessons on brooding. You might very well be the foremost expert on brooding." I was almost surprised at my ability to joke and make light, but I was so genuinely happy to see him. And I was so happy he'd wanted to see me too.

He chuckled again and clasped my hand as we walked.

Five minutes later, we were walking in his front door.

We didn't talk as we walked to his bed. I took off my boots and jacket and then stripped down to my underwear. We'd only been together one time, we'd only touched each other intimately one night, but somehow I already felt comfortable in front of him.

He stripped down to his own underwear and got in under the covers next to me. He pulled my back into his chest and buried his nose in my hair. The exhale that came from him sounded like he'd been storing it up for hours and hours. I pulled his arms around me and held him as he held me.

"Thank you," he said, his voice low and raspy. Something in his tone sounded almost...*desperate*. I turned in his arms, concerned.

He looked at me in the dim light of the room, his eyes filled with some kind of pain. I frowned and put my hand on his cheek.

"Kyland—" I started.

But he shook his head, cutting me off. "I'm sorry."

"Sorry for what?" I whispered.

"Sorry for not being able to stay away from you. Sorry for not being able to stop thinking about you. Sorry for starting to walk over to your trailer every five minutes since I woke up and you were gone. Sorry for being so damn selfish."

My heart soared even as it dropped. "You're not being selfish. I missed you today too. It's okay. I'm not asking you for anything more than you can give. I'm not."

"I'm sorry for that most of all."

"What? *That* what?"

He shook his head slowly again. "That I have nothing to give you. That I can only take from you. And that's wrong."

"It's not wrong if I'm offering it."

"Yes it is. It's still wrong."

I studied the angles of his face in the near-darkness and ran my finger over his cheekbone, down his jaw, and over those full, beautiful lips.

"Well. I'm sorry to render your moral dilemma null and

131

void, but honestly, *I'm* only in this for your body, Kyland Barrett. So you can let yourself off the hook."

He laughed and pulled me into him. I inhaled the scent of his skin, masculine and clean.

After a minute, I asked, "Were you having a bad dream again? Is that why you couldn't sleep?"

He paused and I wondered if he'd answer me, and so when his deep voice filled the silence, I stilled completely. "The dreams aren't the hard part. It's not talking about my family that's been the hardest. And I guess I didn't even realize it until last night." He let out gust of breath. "It was the first time I've talked about my mama, dad, and brother aloud since I lost them. And it sort of, I don't know, brought them back to life in a way I didn't expect."

"A good way or a bad way?" I asked.

"Both I guess."

Yeah, I could understand that. I stroked his cheek again. "I'm so sorry you've been holding all that pain inside for so long." It must be a particular kind of loneliness not to have anyone to share your sorrows with. I had my own hardships, but I also had Marlo.

"I've spent so many lonely nights here in this bed," Kyland said, "and last night, having you here felt so damn good." He made a sound in the back of his throat. "This, you here. It feels so good."

"I know. It feels good to me too," I whispered.

We lay there forehead to forehead, breath to breath, and toes to toes for a few minutes, until I finally got up the nerve to ask, "Will you tell me a little about Silas? I saw him around town now and again, but I never met him."

He released a breath. "He was…" He seemed to take a few seconds to consider. "Full of life. He was a smartass and a practical joker." His lips moved into a smile in the darkened room. "He was always laughing. I can still hear his laugh if I close my eyes. He laughed with his whole body, you know? Like he doubled over and stumbled and it was just..." He laughed a small laugh and I smiled. "He could be such a goofball. The other day when we were sledding, I swore I heard his laughter echoing through the mountains when I was coasting down that hill. I swore I did."

My heart squeezed. And then we were both silent for a minute. I allowed him to gather his thoughts.

"He was five years older than me, but we did everything together. We ran through these mountains pretending we were cowboys and superheroes." He smiled, but it was small and vanished quickly. "We were always afraid of the dark when we were kids. Silas, he always begged our mama to keep the hall light on." He paused again. "He died in the pitch-darkness underground, Tenleigh. The power went out after the cave-in and they were all under there in black-ness. And I can't help...I can't help but think he was afraid. He was probably so scared. I hear him over and over in my mind, whispering to me like he did from his bed when we were kids, 'Get up and turn on the light, Ky.' And there's nothing I can do for him. Nothing at all."

I squeezed my eyes shut against the tears that threatened. "They were together, though, your dad and your brother. All those men. I bet they helped each other cope. All the ones I knew, they were such good men. I bet they were all there for each other in the end."

"Yeah," he said softly.

We lay there in silence for a few minutes until Kyland leaned forward and kissed me slowly and deeply and there was something different in his kiss, but I didn't know exactly what.

He pulled his lips away but moved his body closer to mine. "You drive me crazy," he murmured. He brushed his lips across mine lightly and I shivered. "And you make the darkness go away. You bring me some kind of peace." He let out a harsh exhale of breath and I drank it in. "I don't know what to do with it."

"Take it, Ky," I whispered. "You *deserve* some peace. Let me give it to you."

"And what do I give to you, sweet Tenleigh?" he asked on a broken whisper. "What can I possibly give to you?"

I thought about it for a second. "You help me believe."

"In what?"

"In goodness, in strength."

In the fact that there are good men out there who are honorable.

He smoothed a piece of hair back out of my face.

"Plus, your ass. You have a really great ass," I said.

He gave a short laugh that turned into a sigh. "I know."

I punched him lightly on his shoulder and he grinned, crossing his eyes.

"You're touched," I said, using a word mountain folk use to mean "loopy."

Still grinning, he nuzzled his nose into my neck. "Hmm. I like how your inner hick comes out when you're annoyed."

I laughed, not feeling annoyed at all. "Did you know that mountain dialect can be traced back to Elizabethan English?"

"No, I didn't know that," he said, running his nose along my jaw.

"Mm-hmm. Appalachia and other places have held on to it because there are so many areas that are so remote—cut off from the rest of society in a lot of ways...like how we add a *t* to the end of words like twice and across."

"Ah. So when I go to New York and say, 'Pull up a cheer and set a spell. You look a mite peaked,' they'll think I'm speaking the King's English?"

I laughed. "No, they'll think you need a translator, but you do sound sexy when you talk all hillbilly like."

He made a humming sound and nipped at my jaw. "You like that, huh? Good to know. Because later"—he trailed his lips down my neck—"I reckon I'll go down yonder."

I laughed again and pushed him away, as he laughed too. As our laughter faded, Kyland pushed my hair back out of my face tenderly, his gaze filled with something I wasn't sure how to read, his lips still turned up in a small smile. My eyes moved over his beautiful face, trying to discern what he was feeling.

After a moment, he leaned forward and kissed me lightly. "What are your dreams? Tell me," he whispered.

To fall in love with someone who stays. To stop wishing so hard it could be you.

"Hmm. To see the ocean. To dance in the surf. To go to dinner at a restaurant. To have more than one pair of shoes. To get one of those store-bought birthday cakes with the perfect pink roses in the corners. To get my mama a good doctor who knows how to heal her. To be a teacher—to inspire kids to love books as much as I do. To live in a house with a yard and a garden and my very own bed."

He was quiet for a second. Finally, he said very quietly, "You should have all those things and more."

"What are your dreams, Kyland? Other than leaving here…what things do you hope for?"

He was silent for several beats. "I want to be an engineer. I want to have a refrigerator that's always stocked with food. I want to do something that matters—that really, truly makes

135

a difference. And I want to be wise enough to recognize that thing when it shows up."

I smiled, grateful he had shared that part of his heart with me. "I bet you'll do all those things and even more," I said, feeling just a tinge of sadness. I wanted him to achieve his dreams, but I wondered if, when he did, I would only be a small memory in his head.

He wove his fingers into my hair and put his mouth on mine again and I melted into his kiss.

We found release in each other's bodies like we'd done the night before and then we slept, wrapped around each other—the loneliness and the cold left outside the warm cocoon of our blankets.

CHAPTER FIFTEEN
Tenleigh

I went to Kyland's bed almost every night of Christmas break. He wouldn't make love to me despite my often and shameless begging. But we became experts on each other's bodies nonetheless. We whispered in the dark of night, telling our secrets and revealing our hurts. He told me about his father and his brother and the more he talked, the easier the words seemed to come—the more he smiled and laughed at the memories he shared. He told me about his mama, about the hurt he'd harbored for so long, the confusion and the pain.

"Do you think you'll look for her?" I asked one Saturday morning as we lazed in his bed. "When you leave, I mean?" Just as it always did, pain speared through my heart at the word *leave*.

He seemed to consider my question for a few moments. "I've thought about it. But what would be the point? She left me. She never came back. Even if for some reason she didn't know about the mine accident, it doesn't take those two facts away."

I turned on my side to face him. "Maybe she didn't know, though. Maybe she thinks you were safe and living here with your father and brother. I know she left, but whatever her reasons were, she knew you were with your dad. Maybe she's afraid to come back because she thinks you won't ever forgive her for what she did."

"Do you forgive your father for abandoning you? Do you want to seek him out? What about you?"

His tone was cold and I flinched back from it.

Kyland rolled toward me and squeezed his eyes shut briefly, putting his hand on my cheek. "I'm sorry. That wasn't fair."

I took a deep breath. "No, it's a fair question. The difference is, I never knew my father. I think…I think I *do* forgive him. But to me, he'd be a stranger. Your mama, though, you loved her, and she loved you."

"I thought she did." Pain moved over his face. "But that's not even the worst part—do you want to hear the worst part?"

I nodded slowly. *Yes. I want to hear everything you have to tell me—good, bad, and in-between.*

"The worst part is that as hard as I try, as hurt as I am, I can't stop loving her. Even though I know she doesn't deserve it. She abandoned me and didn't look back, and I still love her. What kind of stupid fool am I?"

"You're not a fool," I said softly. I reached over and held him. There was nothing else I could do.

And as I held him, I thought about how strong and tenacious he was, moving forward, never stopping, never giving up, even though he had all the reason in the world to do just that. I thought about how intelligent he was, how caring, how selfless, how filled with love. "You're going to be just fine. You're so strong," I whispered. "In every way.

You're as strong as a bull and twice as stubborn." I smiled and I felt him smile too. "You've kept that fire burning all this time, despite all you've lost. There's nothing stronger than that. Nothing," I added softly.

We didn't get out of bed that day until the noontime sun was beaming through his window.

When we went back to school two weeks later, I grieved the loss of being in his bed, but it simply wasn't practical. The pressure was on now to start the final semester off right— this was it. This was our last chance to do well enough to win that scholarship. The problem was, for me, suddenly that scholarship was the very thing that was going to take him away from me, or me away from him. I'd been focused on winning for almost four years, and suddenly, I didn't know how I felt about it. I didn't even know if I wanted it anymore. After everything Kyland had been through and as strong as my feelings were for him, how could I hope to take his dream away, even if it meant achieving my own? How could I? He was giving it his all, everything he had, to accomplish the one thing that had kept him going for so many hard, lonely, hungry years.

But Kyland had told me that whether he won it or not, he was going to leave Dennville. And so he had a plan either way. But could I really hope that he would have to walk out of here with not much more than the shirt on his back? Could I really hope that he would have to suffer even more hardship than he already had? Just that thought alone filled me with fear for him and an aching loneliness.

You worry about your own self, Tenleigh Falyn, I thought, admonishing myself. Lord knew no one else was. I wondered, though, if Kyland thought about that scholarship differently too. If he did, he didn't share it with me. It seemed neither one of us wanted to discuss it.

I saw him in school and he grabbed my hand as we passed in the hallway, but we had assigned seating in the classes we shared and ate during different lunch periods, so we didn't spend much time together there. I was filled with turmoil though. I snuck glances at him in class, watching as he concentrated so hard on his assignments. I saw him out the widow of my classes, sitting in the courtyard cramming before a test.

But we quizzed each other as we walked up our mountain back home, and we studied together in the evenings, among other more pleasurable things.

One day in mid-January when I finally got around to checking out a new book in the library, I noticed a small white piece of paper sticking out of the one I had returned several weeks before.

I pulled *The Catcher in the Rye* off the shelf.

Holden Caulfield: A whiny, unlikable narrator. Insults those he calls "phonies," but he's really just one himself.—KB

I laughed softly and scrawled out my own note.

Holden Caulfield: A boy who feels alienated from society, is struggling to understand his place in the world, and is looking for someone he can relate to. A story about loneliness.—TF

Always the optimist, Tenleigh Falyn, even when it comes to unlikable characters.—KB

I smiled at his note. I'd never thought of myself as an optimist, but maybe I was. And maybe we all reacted to stories differently based on our own hearts.

In February, the top four students were announced, the students who were in the running for the Tyton Coal Scholarship. It was down to me, Kyland, and two other girls. I received my letter of admission from San Diego State University and I accepted. It seemed like a cruelty to accept something I may never get the chance to use, but if I won the scholarship, I had to have a school to apply it to. If I didn't win, I'd rescind my acceptance, as would the other two students. I didn't ask Kyland where he'd accepted. I didn't want to know.

All that winter and into early spring, we studied together, we kissed long and slow anywhere and everywhere, we hiked through the hills, and we showed each other the secret spots we loved deep in the Appalachian Mountains, where there was only beauty and only peace. We sat by streams and fished with Kyland's homemade fishing pole, my head on his lap, the sunshine warming our skin, the tall grass whispering in the breeze. We walked through meadows sprinkled with wildflowers and I collected them and put bouquets in old tin cans in my trailer and on Kyland's windowsill. We spent glorious nights exploring each other's bodies, learning every spot that brought pleasure. We read book after book, only discussing them through very short written notes that somehow gave a brief insight into the heart of the other.

I worked when I got the shifts. I struggled, I went hungry some nights, and I scraped together pennies to pay for Mama's medicine.

And I fell in love.

Deep, hard, utter, and complete love.

And he was still leaving. And he still wouldn't look back.

Maybe I'd be leaving too. Anxiety and worry moved through my body whenever I considered it. It wasn't *only* the confusion of the scholarship and how it would impact Kyland if I won it; it was also the thought of leaving my home. I'd dreamed of going to college for so long and, suddenly, leaving my mama, leaving Marlo, leaving everything I knew and...yes, loved—for I did love Dennville, Kentucky, despite the fact that misery lived here too—suddenly, all of it filled me with fear and panic.

Maybe it also had to do with the fact that my mama was doing so much better since she'd been on the new medications. She'd been getting out of bed on her own every day and showering. She'd even started taking walks. She seemed almost normal, and I had never ever used that word to describe my mama. She was *better*, and she was *worse*, but she'd never been normal. It was like Marlo and I were getting a second chance with her. But what would happen when I was no longer here? We were barely scraping together the money it took to buy her prescriptions as it was. When I left, there'd be that much less of an income, as small as it was. Of course, they wouldn't have to feed me anymore either.

But when I thought about *not* winning it, my heart plummeted to my feet. What would I do then? Would I work full-time at Al's like Marlo did? What other choice did I have? There were no jobs here that paid more than minimum wage, and unlike Kyland, I didn't have the courage to start hitchhiking across the country with little more than a knapsack on my back. Plus, I had people here tying me to Dennville. Kyland didn't have anyone...well, anyone except me. And despite the fact that we'd gotten very close, he couldn't stay for me. And I wouldn't ask him to.

Sometimes I caught him looking at me with this strange expression on his face—a mixture of pain and decisiveness. I wasn't sure what it meant, but it made me feel jittery and nervous.

Could I handle getting even closer to Kyland only to have him leave and never look back? Could I handle loving him more deeply? Or could he…*would he* change his mind about cutting all ties now that our relationship had deepened to…well, to more than it had been?

"Stupid Tenleigh," I muttered. I'd gotten myself in this situation despite the fact that Kyland had done everything in his power to warn me away. But I couldn't regret it. I couldn't. I loved him. He was a part of my heart and I hoped desperately that I had become enough of a part of his that it'd be impossible for him to simply leave me behind.

Persuasion by Jane Austen:

"But when pain is over, the remembrance of it often becomes a pleasure." Do you believe this, Tenleigh?—KB

I leaned back on the library bookshelf and put my pen to my lips, considering. Finally, I wrote:

I think that when enough time has passed, when you've survived that which you didn't imagine you could, there's a dignity in that. Something you can own. A pride in knowing the pain made you stronger. The pain made you fight to succeed. Someday, when I'm living my dreams, I'm going to think of all the things that broke my heart and I'm going to be thankful for them.—TF

Even you, Kyland.

CHAPTER SIXTEEN
Kyland

Things were out of hand with Tenleigh. I couldn't stop myself from craving her—her voice, her thoughts, her laughter, her smell, her taste, her delectable body, her lips— just *her*. I'd done the exact thing I'd vowed not to do—I'd formed an attachment that I wouldn't be able to simply leave behind in a couple months. An attachment? Hell, I was practically obsessed with her. I was screwed, completely royally screwed. And yet I *would* leave her behind. That's exactly what I'd do. Because anything else was unthinkable. I felt like I was drowning in her, and just like a drowning person, my instinct was to thrash and resist—*fight*. Fight this thing that had taken over my body and my heart. Fight *her*. I needed to begin spending less time with her to soften the eventual blow. For her, but mostly, for me.

I sat staring blindly out at the town below from the hill Tenleigh and I had sledded on months before...the day I'd started something with her, there was no turning back from.

From here, the town far below looked like it could offer

a life to Tenleigh and me. From here, you couldn't see the garbage and the poverty, the misery, and the unspeakable things that went on behind closed doors in the dark of the night. I put my head in my hands and raked my fingers through my hair. I was crumbling.

"You pierce my soul. I am half agony, half hope."

Oh yes.

I had read those words in *Persuasion* and I'd almost repeated them to her as I gazed at her tender face, her lips swollen and red with my kisses, her eyes full of what I knew was love. I'd stopped myself. It wouldn't be fair. I'd let her in, in ways I'd never let anyone in. But I hadn't made love to her. And I hadn't told her I loved her or let her say it to me, even if it was clear on her face. I vowed to let that be the barrier between us that would allow me to walk out of here with at least a part of my heart intact, still in possession of at least *one* part of me she didn't own. That'd be the part that would spur my feet forward, *away*.

I had tried so hard to resist her, but I was too weak and too selfish. And now we were both going to pay the price when I left.

Maybe we could be together...someday. Someday when I'd seen the world, when I'd made something of myself, when I'd found out what type of life I could have away from here. There had to be places filled with happiness, with hope. Although, it didn't escape me that Tenleigh had given me just a little bit of that back. For so very, very long, I'd pushed the memories of my parents and Silas away. They were too painful, filled with too much grief. And with the bad, I'd had to push away the good. I couldn't separate them in my mind. But then she'd come along, and she'd helped me do that...somehow without even meaning to. And now these hills felt different for the first time in four years. They'd started whispering to me again, the way they did when I was a little boy. It was a feeling, more than a sound. But I pushed it away. These hills should know I was leaving too.

A few weeks ago when I'd been walking home from school, I'd caught sight of a bunny scurrying under a bush, and a memory hit me all at once, so suddenly that I halted and stood there staring off into the woods as if I'd been hit over the head.

One year when I was about ten and Silas was fifteen, we had seen an injured baby bunny hopping across the road. We'd caught it and brought it home, keeping it in the old shed behind our house. We fed it milk from an eye dropper and, eventually, soft vegetables. We named him Bugs, and once he got strong enough, we let him out of the shed, dropping him off on the side of the road near where we'd found him. Silas had said that he'd have a better chance of finding his bunny family that way. I'd cried and Silas had called me a big ol' baby, but he'd put his arm around my shoulders as we'd walked back home.

A few years later, though, Silas and I had been sitting outside one night, my mama and dad inside fighting. Silas had just turned eighteen and was about to graduate, and he was planning on going to work in the mine. My dad did okay; we had what we needed. But we hadn't been able to afford college for Silas even though he was just about the smartest person I knew. "Just a few months, Ky," he'd whispered. "Just until I've got enough money to get us out of here and then we'll leave. We won't look back. Where do you want to go?"

"New York City," I'd answered, just like I always did.

He'd nodded as if it were the first time he'd heard me say it. "Then that's where we'll go. I just need a couple months of my wages and we'll hit the road, baby bro. You'll never work in those mines. You'll do something big, something *great*, something that really matters. And who knows? Maybe I will too."

Suddenly, off to our right, we saw movement and when we swiveled our heads, there was a rabbit. He sat right at the edge of our yard, watching us for a minute and then he limped off. And in my heart, I'd known it was Bugs. And seeing him there was like a sign that everything was going to be okay. Life could injure you, but you could get up again if you were strong enough, and especially if you had the right person to help you out. Silas had put his hand on my shoulder and we'd sat that way until the house was quiet again and it was safe to go back inside.

I owed it not only to myself but also to my brother to make a life somewhere else, to live the dream he'd been denied. And maybe if Tenleigh had to stay here, someday I'd come back for her. Or maybe she'd fade away into a sweet memory. Maybe she'd meet some decent guy in Evansly who worked the mines, and they'd make a couple babies. And sure, they'd struggle and have to scrape together rent money sometimes, and she'd buy her kids clothes from the bargain rack at Walmart, but they'd be happy enough and—

Fuck no.

I wanted to roar with the anger and frustration those thoughts brought me, making me feel more desperate than I'd ever felt in my miserable life. Tenleigh Falyn. Beautiful, hopeful, smart, fiery, tenderhearted Tenleigh Falyn deserved a life better than the scraping and struggling she'd always done. I put my head back in my hands. This was an impossible situation. Picturing her enduring a lifetime of hardship made me feel violent. I picked up a pine cone on the ground next to me and threw it as hard as I could off the hill to the trees below. Distantly, I heard it hit something, but it was a soft, unsatisfying sound.

After a few minutes, I stood up and headed home, my hands stuffed in my pockets. A warm breeze blew, and the ground was scattered with the wildflowers Tenleigh loved so much, the ones she still gasped over even though she'd been seeing them all her life. Spring had officially arrived.

Finals were right around the corner and I had a lot of studying to do. But honestly, I wasn't worried. I knew all the material so well, I could recite it in my sleep. I'd be shocked if I wasn't chosen to win that scholarship. My academic record was nothing less than perfect. I'd made sure of that, despite the fact that I was living in a constant rotating state of euphoria/agony, and despite the fact that most of the time my mind was focused on the constant ache between my legs—an ache that was only going to be satisfied if I plunged into Tenleigh's tight body. "No," I spoke out loud. "Just no." *You think things are bad for you now, Kyland, possess her that way and* then *try to leave her here.* I made a choking sound in my throat as I felt acid rising from my stomach.

Somehow I'd resisted that so far, and I wouldn't back down now. I took a deep cleansing breath of mountain air just as my house came into view. I passed by Tenleigh's trailer and resisted going to her door and knocking, instead, picking up my pace so my traitorous body wouldn't make the choice for me.

She'd probably wondered where I was after school today. I'd been ducking out the back door and taking the long way home—alone—so I could avoid her. She hadn't said anything, but I was sure she was probably hurt. I *needed* to start hurting her in small ways, though. She had to understand what was happening and start pulling away from me like I was pulling away from her. That way, at least it would be easier than ripping the Band-Aid off in a couple months. *A couple months and I'll never see her again.* Desperation raced through my veins.

I heard feminine laughter drifting out of the trailer and something inside me rejoiced as much as it squeezed in pain and longing. Tenleigh.

Half agony, half hope.
Half pain, half ecstasy.
Half grief, half joy.
Half my downfall, half my savior.

CHAPTER SEVENTEEN
Tenleigh

"Why are you avoiding me?" I asked.

Kyland whipped his head around, a look of surprise on his face. "Tenleigh, Jesus, you scared me."

I thought of those first few times he'd startled me in the same way, and my heart dipped. I felt like I was losing him. We'd both been busy lately—and I'd been working at least three times a week, which was good, but as the weeks passed, it had become clear that us not seeing each other as much was purposeful on his part. I looked at him expectantly until he pursed his lips and let out a breath.

"I just have so much to do…finals coming up, figuring out what to do with my house, all the stuff…" He trailed off.

"You're avoiding me," I asserted.

He looked away for a few moments as if gathering himself, but for what, I didn't know. "Tenleigh," he said, "don't you think it'll be easier if we—"

"If we what?" I demanded. We were standing on the trail that led to the main road near the top of the hill, the back way he'd been taking home from school for almost a month now. I looked down at my feet when he didn't answer. "I miss you. We have so little time together. And things are so unclear…" I shook my head. "Neither one of us knows what's going to happen, and maybe—"

"I'm leaving. That's what's going to happen. Did you think this thing between you and me, that it would change my mind somehow?"

I couldn't help wincing. "No. That's not what I thought. But I never expected…I never—"

His eyes flared as he seemed to recognize where I was going with my words. He advanced on me, his body moving into my space until he stood directly in front of me. "Don't," he said almost pleadingly. "Don't. Please don't."

I lifted my gaze, gathering all my courage, refusing to back down. "I never expected to fall in love with you. And I thought maybe…"

…*you could love me back. Even if you leave. You could leave loving me.*

His body was utterly still. Somewhere overhead a hawk called out and the breeze ruffled the trees surrounding us. And still his eyes held mine.

He cursed under his breath and then his lips were on mine, his tongue hot and demanding as it parted my lips and plunged into my mouth. It wasn't exactly the answer I was hoping for, but it was something. *Not enough, but something.*

Kyland broke away, breathing hard and gripping my head in his large hands. He pressed his forehead to mine and we just breathed together for a minute.

"I'm going camping tonight."

"Camping?" I repeated. That hadn't been the response I was expecting.

He pulled away. "Yeah. My family, we...it was something we used to do on my birthday every year. I used to like it—we'd go up to this field filled with lavender and"—he ran his hand through his hair, taming it—"anyway, I've kept doing it every year."

I nodded. "I know where you're talking about. It's where I collect the lavender I use to make that tea...and those sachets..." I trailed off. This felt so awkward and I wanted to cry. *Oh, Kyland, I already miss you desperately and you're not even gone yet.* I stared down at my feet.

He was squinting up at the sky. I watched him, and after a moment, he lowered his eyes to mine. There was something wild and raw in his expression, but he just stood there looking at me for a second before he grabbed my hand and started walking toward home. It felt like it'd been so long since he'd touched me. His hand felt warm and solid in mine. *Still not enough, but something.* And what a pitiful thing to accept. This was all so messed up.

He's been pulling away from me to make it easier. And yet pulling away has only made it hurt more.

We walked in silence, my heart hurting and Kyland seeming to grow more tense by the moment. He didn't let go of my hand when we passed my trailer and so I continued on with him until we got to his house.

I didn't know whether I wanted to cry or throw something, but the sorrow I'd been feeling for weeks now was suddenly heating inside of me to a bubbling anger.

I told him I love him and he hasn't said it back.

Kyland let go of my hand and opened the door to his house. I walked inside with him, not even understanding why I was there.

When I got inside, I gasped, the anger flowing out of me to

be replaced with shocked pain. There were boxes piled every-where and the wood stove that had sat in the middle of the living room was gone. "What? I don't... where's your stove?"

"I sold it for two hundred fifty dollars to some guy in Evansly. He drove up here and bought it, along with my mama's kitchen table set."

I swiped at the tears gathering in my eyes, embarrassed that I was crying.

This is happening. He's leaving.

"Tenleigh," Kyland said, his voice gravelly. "Please don't cry." He stepped toward me. "Anything but that. Please." He sounded desperate. "This is what I've been trying to avoid. *This*. I don't want either of us to feel this way."

"Well, I do! And you don't get to take that from me. I love you, and you don't get to say anything about it. The love I feel for you is mine. And I'll feel it if I want to."

"Tenleigh," he repeated, his voice cracking. "Don't love me. Please don't love me. I can't stay here. Don't love me."

"It's too late." I shook my head back and forth in defiance. "It's too late. I'm not asking you to stay, but it's too late for me not to love you."

"It can't be," he said, shaking his head.

"It is."

His eyes met mine and he walked slowly to me, the look of intensity in his eyes increasing. He stepped right up to my body and his eyes lingered on my mouth for several moments before he pressed his warm lips to my own. The gentleness of the kiss was in direct contrast to the expression on his face and the energy moving between us. I didn't know whether to feel more anger, or more hope.

"I love you, Kyland," I whispered when our lips had parted. "And I'll love you whether you're here in Dennville, or whether you're in New York City, or London, or on Jupiter. I love you."

He squeezed his eyes shut and let out a loud whoosh of air. "This is a mistake."

I shook my head back and forth slowly as I gazed into his troubled eyes. "How can love be a mistake?" I wrapped my arms around his back, sliding my palms up his shirt to feel his smooth, warm skin.

He stepped closer into my embrace. "I love you too, Ten," he finally said softly. "That's why this is so hard." His tone held defeat, as if the words themselves had stolen something from him.

My heart soared as much as it lay bleeding from hearing the distress in his voice and standing among the proof of his imminent departure. I held him tighter. "Whatever you need, Ky. Whatever that is, I'll give it to you."

He let out a long, shuddery breath but remained silent.

The problem was I didn't know if us loving each other changed anything. In fact, after everything Kyland had shared with me over the past months, I understood more than anyone why he needed to leave. He deserved to live a life out of this house of loneliness and loss. He had to picture his torment every day—hear his brother's cries in the very walls, hear his father's voice in every room, feel his mother's absence, her abandonment. I wanted him out of here as much as he did, and yet it still hurt so much. I bit my lip. But maybe...maybe if he won that scholarship, he wouldn't leave me behind. Maybe sometime, *somehow*, we could even make a life together away from here. Maybe he'd allow that—maybe not everything from Dennville, Kentucky, had to hurt. And maybe he'd be willing to take the one thing that didn't—me—with him, in his heart at first, and later...later, into his home, his life. Maybe first he needed some time to live without his demons, to begin to believe that love didn't always have to hurt, that sometimes love was enough. I'd wait. I'd wait as long as he needed me to.

We lay down on the couch together and stayed that way for a long time, Kyland lost in his own mind, and me lost in mine. After a while, he asked if I wanted to stay and study a little bit with him—finals were on Monday. We didn't discuss our feelings anymore.

We ate vegetable soup at his coffee table for dinner and then I kissed him goodbye. Marlo would be leaving for work soon and I needed to get home and make sure my mama was okay.

"I won't see you this weekend," I said sadly. "Be safe camping, okay?"

Kyland nodded, and I thought I saw some kind of sad longing in his eyes. But he was the one going away. That was his choice. And maybe he needed it. Maybe he needed that time in that place where he had a few happy memories of his family. Maybe that was exactly what he needed. Maybe that was exactly what *I* needed. Maybe I simply had to let him go.

I love him. I'll give him whatever he needs.

"It's your birthday tomorrow too," he said softly. "What are your plans?"

I shrugged. "Oh, Marlo will probably bake me a cake as hard as a brick and I'll do some reading." I smiled and he smiled back, brushing a piece of hair off my forehead.

"Happy birthday, Tenleigh."

"Happy birthday, Kyland."

We kissed slowly and deeply for several minutes on his couch and I sensed his desire for me. But when I pulled back, he let me. I kissed him one last time and then I walked back

155

to my trailer. My heart felt as though it was breaking into so many pieces, and for the life of me, I couldn't figure out how to keep them all together. And I wasn't sure I even wanted to.

CHAPTER EIGHTEEN
Kyland

The place where I had camped with my family for years was always a little more peaceful than I remembered it—which was good because I needed a good dose of peace. Tenleigh had told me she loved me, and I'd said it back. It filled me with both joy and fearful desperation. I had nothing to offer her, and now, how would I leave her behind?

I'd almost gone to her trailer and asked her to come with me before I'd left, but I'd resisted. The problem was, I'd been resisting her for over three weeks and I thought it would have gotten easier. Instead, my longing for her had only increased. I *craved* her. It was a hunger deep inside my gut—a burning that only grew fiercer, more demanding without being fed. And I knew I'd loved her for a long time—perhaps even far longer than she'd loved me. When had it happened? When had I let my guard down enough to let her sweetness slip around my heart in a way I'd never untangle myself from? And at this point, what did it even matter?

I looked around. There was a huge, ancient oak that

provided the cover we'd always used for our "campground." We hadn't been able to afford camping gear and so we'd used the same blankets and quilts we always slept with, just with a plastic tarp underneath. My dad would make burgoo, a stew that was a concoction of opossum and squirrel and any other wild game you could catch in a small trap—venison if you had a gun. It was supposed to be a delicacy, but like so many other "delicacies," it was probably born from starvation and the likelihood that calling something a delicacy made it more palatable. As gross as it probably sounded to those not familiar with the dish, it was good. And I made a batch of it every year for this trip, which just happened to be my birthday. I thought my dad would probably like that.

I looked out to the field of lavender. I liked this spot because when the breeze kicked up, you could smell all those purple flowers—sweet and herbal at the same time. Calming. I sat on a huge fallen branch that had been there since I was a kid and regarded the wood for the campfire I'd laid out on the ground in front of me. I'd light it once the sky became dark and heat up the stew and then I'd sleep under the stars in my makeshift sleeping bag in this spot for the very last time. I wouldn't come back here again.

A feeling moved inside me that felt surprisingly like grief, an ache in my guts. I didn't exactly understand it—this place had been so full of pain for me because each time I came, I felt the absence of my family. But at the same time, there had been joy here too, that I was only now remembering. How did I make sense of that? I couldn't stand these conflicting feelings. I wanted to feel hatred for Dennville, Kentucky—nothing more, because then it would be easy to leave and not look back.

Tenleigh. This was because of Tenleigh. She was here

and suddenly, there was beauty. Suddenly Dennville was *her*—the girl who had helped me move through some of the darkness, into the light. I groaned and then sat staring at the grassy ground for several minutes, debating what to do.

How had my life become suddenly so complicated? And so clear?

Tenleigh. Half agony, half hope.

My love for her was fear and pain, and joy and laughter. It was spring flowers and winter frost. How the hell could love feel so damn *crowded*?

I caught movement off to my left and lifted my head, startling slightly, and she was there, walking through the field of purple lavender toward me just like a dream. My heart flipped and I stood, everything inside me buzzing with sudden joy. *Shit.*

She reached me and offered a tentative smile, her hands clasped in front of her. She had her hair loosely braided and was wearing a white sweater that fell off her shoulder, her creamy skin exposed. And I knew I'd never see a more beautiful vision than Tenleigh Falyn standing in a field of lavender.

She stood taller, seeming to gather some courage. When her eyes met mine, she said, "I've been thinking about it since yesterday, and I hoped you might be okay with some company. And I didn't figure you'd turn down my wish today of all days." Her smile was filled with innocent hope and it made my stomach clench.

"You wanted to go camping with me for your birthday?"

She pulled her bottom lip in between her teeth and nodded. "More than anything."

I suddenly felt full of some form of happiness I'd never experienced before. Maybe it was the sudden appearance of the very person I'd been missing. Maybe it was the loneliness

I'd just been feeling floating away as soon as Tenleigh appeared in my line of sight. Maybe it was just *gratefulness*, and God knew I'd had very little to be grateful for in the course of my life. I offered her a bigger smile and said, "This could be dangerous. What if sleeping outside turns me into a caveman and I try to drag you by your hair into my sleeping bag?" I lifted one side of my mouth to let her know I was teasing. We hadn't been lighthearted in what seemed like such a long time, and it felt so good.

"The ones who lived hundreds of thousands of years ago?" she asked, amusement in her eyes as she teased me back. She tilted her head, her expression growing serious. "I wouldn't resist," she said.

"Tenleigh," I breathed. Her lips were so beautiful. I wanted them on my skin. Everywhere. She didn't break eye contact with me. I stepped closer to her and her scent washed over me, distant wildflowers on a summer breeze. Suddenly, I felt like this was the most natural thing in the whole world. Standing outside under the shade of a giant oak tree, the endless sky stretching out around us, not a building in sight, I couldn't remember why I'd ever resisted her. I couldn't for the life of me think why we wouldn't act on the feelings that were swirling through the air around us, feelings only God himself could have invented. It was like there was some kind of magic in the breeze that reduced the world down to just the two of us, standing there. I closed my eyes, growing dizzy with the feeling of need coursing through my system, and let my instincts take over. I leaned in and she tilted her head back, lifting her lips to mine, parting them to permit me access. I groaned and pressed my lips to hers, any fleeting thoughts of why this shouldn't happen lost in the mingled sound of our moans and the wet sound of our tongues dancing.

I ran my hands down the sides of her body, moving slowly over her feminine curves, marveling at how differently she was made from me, how perfectly we fit together. "I want to feel your skin, Tenleigh," I said as I broke away from her lips and gazed down into her eyes—eyes filled with lust...and love.

The sun was just setting, twilight moving swiftly across the mountains.

Tenleigh glanced at the makeshift bed I'd set up on the ground under the far-reaching branches of the tree, before she took my hand and led me to stand beside it.

"Tenleigh, I—" She reached up and put two fingers on my lips to stop my words. I went silent. Truthfully, I didn't know what I'd been about to say anyway. Another warning about how this wouldn't change anything? Another reminder I was still leaving? Surely she'd heard those words from me enough—she probably didn't want to hear them in this moment. And I didn't really want to say them anyway. I was starting to wonder if I even meant them. I was starting to wonder a lot of things.

We kissed and kissed and kissed. We kissed for what seemed a lifetime. Tenleigh was the only girl I had ever kissed like that. Always before, I had quickly tried to move things to the next level. But with her, I let myself melt into the pleasure of her mouth, my body heating slowly. I memorized the feel of her soft body pressing into mine, the sweet taste of her lips, her tongue, her breath.

After a while she pulled back, her cheeks flushed and her lips wet and red, dark hair falling loose from her braid to frame her face. As I looked at her, it was as if the vision of her just like this sunk through my skin, into my blood, my soul. My body pulsed with need.

"I'm going to try to be gentle," I said. Her eyes flared, but she only nodded. Visions were assaulting my brain—visions I'd pushed away before, but now I let swirl inside my mind—pictures of Tenleigh's head thrown back in passion, her legs wrapped around my hips as I drove into her.

I let myself imagine it. I let myself anticipate it because it was about to happen.

Slowly, we stripped off our clothes as the other watched. I'd never experienced anything more erotic than watching Tenleigh bare herself to me knowing that very soon I was going to be inside her. When she was completely nude, I let my eyes do a slow perusal of her body, although I'd seen her naked before. But that had always been inside the dim walls of my room. This, this was under the setting sun, the golden light shining on her skin, the cool air pebbling her rose-colored nipples.

"You're stunning," I told her.

Her own gaze ran over me, and my erection pulsed when her eyes landed on it. She raised her eyes to mine and said, "You're stunning too. And I don't want you to be gentle with me. I want to feel *you*. I want all you have to give me."

I let out a groan and moved in close to her, my cock aching, my blood boiling under my skin.

I laid her down on the ground, feeling the first twinge of regret. She was beautiful and desirable. She deserved to be laid down on something better than old musty blankets under a tree. "Kyland," she whispered, taking my face in her hands and looking into my eyes as if she knew what I was thinking. "This is the best birthday of my life." God, she was sweetness. Sweetness and beauty.

I smoothed her hair back. "Mine too."

She arched her back as my mouth found her nipple. She

moaned and pressed her body up into mine, her skin warm, her body soft. Her responsiveness, her wonder, her sweet innocence was something I had no experience with and it changed me inside in some essential way I couldn't focus on figuring out right then. I simply absorbed it, enjoyed it. Revered it.

Before long, we were both moaning and writhing and I was so turned on, I was praying I'd last long enough to make the experience at least somewhat noteworthy for her.

I reached down between her legs and felt her slippery liquid, running it up to her clit and circling gently. She gasped and pressed herself up into my hand. I lowered my head back to her breast and suckled gently. She moaned out my name, and after a minute, I felt her pulse and shudder under my hand.

I looked into her lust-fogged eyes and took myself in my hand and gently used my erection to open her. In response she parted her legs. *Oh, Tenleigh, you're so perfect.* I grunted, trying to go as slowly as I could while my body was screaming at me to plunge inside her and rut like an animal. I wanted her so badly.

Tenleigh's hands came to my shoulders and she closed her eyes as I moved more deeply inside, her warmth surrounding the head of me and making me lose another portion of the control I was trying to hold to so tightly.

"Open your eyes, Ten," I gritted out. "Look at me." Look at me what? When I claim you? When I make you mine? *Yes,* my heart screamed. But I shut it down. No. We were each other's for tonight. But this didn't change anything. It couldn't.

Her eyes opened, gazing into mine as I plunged inside her in one smooth thrust. Her face flinched in pain and I felt my own flesh tear through hers, but she didn't cry out. And it was done. I had been so resistant to taking Tenleigh's virginity, but now I wasn't sorry. Whatever else happened, this part of her would always be mine. It would *never* belong to another man. Never. I watched her face closely as I began to move inside her, the bliss swirling through my balls, my abdomen, but she didn't flinch again. She ran her hands down my back, over my ass as I stroked inside of her, slowly at first and then with more desperation. She felt so good, so good. "I'm gonna come," I breathed out, taking one last blissful thrust into her as I erupted in pleasure, collapsing and moaning my orgasm into her neck.

After a moment, I rolled slightly to the side so I wouldn't crush her. We lay like that for several minutes, Tenleigh running her nails up and down my back and me getting control of my breathing.

I fell back on the blankets in awe.

"That was amazing," I breathed. "God, Tenleigh, that was so amazing."

She smiled sweetly at me and nodded. "Yes." She sighed. "Yes, it was."

We didn't sleep much that night. She was a drug and I couldn't get enough of her. I wanted to live forever planted deep inside her. She must have been sore, but she never said anything. That night was made of damp skin and cries of pleasure that echoed through the hills. And I knew for the rest of my life, wherever I was, whoever I was with, when I thought of Tenleigh, I'd think of warmth and lavender and the wide-open sky.

Sometime later, when a luminous crescent moon hung suspended above us, I finally untangled myself from her and built a fire. We sat on the fallen tree trunk wrapped in quilts and I fed her burgoo heated over the open flame. An owl hooted incessantly in the background and Tenleigh's laughter rang out over the meadow as I told her story after story of some of the trouble Silas and I had gotten into as kids— stories that up until then, no one knew except my brother and me. And somehow it felt like I had brought another piece of him back to life.

We danced briefly under the starlight, Tenleigh laughing as I dipped her. "I'd take you to the prom if I could," I said softly, regretfully, bringing her back up so her body pressed against mine. "I'd do so many things if I could."

"I know," she answered, cupping my cheek in her palm and kissing my lips sweetly.

So many things were swirling through my mind, emotions I was unfamiliar with, feelings I couldn't organize. But as the embers died and the first rays of daylight rose over the mountains, I looked next to me at a sleeping Tenleigh, her beauty soft and vulnerable under the early morning sky, and I knew what I had to do. I knew it was wrong, and I knew it would shatter me to do it. And I knew despite all that, I would do it anyway.

Someday, when I'm living my dreams, I'm going to think of all the things that broke my heart and I'm going to be thankful for them.

I knew I had to. Because I had been wrong.

Everything had changed. In one night, nothing was the same.

CHAPTER NINETEEN
Tenleigh

We took our finals a week later. I looked for Kyland after school but was relieved when I didn't see him. I didn't really want to talk about how he'd done. Not that I didn't already know—I was sure he had aced them. He hadn't seemed concerned in the least, and when we'd studied, even though he'd been distracted, he'd answered every question I'd asked him from his study guides with unflinching certainty. And I definitely didn't want to talk about how I'd done. I shifted my shoulders back, swallowing down the lump in my throat.

I had to hurry to get home and drop off my stuff so I could get going to Al's, where I had a shift. Al had said he'd have more shifts available now that summer was almost here. The clientele picked up in the warmer months when he opened the outdoor patio and he had lost a couple girls to the new bar that had opened in Evansly. So that was great news. I had insider information I'd be staying in Dennville and so it was good I was going to have a regular income, at least for the summer. After that, I'd figure something out.

I'd come up with my life plan B. Disappointment filled my chest, but I dismissed it. *I'd done this.* I'd made the choice and I'd followed through with it. There was no going back now.

As I walked up the main road through Dennville, lost in my own thoughts, I looked to my left and saw Shelly talking to Kyland in the doorway of an abandoned building. She was standing in his space and looking up at him just like she owned him. A pang of jealousy made my stomach cramp. He leaned his hip on the doorframe as she said something I couldn't hear. I stepped backward so that I was being hidden by a thick, wooden telephone pole and peeked out at them.

Great. Now I was a stalker.

What was I doing? I bit my lip and debated whether to walk over and join them. We'd only been together the one beautiful night in the lavender field, but I knew it had meant something to both of us. *Didn't it?* I glanced back over at Shelly and Kyland. Why did some part of me feel like I would be interfering in whatever they had going on between them if I approached? Like I was the interloper? I recalled the kiss I had witnessed between them, the groping in the theater all those months ago, and suddenly I felt like I'd be sick to my stomach. When I looked back again, they were gone. I looked around and spied them walking up ahead, Shelly pulling him along by the hand as he followed her.

My heart dropped. I didn't know how to feel. Was he mine? Did I have any right to claim him in some public way? He had asserted again and again that he was leaving and he could make me no promises. How could I talk to him about it now, demand things, when I had been the one to tell him it was okay with me if he slept with me and still left? But he'd told me he loved me. If love wasn't a sort of claiming in itself, then what was it? Could he love me, be intimate with me, but still feel free to be with other girls? I was upset and confused. I felt hot yet empty—my skin prickly. No, he wouldn't. That wasn't Kyland. If I knew anything of him, I knew he was honorable. Didn't I?

I walked home slowly when I should have been hurrying. We'd spent what I thought had been such a beautiful night together, one that had changed me. I had given him all of me—my body and my heart. And suddenly, because I hadn't spent time with him for the last few days, I felt doubtful and insecure again.

"I hate love," I muttered.

I rushed into our trailer and threw my school stuff on the couch. Marlo came out of the bathroom, buttoning up her white shirt.

"Hey." She smiled. "How'd finals go?"

I didn't look at her as I grabbed my work clothes out of the closet. "Oh, um, fine I think," I lied. "I'm just glad they're over." I turned to her and gave her a big smile, one I hoped was distracting.

She nodded her head slowly. "Okay, good. Well, are you ready? If we leave now, we won't be late."

"Yeah, just give me two minutes," I said, rushing into the bathroom.

Five minutes later, we were walking back down the road toward town.

There was a big basketball game on television today and the place would be packed, so we were both eager to get there. The extra customers would bring in extra money, and now that we'd both be working a shift, we'd bring in double. At least this day offered some sort of silver lining. I didn't get a lot of tips, but if the customers got drunk enough, a few of them would confuse me with a waitress and I'd make a little bit of cash, too. My usual MO was to stay out of the way as much as possible, especially when it came to the drunk executives who worked at the mine company headquarters in Evansly, but not today. Today I'd stay right in the way.

I scowled down at my moving feet, thinking of those men who found it amusing to slum it at Al's. They might look classy in their suits and gold jewelry, but down deep, they were just entitled scums who acted as if we backwoods women were damn lucky to get their attention at all. Of course, plenty of the girls around here thought just that and acted accordingly. I'd heard a particularly loud executive yell drunkenly to his group of out-of-town coworkers, "Take your pick, gentlemen, they come cheap," and then guffaw loudly. Problem was, food and heat *didn't* come cheap, and sometimes you did what you had to do. And sometimes, you got it in your fool head that one of them wanted to save you from the miserable life you were living.

By six o'clock that night, the shift was in full swing, the bar packed with boisterous men cheering and yelling at the large flat screen on the wall.

I moved through the crowd, gathering empty glasses onto my tray and delivering food to the tables that had ordered it. A particularly drunk guy in a red shirt kept grabbing my ass whenever I walked close and so I went the long way around the tables each time to avoid him.

"Come on, gorgeous!" he yelled as I made my way back to the kitchen to drop the dirty glasses off to the dishwasher. "Bring that sweet little ass back over here."

"He giving you trouble, honey?" Brenda, an older waitress, pretty in a beat-down kind of way, who had been working at Al's forever, asked when I'd returned to the bar. She nodded her head in Red Shirt's direction.

I glanced over at him. "I can handle it, Brenda," I said, giving her a small smile.

"You let me know if you need me to take over your section. I've got plenty of extra to grope. I don't mind sharing a little." She squeezed a handful of her generous backside and winked at me. I laughed.

I successfully avoided Red Shirt for the rest of my shift and he left with his group of friends as the game ended and the bar started clearing out a little bit.

As I wiped down a table near the back, Marlo came over to me. "Hey, Ten, I asked Brenda and she said she could give you a lift home."

I stopped wiping and looked up at her. She fidgeted slightly. "Why?" I asked, suspiciously.

"Uh." She glanced back to a guy sitting at a table near the door. I didn't recognize him—probably another guy in town on business. I narrowed my eyes, taking him in from across the room. "That's Corey. He asked if I wanted to go to dinner with him tonight and..."

Dinner? It was way too late for *dinner*. I moved to the side so her body was blocking me from *Corey*. "Do not go home with some guy you just met at this bar, Mar. Have you already forgotten how that turned out—"

She straightened her spine. "No, I haven't forgotten." She glanced over her shoulder at Corey and gave him a small smile, and then turned back to me. "I'm not stupid, Ten. I know what Corey wants. I don't have delusions that he's going to marry me and we're going to go riding off into the sunset. I just want some company, is that so bad?"

I sighed, my shoulders drooping. "What about Sam?"

Marlo bristled. "What *about* Sam? We're just friends. Sam doesn't own me."

"He'd care that you went home with Corey."

"Well, he shouldn't. That would be stupid of him."

I sighed. "Yeah." I studied her pretty face for a moment. "Just be careful, okay? And stay in public with him, well-lit areas that—"

Marlo laughed and leaned forward, hugging me. "I will. I'll be home in a couple hours."

"Okay."

I went back to wiping down the last of the tables as Marlo clocked out and then waved at me as she and Corey walked out the front door of Al's.

I went to clock out and when I saw Brenda, she said, "Honey, I'm sorry. I just went out to warm my car up and it won't start. Dave's coming by in about an hour to pick me up. Do you mind waiting?"

I really didn't want to hang out in this smoky bar for another couple hours waiting for Brenda's husband. "That's okay, I'm used to walking and it's not cold."

"You sure?"

"Yeah." I smiled and after calling goodbye to everyone, I walked outside. It was a mild spring night, but I still pulled my sweater on and folded my arms over my chest. I was going to have to buy a few new things soon. Some of my clothes had actual holes in them. I'd talk to Marlo and see what we could afford.

Pine needles picked up and blew in the wind at my feet as I trudged through the dirt and leaves on the side of the highway. A breeze blew gently through my hair. I looked up at the moon, recalling what it'd looked like hanging over us in the meadow as Kyland moved above me, his skin damp with passion. I shivered in want, my steps speeding up. Maybe I'd stop at his house. Surely he wouldn't mind. I heard a car coming behind me and moved as far as I could away from the road. The car went whizzing by and then I looked up as I heard it slow and pull to the side of the embankment.

My steps faltered and I squinted as I walked toward the silver car. Was that Jemma Clark's brother's car? As I got closer, I realized that, no, this car was in much better shape than his, still running, but no one emerging. Then the door opened and Red Shirt stepped out from behind the wheel, swaying slightly. "Hey, pretty girl, I've been waiting for you." He smiled a droopy-lidded smile and began walking toward where I now stood still, nerves assaulting me. I looked up and down the highway. It was deserted.

"My ride should be along any minute. Nice to see you, though," I said as I began walking around the vehicle.

As I walked moved by the passenger side of his car, he started coming around the front and I increased my speed, breaking into a jog when he increased his speed too. Fear pounded through my blood as he took up chase behind me. I let out a small yelp as his hand made contact with my shoulder, but then I pulled ahead and for a brief second, I thought he'd give it up and walk back to his car. I dared to glance behind me and in that instant, his hand grabbed hold of my sweater and he yanked. I went flying backward, hitting his chest with my back as his arms went around me and he let out a loud half-laugh–half-victory cry.

"Let me go!" I yelled, panic causing tears to spring to my eyes as I sucked in a sob.

A car drove slowly by us and I yelled out, "Help!" as my eyes connected with those of the driver's, a woman. But she looked away and sped off down the highway.

Red Shirt's hot breath was at my ear. "Relax, pretty

thing, I've got you. Feisty, aren't you? I just wanna get to know you. You kept running away from me at the bar. Let's go somewhere where we can get acquainted." His hand ran up my rib cage and cupped my breast, squeezing it harshly.

"No!" I screamed, kicking backward with my legs, connecting with his shins. He let out a pained grunt and let go of me. I whirled around and struck with my fist, connecting with the side of his head. He released an enraged growl and struck back at me. Pain exploded behind my eye and I stumbled, off balance, my butt landing in the dirt, a whoosh of air escaping my mouth. I crab-crawled backward in the dirt as Red Shirt stalked toward me and then sprang to my feet just in time to see a car pull up right behind Red Shirt's.

From my peripheral vision, I saw a man jump out of the driver's seat and when I turned to run, the man called out, "Tenleigh! It's okay." I whipped my head back around and saw it was Jamie Kearney heading toward Red Shirt. I halted, tears running down my cheeks as I heaved in big breaths of air.

Jamie Kearny, Edward Kearny's son and the boy who had watched from the window as his father spit on my mama. *Just great.*

"Hey, man," Red Shirt said, taking a step toward him. "We got this covered—"

Jamie punched him in the face and Red Shirt went down hard in the gravel, not even breaking his own fall. I cried out, bringing my hands up to my mouth. I was shaking all over. As Jamie hefted Red Shirt up and dragged him under his armpits to his car, I quickly took stock of myself. My sweater was torn and hanging where Red Shirt had grabbed it, and my eye felt like it was quickly swelling closed. I brought my finger up to my mouth, and when I took it away, there was blood on it.

Jamie threw an unconscious Red Shirt into his still-idling car and then reached in and pulled the keys out of the ignition. He leaned in and did something I couldn't see, and when he leaned back up, he was holding a pair of jeans in one hand and the keys in the other. He slammed the door shut and brought his arm back, throwing the keys into the forest next to the highway.

"You all right?" he asked, throwing the jeans over his arm and turning toward me.

I nodded my head shakily as he approached me. His lips thinned as his gaze moved over my face, but he didn't touch me. "Come on, I'll drive you home."

I hesitated. True, I'd gone to school with Jamie for the last four years, but I didn't really know him, and I tried not to think about him at all. In fact, I avoided him whenever possible—I could only figure he didn't look too fondly on any member of my family, including me after what he'd witnessed.

He watched me now as I hesitated and then he reached in his pocket, bringing something red and shiny out. He walked it over to me, holding it out so that I could take it from his outstretched hand. It was a Swiss Army knife.

"If I try anything that makes you uncomfortable, you stab me in the eye with that," he said, a glimmer of a smile on his lips.

I released a breath, my racing heart slowing enough that I could get a full breath through my body again. I took the knife from him. I didn't say anything, but I followed him to his car and got in the passenger side. He got in and threw the jeans in the back seat. I glanced back at them, confused, and then sat huddled against the passenger door as Jamie pulled out onto the highway. I looked out the back window—Red Shirt still hadn't sat up in his car.

"What if he's dead?" I asked.

Jamie glanced in his rearview mirror. "He's not dead. He's just going to wake up with a big headache and a massive hangover…and he'll have to walk himself back to his hotel… pantless." He looked over at me, and the side of his lip quirked up slightly. I stared at him, my own lip quirking up too, as I pictured Red Shirt walking along the highway naked from the waist down. But then my expression sobered.

"He might come back to Al's," I said.

Jamie glanced at me before he turned off onto the road leading up into the hills. "You live up here, right?"

"Yeah. I'll show you where to turn."

"That man," Jamie said, "he won't bother you. I'll make sure of it, okay?"

I glanced at him. "Okay." I don't know why I trusted that he would, but for some strange reason, I did. The way he'd said it had been so incredibly sincere.

I thought about what little I did know of Jamie, other than that he was a Kearny. I knew he hung with the popular kids, the small group at our high school who lived in Evansly and had parents who were executives at the mines—the rich kids. I didn't know if he'd be considered "rich" by *all* standards, but by mine, he most definitely was. Our lives were legions apart.

I directed him up the hill to my trailer, and when he pulled up in front of it, he sat staring at it for several moments. I was too achy and numb to care. In that moment, my little trailer looked good to me and I wanted to get inside and lie down on the small couch I slept on. I pulled the door handle and the door clicked open.

"Hey, Tenleigh," Jamie said and I paused, but didn't turn toward him. "This is kinda weird timing, but would you, uh, want to go to the prom next week? I mean, with me?"

I looked back over my shoulder. Jamie was good-looking—not in the same way Kyland was—but he had a nice face, a kind face, actually, now that I was really looking at him. "Thanks, Jamie, but uh, no. I don't dance, and…" *I can't afford a dress or shoes and I'm kinda desperately in love with someone.*

"Come on, you sorta owe me." My eyes snapped to his and I saw he was kidding.

I let out a breath and offered him a smile. "Thank you, Jamie, really, for what you did. But no, I'm, um, kind of seeing someone and—" Tears started leaking out of my eyes at my own words. Was I seeing someone? God, it was all so confusing. And somehow, my heart felt as bruised as my eye.

"Hey," he said gently, "I understand. I just thought…you know, you and I…" He thinned his lips, looking as if he was considering his words. "I've never really made an effort to get to know you, and I'm sorry for that. I realize there's not much time now, but I thought maybe a dance…" His eyes moved over my face. "But you're involved with someone and so I understand that he probably wants to take you to the prom."

I looked down at my lap and shook my head, but I didn't speak. Would this boy even understand what it was like to have so little that some days you were just thankful you had enough food to eat? Dances, dates…those things were so far outside my realm of experiences. I had no idea what it was like to do any of that. I had no idea what it was like to live a life where you had the luxury of caring about that kind of stuff.

"Thanks again," I said.

"Tenleigh?" I turned back around. "I…Well, see, I…"

"Spit it out, Jamie."

"I'm gay."

Oh. I turned all the way toward him. "So why'd you ask me to the dance then?"

"I just wanted to spend time with you."

I attempted to lift a brow, but it made my face hurt. "What if I'd said yes and had hope that you liked me?" I asked.

"I...I guess I didn't really think that part through. Sorry."

I studied him for a second and then sighed. "No harm done."

"I can't tell my parents. I mean, I can. I'm going to. Soon. I think. Maybe." He looked out the driver's side window.

I took a deep breath and sat back. I was surprised Jamie Kearney was opening up to me like this. I pictured him again staring out the window as his father humiliated us, and wondered if he might be attempting to make up for what he'd watched by telling me one of his secrets. To put us some sort of equal footing. Which was very kind actually. And unexpected. "I'm sure it'll be okay," I said.

"No, it won't be. It won't be okay. But I guess I have to do it anyway. I thought maybe before I go off to college. That way they'll have some time to digest it while I'm away, you know?"

I nodded. "Yeah." I reached over and squeezed his shoulder. "Well, good luck."

"My dad, he grew up like you," he said, glancing over at my trailer. "In his office, he has a picture of the shack where he lived in West Virginia when he was a boy."

I pressed my lips together and scratched at my thigh. "Well, that makes it worse."

"What?" he asked.

"He knows how painful it is to live like this—and for us, he made it worse." *For him, it was a sick, thrilling way to*

177

remind himself of how far he'd risen—and how far others were now beneath him.

Jamie flinched slightly, his eyes flitting away and then back. "I know." He paused for a second. "If it makes you feel any better, I don't like where I live either, despite everything I have." He frowned as he looked out the window behind me. "That day"—his eyes met mine—"that day my dad... told you to leave our house, I was watching. I saw. I think you saw me too. But what you didn't know is that I wanted to go with you. I wanted to run downstairs and catch up. I saw the way all three of you gripped hands and walked away, the way you leaned on your sister, and...as stupid and probably insensitive as it sounds to you to hear me say this, I wanted to go with you. I wanted what you had. A *family*."

I stared at him, shocked. "I wanted what you had. Not only a family, but"—I laughed softly—"some food in the fridge."

His short laugh ended in a grimace.

"Well," I said on a sigh, "as it turns out, things are tough all over, Ponyboy."

"What?"

"Nothing. Thanks again, Jamie. Good night."

"Good night, Tenleigh. Make sure you ice that eye."

"I will." I handed him his knife and then opened the car door and got out.

I watched him as he turned around and drove back down the road toward town. I stood there for a minute, breathing in the fresh night air, thinking about what I was going to tell my mama. I wouldn't tell her the truth. It wouldn't be helpful—there was nothing she could do about it, and it would only make her worse. I'd tell her I ran into the swinging door at work.

But as I stood there, emotion overwhelmed me. I didn't want to lie. I wanted someone to hold me as I cried. I wanted someone to tell me everything was going to be okay. Tears streaked down my face as I looked up at the sky.

"Ten?" My head whipped around at his voice. Kyland.

I swiped at my tears and turned to see him walking toward me. As he came close enough that I could make out his features, he hesitated, his face contorting first in confusion and then in anger. "What the fuck?" he hissed out, moving to me quickly and tilting my face up toward the moon, toward the light.

"Who did this?" he demanded.

"Kyland," I choked out, all the fight draining out of me. He wrapped his arms around me and pulled me into his solid, safe body. I melted into him, holding the front of his shirt in my fists as I cried. I cried not just for my battered face but because this could happen again. I cried because I was scared and hopeless and because even though Kyland was holding me, and despite all we'd shared, I sensed a withdrawal of his emotions. I sensed him stiffening as my tears fell and I clung to him.

"Who did this to you?" he repeated, only his voice was calmer this time.

I sniffled and wiped at my cheeks as I pulled back. "Just some guy," I whispered.

"A guy at Al's?"

I nodded. "I wouldn't get in his car and he didn't like that."

He didn't say anything, his jaw tense, his gaze focused somewhere beyond me. "Did you get his name?"

I shook my head. "It doesn't matter, Ky. Jamie Kearney knocked him out and then drove me home. He said he'd make sure that guy didn't bother me again..." I trailed off. I had no idea what Jamie planned to do, if anything.

Kyland didn't speak for several beats. Finally, he nodded. "That's good." He smoothed a piece of hair behind my ear. "I'm so sorry *I* can't do anything. I'm sorry I'm so useless," he said.

I hesitated at the tone in his voice. "You're not useless, Kyland. Don't ever say that."

He gazed down at me, a look that was raw and pained on his face. "Go inside and put some ice on your eye," he said. "Do you have any Tylenol or anything?"

I nodded. "I thought maybe I could come to your house?" I said hopefully, wanting nothing more than for him to hold me.

"That's not a good idea," he said, his words short. "We can't do that anymore."

"Why?" I asked, my voice cracking as a ribbon of hurt wound through me.

"Because I sold my bed. I'm sleeping on the floor."

Oh.

"That's okay. I'll sleep on the floor with you."

I need you, Ky.

He shook his head, his jaw hard again. "No. You won't sleep on the damn floor, Tenleigh." He let out a long, controlled breath. "No, you won't sleep on the floor. Go inside your trailer and get in bed. I'll check on you in the morning, okay?"

I wanted to scream at him. I wanted to beg him to stay with me, take me with him, something. I pictured my mother in that auditorium screaming at Edward and I looked down at my feet, a sudden understanding of some of the deep pain she must carry inside her damaged brain. "I saw you earlier with Shelly," I said. "I waited for you to walk me home, but you were with her." I couldn't hide the accusation in my voice. *Was I expecting too much?*

He regarded me silently for a few beats. "Sorry, Ten, she just wanted to show me the car her brother fixed up for her. It was nothing."

My eyes moved over his features for a minute. I didn't feel better. "Okay," I said. "I love you."

"I love you too. Go inside. I want to hear the door lock behind you."

The lock was useless and we both knew it. If someone had a mind to, they could kick it in without even trying too hard. I turned and walked on wooden legs to the door of my trailer, unlocking it, and opening the door. I glanced behind me before I stepped inside. Kyland was standing just a little distance away, still and watching me. He nodded and I hesitated, feeling something like *fear* at the resolute expression on his face. I didn't know what it meant exactly, but I sensed it wasn't good.

I closed the door behind me and locked it, sinking down on the couch, and then I put my face in my hands and sobbed.

CHAPTER TWENTY
Tenleigh

Kyland did come to check on me the next morning, but his demeanor was distant, distracted, almost cold, and it did nothing to comfort me. I was desperately hurt. The pain in my body was the least of my aches.

Marlo had come home a couple hours after me and she must have noticed my bruised face because she'd woken me from sleep and demanded I tell her what happened. I cried in her arms just like she'd cried in mine after being dumped at the bottom of the hill by the man who'd taken her virginity and discarded her.

Physically, the boy who had taken my virginity hadn't hurt me, and I wasn't crying for the pain in my face anyway. I was crying for the pain in my heart.

The minutes ticked by that weekend. I stayed holed up in my trailer, jumping at every sound, hoping against hope it was Kyland. But after that first morning, he didn't come back, and I didn't go to him. He had made his choice clear, and although we'd gotten closer physically, for him it hadn't changed his resolve. In his mind, he'd already left. Somehow I understood that. And it broke my heart.

The following week and through the next weekend, I didn't see him at all. I went to his house a couple times, but he wasn't home—or he wasn't answering his door.

They'd be announcing the winner of the scholarship on Monday. I tried to feel something about that, but I couldn't. I knew what was going to happen; it was a foregone conclusion—Kyland would win it. I had purposely bombed my finals. I knew the contest was between him and me. And I knew he needed it more than I did. I understood why now. And I loved him. And other than my virginity, it was all I had to give. And I understood now that whether he deserved it or not, I would lay everything I had at his feet. I felt desperate and crazy, half out of my head with the fear of losing him forever. Grief pounded in my chest.

On Monday morning, as I walked down the road toward school, I was surprised to see Kyland waiting for me in front of his house. Despite all the hurt of the past week, the smile in my heart at seeing him made its way instantly to my face. "Hi," I said.

He smiled at me too. "Hi. Your eye looks a lot better." But his gaze lingered on my bruise, still slightly yellow.

"It doesn't even hurt anymore," I told him.

He looked at me as if he wondered if I was lying, but he didn't say it.

"I came to your house a few times this week," I said. "You weren't home." I glanced nervously at him, hoping he would say something to make me feel better—anything.

"I needed to make some money, Ten. With all the studying I've been doing, I've neglected some bills. And I have to eat."

My heart dropped. "Kyland, we had a little extra. I could have spared some food."

He was silent for so long, I didn't think he'd say anything. But finally he muttered, "There's no need. I'm fine now."

So much unsaid between us suddenly. Another crack formed in my heart. I wasn't sure how many cracks it could take. I didn't want to know.

We walked in silence for a while, the morning filled with the sound of birdsong, the warm spring air caressing my face and my bare arms. The rhododendrons were in bloom—we passed by one that was so heavy with blossoms it looked like a blazing inferno of flowers. Everything in nature felt new. I inhaled deeply and smelled the mixture of fresh soil and new leaves. Maybe *we* could be new too. Very suddenly, the world seemed rife with possibility as the boy I loved walked solemnly next to me. Maybe we both just needed to get over ourselves, have a little hope. Plus, this was going to be a good day for him—he just didn't know it yet. I squinted up at him. "So, big day today."

He frowned down at me. "Yeah." The smile disappeared from my face. He stopped in the road and turned to me. "Tenleigh, whatever happens today, I…" He ran his hand through his hair in that sexy, unsure way that he did. "It's the way it's meant to be, okay?"

My brows dipped. I didn't understand exactly what that meant. "Okay." I agreed anyway. I already knew what was going to happen today. I had made peace with it.

We walked the rest of the way mostly in silence but a pleasant enough one. I couldn't read his mood, but I figured that was to be expected. I left him alone with his thoughts. He was probably nervous, anxious, and afraid. The last four years of his life, all the suffering, all the pain, all the work, all the sacrifice, all the *hunger*, it was going to come down to one moment at the school assembly we were walking into in only a few hours. I wanted to reassure him, but I didn't. He couldn't know what I'd done.

So many things hung between us in the air that morning, so many things neither of us spoke of. So many secrets, so many half-truths, so much pain.

When we got to the door of the school, he leaned forward and took my face in his hands and kissed my forehead, his lips lingering there as if he was gathering himself. And then he backed up and looked at me, smiling a small smile, his eyes moving over my face as if he was memorizing me—as if he was saying goodbye.

I opened my mouth to speak, to beg him to do something, to ask him to explain what was happening. But I had no idea what. He turned and walked into the school. He didn't look back.

———

Later, when I recalled that assembly, it seemed like a dream, like I hadn't really been there in the flesh when they called my name. I had been so ready to hear the name *Kyland Barrett* called when the winner of the scholarship was awarded, that my brain didn't hear my own name instead. And so I sat there, smiling and clapping with the rest of the student body. The girl next to me laughed and elbowed me, smiling kindly as she said, "Get up there."

I had blinked and looked around, shock cascading through me like an icy waterfall. No! No, this wasn't right. I even whispered it, "No," as I was pulled up and pushed along the aisle, faces smiling at me and congratulations being called out as I moved along the row of students, drawing their legs to the side to make room. I looked around wildly for Kyland and finally spotted him, sitting with his last period class, the look on his face strangely blank. "No," I whispered again.

"Tenleigh Falyn," Edward Kearney announced again, beaming at me from the stage. I didn't remember walking up there, but suddenly I was in front of him and his large, capped smile was right in front of me. He laughed, a deep chuckle, the same one I recalled coming from the small bedroom of our trailer as the bed squeaked and my mama moaned.

I looked back at Kyland's seat, but he wasn't there. He had gone.

"Well, congratulations," Mr. Kearny said. "I can see this is quite a shock." I looked over to our principal, Mrs. Branson, and she grinned widely at me, but I couldn't manage to smile back.

The rest of that hour went by in a haze. I wanted to jump up and run out of there. I wanted to chase after Kyland. I wanted to comfort him, talk to him, be with him. What was he feeling right now? *Oh, Kyland.* I wanted to scream.

How did this happen? How could it be that I was getting the one thing I had dreamed of more than any other over my high school career and it was like a nightmare? Funny how our dreams can shift in what seems like an instant.

When it was over, when there had been applause and congratulations, when I'd been handed the paperwork telling me that my tuition at San Diego State University had been paid in full, including my dorm room, and an account opened in my name that would pay for my meals, when all my dreams had supposedly come true, I went tearing out of there straight to Mrs. Branson's office.

"Tenleigh," she said, surprised laughter bubbling from

her when I barged into her office and shut the door behind me, probably looking crazed.

"I can't take the scholarship," I blurted out. "There's been a mistake."

Mrs. Branson laughed again, but her brows furrowed. "Tenleigh, my dear, there hasn't been a mistake. Mr. Kearney had all that paperwork drawn up already. It's all set, all in your name. Mistakes aren't made when it comes to something important like that. You won it, honey. Fair and square."

I shook my head, collapsing in the chair across from her desk. "I bombed my finals," I said. "I did terribly."

I did it for Kyland. I did it so he'd win.

This is all wrong. This is all wrong.

She regarded me quizzically. "I did see that you choked on those tests, Tenleigh. I was surprised. You've always been such a good test taker." She waved her hand in the air. "But evidently, the scholarship is based on more than final test scores—you have to understand that your whole four years here is taken into consideration…how many AP classes you took, what extracurricular activities you were involved in, things of that nature."

The truth was, I hadn't been involved in many extra-curricular activities. We couldn't afford them, and I'd had to work. This couldn't be right.

I wondered briefly if this had anything to do with my mother. I sat up straight in the chair. Had Mr. Kearney given me this scholarship to get our family out of town? But how would that work? It's not like I could take anyone with me. What? Would my mama and Marlo sleep in my dorm room bunk bed with me? *Of course not.* I was desperate and so confused.

"I want to transfer it into someone else's name," I said, looking at her pointedly.

She frowned. "That's not possible. I'm sorry, but that's absolutely not possible. It's all been arranged." She stood up and came around her desk and took my hands in hers, looking at me kindly. "Tenleigh, you won this. It's yours. I know"—she bit her lip—"well, I know sometimes it's hard to accept things when you're not used to having a lot, but please, dear Tenleigh, let yourself feel happiness and pride in this. You did it. You did all the work involved to win. You deserve it. It's yours."

My shoulders sagged, but I nodded. "Thank you, Mrs. Branson." I got up and walked out of her office. Yes, I earned it, but I no longer wanted it. It had to go to Kyland. He needed this more than I did.

I left school and fast-walked all the way back to Dennville. This wasn't right. I wouldn't leave him. We'd make other plans. I didn't want to leave Kentucky. I didn't want to go to college. I wanted Kyland's love and I wouldn't let it go, not for a college education, not for anything. I wouldn't. It was foolish, but I didn't care. The only thing I wanted in this world was him. Near the base of our hill, I stopped and sat down on a rock on the side of the dirt road, taking a piece of paper out of my backpack and scrawling out a quick list. Then I got up and ran the rest of the way.

I was huffing and sweaty when I got to Kyland's door and pounded on it. He had left the assembly, so surely he'd come back here? I heard footsteps and waited. After a minute, he opened his door slowly, staring out at me. I stared back at him, my breath coming out in ragged exhales.

"Can I come in?" I asked.

He smiled stiffly and opened it wider, inviting me inside. He still hadn't spoken.

When he closed the door behind me and I turned to

him, I couldn't help it, I burst into tears. He moved toward me instantly and wrapped me in his arms. "Shh, Tenleigh, why are you crying? I'm so proud of you. You earned this. You earned it." He pulled back and smoothed my hair away from my face. "You're going to go to college." He smiled and it looked sincere and tender—*proud*. It made me cry harder.

"I don't want to go to college," I cried. "I want *you* to go to college."

He pulled back. "Well, that's not the way it happened. It just didn't. You're going to go—and you're going to get an education. You're going to get out of here, Tenleigh. You're going to have such a beautiful life—a life filled with books and nice clothes and a house that's heated in the winter, a *car*, and plenty of food in your refrigerator. You're going to see the ocean." His voice was filled with passion…and heartbreak. My own heart felt like it was bleeding in my chest and my eyes filled with tears.

"Kyland." I went toward him and put my hand on his cheek. "I don't care about any of that. I want…I want *you*. I know the last few weeks have been…tense, but we can get back to the way it was. I know we can. And I already have books. If I'm cold, we'll warm each other. If I'm hungry, we'll find a way just like we always have." Hope gripped me. *Love*, that's what I wanted. And I was willing to fight for it. I was willing to be a fool for it. Suddenly, I realized, nothing on this whole earth was more important than love. I moved closer to him. "We'll both get jobs somewhere—who cares where—and we'll rent a little house. We'll plant a garden." My voice rose as I pictured it, the words spilling out faster and faster. I realized I sounded desperate, but I didn't care.

I grabbed my backpack and took the list out that I'd written on the side of the road. "I made a list," I said hopefully. "All the things we'll need to save up for before we can move into town. Sometimes writing things down, you know, makes it easier to picture, makes it seem more possible." I glanced down at the piece of paper, shaking in my trembling grasp. "I figure it'll only take us..." My words faded away when I noticed Kyland was looking at me with deep pity in his eyes. I stopped talking as his look of pity morphed into anger. I dropped my arms, the piece of paper floating to the floor forlornly.

"Don't you dare even say that, Tenleigh," Kyland gritted out. "You have a chance here, a chance at a real *life*, and you'd turn it down for a shitty little *existence* with me? Both of us struggling and scrimping and going without until we both hated each other?"

"No," I squeaked. "That's not how it would be. And I *would* turn it all down for you." Because it was true. I realized in that instant that I'd throw it all away for him. And I knew maybe that was stupid and reckless and wrong, but it was how I felt. I wouldn't leave him here in this little house or on a lonely highway somewhere hitchhiking out of town. I wouldn't let him suffer and scrounge for food one more day of his life. *I wouldn't.* Nothing on earth could make me.

He barked out a sharp laugh and I winced. "Love will keep us alive?" he asked, his voice dripping with ugly sarcasm. "You of all people should know what a *stupid* thing that is to say. Love doesn't keep anyone alive. Food does. Warmth does. Have you, your sister, and your mama been barely surviving on *love* all this time, Tenleigh?"

I swallowed down a lump of hurt. "I just... No." I shook my head. "Why don't you come with me, then?"

"What?"

I moved closer to him. "Come with me. You said you

190

were going to walk out of here. Make your way to California. I'll wait for you. You won't be able to stay with me, but… you can get a job, find a place of your own. We can be together there."

I swore I saw longing flit through his expression, but then he turned from me again. "I can't do that."

I looked down as I chewed at my lip. The truth was, that would be difficult. He barely had any money at all. To hitch-hike all the way across the country without stopping…and then what would he do? Live in a homeless shelter until he got a job? Could you even get a job from a homeless shelter? Where would he get clothes? Could I keep him hidden in my dorm room? Would that risk my scholarship? Okay, so the logistics weren't exactly adding up…

"Okay, then listen, I'll go to California, Ky, and when I'm done, I'll come back here and—"

"Don't you dare ever come back here," he yelled, startling me with the intensity of anger in his voice, his eyes fiery. "Don't you dare go to college and then come back here. Why would you ever even consider that? This is your *chance*, Tenleigh. Why would you ever come back here? The whole point of this scholarship is that you can get out of Dennville. It's the whole point. There are no jobs here—there's no reason on earth to come back."

"The people I love are here—you're here, my mama's here, my sister."

He shook his head. "You finish college and then you get a good job and you pay for them to move to California with you. Then all *three* of you will have a chance at life."

"I'd come back here for *you*," I said. "Or you could work for a year, save some money, and then you could come to California. If we have to wait—"

"I can't do that."

"Of course you can," I said. "Anything's possible. We can make it happen. Why can't we?"

His eyes met mine. "Because Shelly's pregnant."

For a brief second, the words didn't compute. "Shelly's..." I trailed off. "What? What does that have to do with you, Kyland?" I asked, my voice breaking on his name.

"I have to stay here," he said in barely more than a whisper.

The world around me swayed, and my face turned hot. "I don't understand," I said. "How could... It's yours? I don't..." I backed up and when I felt the wall behind me, I leaned against it. Kyland watched me, his expression wary, unreadable. "You had sex with her?"

He let out a long, shuddery breath. "I'm sorry. Things were getting too intense with us. I just needed to remind myself that—"

"That what?" I sobbed. Kyland winced. "That it was going to be possible to dismiss me when the time came?" Devastation hit me in the gut like a body blow and I weaved. This couldn't be happening. Oh God, oh God. *No. No. No. No. No.* I realized I was moving my head along with my inner screaming.

"You said you loved me," I croaked out. I put my hand to my head. This couldn't be real. Make it *stop*.

"I—"

I stuck my hand up to halt his words. I held it out in front of me, shaking, warding off whatever he'd been about to say, whether to confirm or deny. Either one would be equally as bad. A sob came up my throat.

Suddenly Kyland advanced on me. "You listen to me, Tenleigh. You are going to leave here. You are going to forget all about Dennville, Kentucky. Leave here and don't ever look back. And when the time comes, you'll make a life for yourself, your mama, and your sister. All three of you are getting out of here. Do you know how fucking *rare* it is for people like us to get out from under the poverty of a place like this? You have a chance. Take it."

I was still shaking my head back and forth, looking at him in horror. This wasn't happening.

"It was meant to be that you won the scholarship. It's for the best that I didn't. Because I wouldn't have been able to use it anyway."

"You touched her," I choked out in a horrified whisper. "You touched me and then you touched her. Or did you touch her and then still..." I let out a sob. "In what order did it happen, Kyland? Tell me!" I screamed, hot tears finally starting to fall.

"I, what?" he asked, looking confused.

"Did you betray me with her before or after you took my virginity?" I voice shook. I was trembling all over now.

"Does it matter?" he asked.

I slapped him across his face. Hard. Deep hurt flashed in his expression for a second before he met my eyes. *Good*. I wanted to hurt him to his core right then. Just like he'd hurt me to my core. Just like he'd destroyed me with three words: *Because Shelly's pregnant.*

I beat at his chest with my fists. He never raised his hands to push me away or to stop me. He just let me hit him—again and again and again, his face, his chest, his shoulders. This couldn't be happening. I choked out another sob, feeling sick and dizzy. I fell back against the wall again and cried out my misery and confusion, the very last piece of my stupid, unguarded heart crumbling away.

He stood, looking down at the floor, his hands in his pockets, a drop of blood dripping from his lip where the cheap metal ring I was wearing on my right index finger must have cut him. I watched that drop of blood fall to the floor as if in slow motion and splash on the hardwood right next to the ridiculous list I'd made, both lying there, the last remnants of us. My eyes moved slowly to his face. It was filled with sorrow. I wanted to spit on him. He'd done this. How *dare* he feel sorrowful?

I drew my shoulders back, gathering myself. Kyland finally raised his eyes to mine, red rimmed and pleading me for something. Forgiveness? I'd never give him that.

"You leave Dennville," he said, his voice raspy. "Leave here and don't look back."

I regarded him for a second, suddenly feeling strangely empty, numb. "You're the biggest disappointment of my life," I said. "I'll never forgive you—not as long as I live."

He nodded as if that was the best idea I'd ever come up with. "Good," he said, and then he turned his back on me.

I walked on legs that felt like they were made of jelly to his front door. I picked up my backpack and the scholarship packet I'd left on the floor, and I walked out of Kyland Barrett's house and out of his life, leaving behind the man I'd been stupid enough to give my whole heart to, the one who didn't want to love or keep me, the one who had betrayed me in the cruelest way possible. The pitiful words I'd begged him with echoed in my mind, shameful and humiliating.

I didn't go back to my trailer. I went into the woods, not bothering to push aside the tree branches that slapped me in the face as I walked, causing small, burning cuts across my cheeks. The pain brought me out of my fog, and again, I recalled Kyland's words. *Because Shelly's pregnant.* I stopped by a vine of wild honeysuckle and vomited on the forest floor. And then I walked, all the while clutching that scholarship to my chest like it was a lifeline—because now, it was. I didn't know how long I walked, but even in my half-shocked state, my body knew right where I was and eventually, I'd circled back around to my trailer.

That night my sister rocked me in her arms like I was a baby and she was a mama. I was still so shocked and heartbroken I couldn't even cry.

The very next day I went to the principal, Mrs. Branson, and asked her if there was any way I could move to San Diego immediately. Mrs. Branson knew my home situation and I'd made it seem like I couldn't stand it one more minute. She probably thought I was all over the map, trying to reject the scholarship one minute, and begging her to help me use it as quickly as possible the next. The truth was, I couldn't live in the same town as Kyland Barrett after that day—not for any longer than I had to.

Mrs. Branson told me I couldn't move into the dorm, but it turned out she had a niece who lived there and she called and asked if I could stay with her for a couple months until school started. Her niece very kindly agreed, and so I went home and numbly started packing up my few belongings in preparation of leaving the only place I'd ever known. I'd never even set foot out of Kentucky, and here I was about to board a plane for the first time and fly to California. And yet somehow, the excitement of that didn't penetrate the emotional stupor I was still in.

The night before I was scheduled to leave, I went outside our trailer and sat on the steps, looking blankly out at the sunset. I listened to the familiar sounds of home—the sway of trees, the whistling wind, the far-off scream-like noise bobcats make. Thoughts of bobcats made my heart dip and right then and there, I decided two things: one, I was going to succeed in California, no matter how hard it was, and two, I'd never fall in love again. Not *ever*.

CHAPTER TWENTY-ONE
Tenleigh

Four Years Later

There's nothing like going home again, or so the saying goes. It was late afternoon when I got the first glimpse of those Appalachian Mountains outside the window of my car. I gripped the steering wheel. Despite nervousness and anxiety and a somewhat uncertain future, there was also a faint current of excitement flowing through my veins—a feeling that I was back where I belonged.

I rolled the window down as I turned off the highway and took a deep breath of the cool, pine-scented mountain air, so different from the warm, salty San Diego breezes I'd been breathing for the past four years while I was away at college. I hadn't come home for summer or winter breaks, choosing instead to take classes year-round and graduate early. I'd stayed in San Diego a couple extra months to wrap up a few things with my student teaching and so I didn't have to drive through winter weather to get home. And now here I was, the mountains just barely coming alive with spring. God, I'd missed Kentucky. An unexpected peace fell over me and my lips tipped in a smile when I turned up the mountain road to our trailer.

"Home," I whispered. Everything was going to be okay. I was back because I had a goal. I had a purpose. And in that, I had succeeded.

As I drove uphill, my gaze flitted over the small, rundown houses sitting to the sides of the road. Surprisingly, some of them looked better than I'd remembered. Several of the people on the mountain had cleaned up their yards. Well, that was a welcome sight.

But all too soon, the anxiety hit full force as I turned the bend in the road, knowing I'd be driving past Kyland's home in another minute. I purposely kept my eyes straight, not daring even a glance at the little blue house I knew was on my left. I turned at the next bend in the road and let out a long exhale as I pulled into the dirt clearing next to our trailer and sat in the car for several minutes, just looking at the only home I'd ever known until just a few years ago. But, oh, what a difference four years could make.

I'd left Kentucky broken and bruised, crushed in a way I thought I'd never recover from. But if time didn't heal all wounds, at least it made them bearable. And I'd survived. I shut off the engine and then stretched my limbs as I stepped out of my small beater of a car—a dull red VW Rabbit that I'd bought for three thousand dollars. It wasn't exactly pretty, but it was all I'd been able to afford. The truth was, I loved it. It was mine. It was the first thing I'd ever owned outright. I'd waited tables at a large chain restaurant in the evenings after classes, finally saving up enough money to buy my own transportation. It had just made the two-thousand–mile trip from California to Kentucky. I'd say I'd done a decent job picking a good one. Or more likely, I'd gotten lucky, but that was okay too.

I took a minute to look around, taking everything in as if it were the first time I was seeing it. The trailer looked just about the same as I remembered it—small and sad. But I felt a twinge of happiness nonetheless. "Be it ever so humble, there's no place like home," I whispered. *Humble* was probably a generous word for our trailer, but it was still a soft enough place to land. And everyone had to land somewhere.

Still, I planned on getting my mama and sister out of here as soon as I could—somewhere bigger, more comfortable, somewhere where we could all have our own rooms.

My mama was in a psychiatric hospital in Lexington. Three years after I'd left, she'd had a particularly bad episode and thankfully, Sam had stepped in and offered to pay for her care in a really great facility. That was a relief because when I heard the news, I had planned to come home. There was no way Marlo could handle that by herself. I was actually surprised not only that Sam was still in Marlo's life, but that she had agreed to let him pay, which spoke volumes about how bad it had been. *Oh, Mama...*

The aged handle squeaked as I turned it and pushed the door open, the old familiar noise making me feel like a little girl again. "Hello," I called out. I heard a loud, excited yelp from the bedroom and suddenly the door was flying open as Marlo danced out and launched herself at me. I squealed as she picked me up and jumped around with me, laughing out loud. "Stop! Stop!" I demanded. "I haven't peed in hours. I'm going to wet my pants."

Marlo set me down, laughing. She grinned and wrapped

her arms around me, saying, "Welcome home, baby sister. College graduate."

I grinned back, squeezing her tightly, holding back tears. Marlo hated it when I cried. I went and used the restroom quickly and when I came back out, she smiled and took my hands again. "Let me look at you." Her eyes ran over me for a minute and she shook her head. "You always were pretty, Ten, but wow, you're a class act."

"I'm the same," I said, disagreeing. "Just some new clothes and a haircut."

"No, no, it's not just the clothes and the hair. It's you. You look all grown up. You're too skinny, though. Is everyone on a diet in California?"

I snorted. "Yeah. A little different than the starvation diet we were always on. There, they do it on purpose."

She let out a half laugh–half groan and brought her hand to her forehead. "How are you? Really?" she asked, sitting down on the couch. "Is it weird to be back?"

I sat down next to her. "Yeah. Kind of. I mean, I'm not sure yet."

Her forehead creased as she studied me for a moment. "Have you seen him?"

"Who?" I asked flippantly, as if I didn't know exactly whom she was referring to.

She just raised her eyebrows.

I sighed. "No. I literally drove straight here."

"Well, it's going to be fine. It's been a long time. And you know, he gained about two hundred pounds, lost all his hair, and came down with a really bad skin disease, so…he's hideous, unsightly. Honestly? Disgusting." She shivered.

I gaped at her and the corner of her lip quivered into a smile. "What?" Then I laughed. "You're lying. He did not.

199

I mean, God, that'd be a stroke of luck on my part, but..." I shook my head. "You're right. It's going to be fine. I have a job to do here. It's been almost four full years, and I'm just going to have to look past the fact that someone I loathe lives right up the road. We'll just steer clear of each other, I'm sure."

"Do you really still loathe him, Ten?"

I thought about that for a second. Loathing Kyland was just a step below hating him, and I found it hard to completely hate him, as I still knew who he was capable of being. Still, I needed something to hold on to. "Yeah. Yeah, I do. And no one's going to take that from me. At least, not yet. When it comes to men, never forgive, never forget—that's my life motto."

She looked at me dubiously. "That's *my* life motto."

"Well, I've adopted it."

"That's good," she said. "You should. *All* women should."

I'd only ever asked Marlo about Kyland once, or rather, about Shelly. A couple months after I'd left, I'd woken up in the middle of the night, something from a dream or a half-formed thought convincing me everything he'd said to me that horrible day had been a lie. In the dark of the night, it'd seemed so possible, likely even, that he hadn't been telling the truth. I'd *known* who he was. And that wasn't him. *It wasn't.* The pieces of some puzzle I couldn't fathom once I was awake had come together in my head in the bleariness of sleep. But in the morning when I'd called Marlo asking her if she'd seen Shelly around town recently, she'd haltingly confirmed that she had and that she looked like she was just a few months pregnant. *A few months.* Meaning Kyland *had* been with her right about the time he'd slept with me. I'd spent that day in bed, curled up, staring at the wall, contemplating how slowly an hour could tick by, my heart breaking all over again.

I'd vowed not to ask about him again and I hadn't. Not once. Even the month I'd calculated in my head that his baby would probably have been born, I didn't ask Marlo a thing. It'd taken an act of willpower unlike any I'd shown before, but I'd done it.

The day four years earlier that he'd told me what he'd done, the day I ran from his house back to my own, was the last time I'd seen him.

"I think you should know…"

"What?" I asked.

"Well, he works belowground at the mine. I've seen him coming home, covered in coal dust."

Shock momentarily rendered me mute, the vision of what Kyland would look like with the blackened face of a miner, only his teeth and the whites of his eyes showing blossoming in my mind. *No way.* She was obviously mistaken. "The mine? Belowground? He can't." I recalled Kyland's fear of small spaces, how he feared the dark…his father… his brother… I shook my head. *He'd never work that job.* I felt almost sick to my stomach at the very thought of Kyland down there in those dark tunnels, the weight of the earth pressing down… I knew he'd have to work *somewhere*, but I never for one second imagined he'd work at Tyton Coal. "It's not possible that he works there," I insisted.

"Well," she said gently, "it is, because he does. I know I'm not supposed to talk about him, but I just thought you might want to know." She watched me with a sensitive expression in her eyes. "In case you were going to go see Jamie at the mine, I wouldn't want you getting blindsided."

"Thanks, Mar," I whispered.

"How is Jamie by the way?" she asked, clearly to move my mind away from Kyland.

"He's good," I said, my breath coming easier as I thought of my friend. While I'd been in San Diego, my friendship with Jamie had blossomed. He'd gone to school in California as well, at Harvey Mudd, just a couple hours from me, and when I'd been heavily involved in applying for grants, I'd reached out to him for some information about Tyton Coal that I thought would be applicable to my cause. We'd gotten together several times over lunch that turned into dinner. Over a few too many glasses of wine, I'd told him about Kyland and how he'd broken my heart. Truthfully, it'd been a really healing friendship for me, considering everything. Jamie had also told me he'd come out to his parents right before he left for college and it had not gone well. He wasn't sure he was going to be welcomed back into his parents' lives. He already had a job waiting for him back at the mine, though, so he'd have to have at least some interaction with his father. And at least he hadn't been cut off financially. But he'd stayed away during the summers like me and graduated a little earlier as well. Funny how different our lives were and yet how similar our hearts felt. "You should get to know him, Mar," I said. "He's a really nice guy. I know it seems kinda weird with the history between our parents, but he's never judged me by that, and I don't judge him by it either. Seriously, he's had things rough in his own way."

She gave a non-committal shrug. My eyes shifted away as my mind insisted on returning to the imagined picture of Kyland with coal dust on his face.

When I looked back at Marlo, she was watching me knowingly. My sister had always had me pegged. Some things never changed. "So," she said brightly, patting me on the knee, "tell me more about this school you're building."

I took a deep breath and forced a smile. Marlo and I had talked as often as possible—I'd even shipped her a cell phone that she could load with minutes so I could get ahold of her when I wanted or needed to. Unfortunately, she didn't always keep it full, and if she was at the trailer, there was no reception anyway. If she was at Al's, we could only talk for a few minutes before someone, usually Al, was yelling at her to get back to work. So we still had a lot to catch up on.

"It's going to be right on the edge of town where Zippy's Ice Cream Parlor used to be before the mine cave-in."

"Isn't the library on that lot?"

I nodded, melancholy moving through me. That small building—practically a shed really—had been my sanctuary at one point...and the place where I'd received my very first kiss...the place where—

I cut those thoughts short, focusing back on Marlo. "The building is going to be torn down to make room for the school, but I'll pack the books up." I took a deep breath. "Anyway, I've already started spending the money from the grants. I have a construction crew lined up. It's going to be a lot of work, but I'm excited about it. And it's going to make such a difference for the kids who live on this mountain and the ones who still live in Dennville."

"That's for sure. I can't even imagine what it would have been like not having to walk six miles to school every morning and then back home again."

I nodded. I knew a lot of the kids on the mountain didn't make the effort most of the time—hence the never-ending cycle of illiteracy, poverty, unemployment, and hopelessness.

But I was hoping to change some of that. At least for a few—hell, even for one.

It would even help the kids who lived in Evansly and went to school there. As it stood, the public school system there was so overcrowded, and the ones who needed it, didn't get any individual attention.

When I'd started college in San Diego, I'd thrown myself into my studies full force. I'd been in survival mode, just trying to get from one day to the next, my heart so cracked and battered, some days I felt like I was too broken to move.

Having something other than Kyland to occupy my mind had been my saving grace. One late fall day my first year, I'd gotten into a discussion about education and poverty rates in Kentucky in a small study group I was in. I'd told them how the kids like me who lived on the mountain walked six miles or more to school every day. I'd held back from telling them the worst of it, but the group had been astonished that where I lived, very few people had cars or even heat. There had been a boy in that class, Howard, who mentioned offhand that I should look into grants for building schools. That comment had lived in the back of my head for several months until I'd finally decided to actually look into it.

I'd spent the next few years getting my teaching degree in English literature and applying for grant after grant—both public and private—to build a school in the poverty-stricken town of Dennville, Kentucky. Much to my surprise and joy, I'd secured a few grants from several private investors right before I'd graduated a few months ago. The funding would pay for the building, all the operating costs, and a very small staff.

And so I was home. Home to give back.

"So once this school is built, do you think that's where you'll work?" Marlo asked.

"I'm not sure," I said quietly, running my finger along my lower lip. "Maybe. I wanted to talk to you about that, though, Mar. I mean, me coming back here, well, it means that you and Mama will have to wait just a little longer to get out of this trailer." I frowned. "I'm going to see if I can work at Al's while construction is underway, and I've saved up a little bit of money while I've been gone, since my expenses were paid for. I used some on my car, but whatever else I didn't send to you and Mama, I put away in a bank account. But whether I work here in Dennville at the school or whether we all decide to move away so I can work somewhere else, that affects you."

Marlo put her hand on my knee. "First of all, Tenleigh, Mama's away for a little longer at least. Her doctors say another three months there would be ideal. You only took three and a half years to graduate. We didn't even expect you home until this summer. We can wait—we can wait for you to decide, to build your dream. We're so proud of you." She pulled her hand back and studied her fingernails. "Also, I… well, I don't spend very much time here."

I cocked an eyebrow. "Sam?"

"Yeah, his place is nice. It's warm. He's warm."

"Why, Marlo, I do believe you're blushing." I ribbed her. "You love him, don't you?"

She made a sputtering sound. "No, no, it's still just casual. But why stay here"—she waved her arm around our small, run-down trailer—"if I can stay there? It's closer to work too."

I didn't buy it. It'd been *four* years. "Well, okay, whatever you say." I stood up. "I actually need to get going. I'm meeting Jamie at the site in half an hour."

"Okay. I'm so glad to have you back, baby sister. I've missed you so much."

"Me too. You have no idea, Mar." She stood up and I squeezed her tight, sinking in to the comfort of her embrace, so happy to be back with my best friend.

When I pulled away, she said, "So, you up for visiting Mama next week? She's expecting us."

"Of course," I said. "I wish we could go sooner."

Marlo shook her head. "She does really well on a specific schedule. She's so much better, Tenleigh. Wait until you see her." Her eyes lit up in a way I hadn't seen since we were kids. "Wait until you talk to her. It's..." She became teary and started laughing, like Marlo usually did when she was about to cry, which was rarely. "Anyway..."

"I can't wait." I smiled. "Okay, I'm off. I know you have to work late. I'll see you in the morning?"

"Yeah, I'll see you in the morning." I hugged her again tightly and with that, I was out the door, and a few making later, I was driving back down the mountain.

As I drove down Main Street toward the lot the school would be built on, I felt the same happiness from when I'd caught sight of the mountains for the first time earlier today. Yes, I was home. And it was going to be good—it was going to be just fine.

But that feeling was short-lived when I glanced to my left and saw the figure of the person who had haunted me for almost four years: *Kyland*. My heart bounced around in my chest like a ping pong ball and I sucked in a breath. He had a little boy on his shoulders and Shelly was behind him, laughing at something the boy was saying. Kyland turned around and said something to her too, and then laughed. I watched as he swung the boy to the ground, the boy squealing and laughing. He took his hand as they continued on.

I clutched the steering wheel as my eyes filled with tears. The air felt sharp, as if it were made of a million tiny razor blades. It hurt to breathe. Oh God, it hurt to breathe. All these years I'd tortured myself with the picture of Kyland as a dad—Kyland as the dad to someone else's kid—but the reality of it pierced me so deeply, it was a physical pain. It was true. Kyland had a child—a son.

Breathe, Ten. Breathe. I sucked in another small, tortured breath.

What the *hell* had I been thinking coming back here?

CHAPTER TWENTY-TWO
Tenleigh

I didn't run into Kyland again that week. Not that I'd run into him exactly—I didn't think he'd seen me, but I made it a point to steer clear of anywhere I thought he might be and that included Main Street.

I'd pulled off the road that day and spent twenty minutes in my car, just trying to breathe normally again. And then I'd gathered myself together and driven to the lot where the school would be built. Jamie was already there, waiting for me. He had taken one look at my face, asked, "Kyland?" and when I'd nodded, he had wrapped me in his arms. I hadn't truly suffered over Kyland Barrett in years, and suddenly just a brief glimpse of him and I was a mess. So yes, taking the back roads might seem cowardly and slightly pitiful, but at least for the time being, I was just fine with being a pitiful coward. Hiding was less painful.

With new perspective, I saw how dinky and sad the small library, that had once been my refuge, really was. I stood looking around, hardly able to fathom that a construction crew would be here in less than a week to tear the shed-sized building down and start pouring the foundation for my school. Today, I was going to start clearing out the books that the high school in Evansly had agreed to donate to the new school library.

Truthfully, it didn't look like anyone had set foot in this place since I'd been gone. It wasn't even worth having someone lock and unlock it.

So many years ago, I'd lobbied for a library in Dennville and helped it become a reality. How surreal that the school I'd lobbied for would be built on the same lot. And yet so perfectly fitting.

I took a moment to picture the building that was planned. I had a drawing of it back at the trailer and I looked at it when I needed to remind myself why this was going to be worth the emotional hardship I might have to endure by being back in Dennville.

A deep, fortifying breath buoyed my resolve. This wasn't about me. This was about the kids who might have more choices because of this school. This was about giving someone else the same opportunities I'd been given when I won the Tyton Coal Scholarship. This was about remembering that, although it was hard for me to be here now and it had been hard for me to grow up in a place so lacking in so many ways, because of that scholarship, I had *choices*. I could do anything I wanted with my life—I could go anywhere I wanted to go. That scholarship had set me free—from poverty, from hopelessness, from the limited opportunities of the life I'd been born into.

I stepped into the library, a box in my arms, the smell of dust and old paperback books transporting me back. For just a moment I was seventeen again, sitting at the desk right there at the back of the room, dressed in old, worn clothes, homework spread out...

At the back wall, I set the box down and ran my hand along the books, almost expecting to see a small piece of white paper sticking out of one. Memories bombarded me and I shut my eyes, holding back the tears that threatened.

"This place still smells the same," I heard behind me in a low voice.

I whirled around and sucked in a breath. *Kyland*. My heart practically jumped out of my chest.

Our gazes held for several long beats.

"H-Hello," I finally said.

Hello? That's what you come up with after all this time? Hello? Excellent job.

Kyland just lifted his chin and then leaned indifferently against the doorframe. And God, *why?* How did someone evil and cruel get to be so beautiful? It didn't seem like karma should work that way. He had been a boy the last time I'd seen him and it was easy to see that he was a man now, all chiseled cheekbones and strong jaw. His hair was shorter, almost a buzz cut, and his frame seemed even bigger, taller and more muscular. His jaw ticked. I straightened my spine and crossed my arms. I was a woman now, and I could handle this.

"You're back," he finally said.

"It appears so."

"Why?" he grated out. "What the fuck are you thinking, Tenleigh?"

Hurt slammed into me, and I flinched slightly before I quickly got control of myself.

Kyland stared back unapologetically.

"What business is it of yours?" I asked, turning and

pulling a stack of books from the shelf and dropping them into the box sitting on the floor at my feet.

Just as quick as that, he was behind me and his hand was on my arm. I looked down at it, anger rising in me just as quickly as the hurt had. I turned slightly and shook him off me violently, hissing out, "Don't touch me. Don't *ever* touch me."

For the briefest second, shock and what looked like hurt flashed in his eyes, but then it was gone. The air sizzled between us, our wills clashing as my skin prickled. Kyland flinched and took a step backward as if he felt it too and it pained him in some way.

"I saw you the other day," I said. "With Shelly and your son." I wanted to kick myself for the way my voice hitched on the final word. "It's overdue I suppose, but... congratulations."

Kyland froze and something faltered in his expression, but he didn't say anything.

I waited, but when he remained silent, I sighed. I turned to him fully. "Is there something you want, Kyland? Why are you here?"

"I want you to turn around and drive back out of town."

I tilted my chin up, determined not to cry. *Asshole.* What had I ever done to him except give him my whole heart? I'd also given him my body—let's not forget that small fact. And he was treating *me* this way? "What? This town isn't big enough for the both of us? Why don't *you* leave?"

He leaned in toward me and I had a brief flash of him leaning in to kiss me, right here, right where we were now standing. I drew in a quick breath. "Because I *can't*," he gritted out.

I leaned back against the bookshelf behind me, trying

to create space between us. "Right." *Your son. Your family.* I narrowed my eyes at him. "Which brings us back to the reason why what *I* do with my life has zero to do with you. Go to hell, Kyland," I hissed.

His eyes flared and he leaned in even closer. I smelled clean breath and salty, masculine skin and I sucked in a big breath of his air, as though the oxygen I'd been breathing for the last four years had only barely sustained me, lacking the one element that filled me with actual *life*. He smelled delicious and achingly familiar.

He stared down at me for several long beats before he rasped, "I do go to hell. Every day. For you." And then he whirled around and stalked out of the library, leaving me trembling and confused, angry and hurt. But I didn't cry. I refused to cry another tear over Kyland Barrett.

"Hey, Al," I said, entering the smoky bar a few days later. "You know there's a smoking ban in bars in Kentucky, right?" I gave him a small smirk.

"Yeah, I know, smart-ass," Al said. "But this is my bar. They can come cite me if they want."

"You're a rebel, Al," I said. Truthfully, I wished Al would follow the law, considering my sister and her lungs worked here and had for quite some time. But Al was Al and what he lacked in workplace health practices, he made up for in other qualities. He paid a fair wage and he protected his girls to the best of his ability.

I'd come into the bar a few days before and asked if I could pick up some shifts. Al had welcomed me back. And luckily for me, one of his regular waitresses had recently quit.

So here I was—back in Dennville, Kentucky, living in

the same rickety trailer, and working in the same smoke-filled bar, overcome with sadness and despair over the same lying, cheating boy. "You've come a real long way, Tenleigh," I murmured to myself as I wiped down a table and cleared the beer bottles. Only in actuality, I had. I had a college degree now. It changed everything. I took a deep breath, determined not to let the run-in of earlier that week completely ruin me. I had chosen this. I had chosen to come back. And I needed to deal with it. I'd never really faced it because I hadn't had to—the distance between Kyland and me had made it a little easier to pretend he didn't exist. But now it was utterly clear that he did exist. And for some unknown reason, he was angry and bitter with me for returning. I snorted. "Asshole," I murmured again to myself.

The rest of the early evening went by quickly. It was Friday night so I expected it would be crowded. Since I'd been gone, Al had added a small platform area that worked as a stage and a dance floor in front of it. Tonight he had a local band performing live. By nine o'clock the bar was filled with people drinking, dancing, and laughing boisterously. Marlo was working too, and Sam had come by to listen to the band. When he walked in, I gave him a big hug and showed him to Marlo's section.

"You look great, Tenleigh," he shouted over the noise.

"Thanks, Sam." I grinned at him. "You treating my sister good?"

He got a shy, lovesick look on his face. *Oh boy.* "I try my best," he said.

I grinned and walked him to a table and then leaned on the back of the chair facing him at the table. "Hey, Sam, before I grab you a beer, I wanted to thank you for what you're doing for our mama. Marlo says she's doing really great, and that's all because of you."

He glanced away for a minute, something shifting in his expression. Had I embarrassed him? "I'd do anything for your family, for Marlo," he said after a beat.

I smiled. "I've always liked you, Sam."

He smiled back and pushed his glasses up on his nose and I and went to get him a beer. The guy wasn't giving up on my hardheaded sister, and he was doing something wonderful for our mama. I couldn't help but like him—he was one of the few good ones. As happy as I was for Marlo and as much as she deserved a good man who was willing to fight for her, I couldn't help the despondency I felt as I stood at the bar waiting for Sam's beer. *Would I ever have that?* Would someone ever love me that way? Would I ever love someone like I'd loved Kyland? Did I *want* to ever love someone that intensely again? I'd sworn off love forever after Kyland broke my heart, but that vow hadn't been sustainable. I still longed for love. I ached for someone to hold me tight and tell me everything was going to be okay, to kiss my forehead tenderly, and reach for me in the darkness.

"Looks like you could use this," Al said, sliding a shot down the bar to me.

I was jolted out of my reverie. "What is it?"

"Don't ask stupid questions, just bottoms up."

I laughed. Al was not opposed to his waitresses doing a shot or two during a shift. Sometimes you needed a little something to get you through a night of being jostled and groped by drunks. Ah, hell, why not? I did need a drink. I needed to quiet my own brain. I threw the shot back and grimaced as the fiery liquid burned down my throat, and then leaned over the bar and grabbed a lime. I bit down on it and turned away from the bar as I sucked out the sour liquid.

For the second time that week, my eyes met with stony gray ones. Kyland. My body froze and I just stared at him, my heart pounding in my ears. Geez, maybe this town really wasn't big enough for the both of us.

He was standing stock-still right at the doorway, glaring across the space at me, his mouth hanging open before he snapped it shut. And suddenly all the air in the place seemed to be sucked right out the door.

The raucous noise of the bar faded away as we held eye contact. And then, from behind him, Shelly appeared. I took a step backward, the bar hitting my back. Her appearance felt like a punch to the gut. Shelly looked at Kyland and then followed his eyes to me. Something that looked like sympathy came into her expression and I looked away, turning back around to the bar. I took several deep breaths, trying to calm myself. I grabbed Sam's beer and put it on my tray and walked it toward his table, not glancing toward the door again. Hopefully when Kyland had seen me, he'd left.

Marlo pulled me aside as I was heading back to the bar. "Kyland's here. You okay?" Her expressive eyes were wide with concern.

"I'm fine," I insisted, even though I wasn't exactly sure. "I thought I was the one who was angry, but he seems to *hate* me."

"Why would *he* hate you? For getting out of here when *he* screwed his life up?"

I chewed on my lip. "I don't know. Do Kyland and Shelly come in here often?"

"I've never seen them in here."

"Huh. Well, we both have to live in this town. Or rather,

I've decided to live in this town for now. And so he can deal with it—whatever his problem is."

Marlo nodded but looked unsure. "Okay. If you need me to pour a beer on him or something, I will. That'll get him out of here."

I laughed, but she didn't.

"I'm serious."

"I know you are, Mar." I hugged her quickly.

As I served a few more drinks, I noticed that Kyland and Shelly hadn't left. In fact, they'd gotten a table up by the dance floor. I watched them from the corner of my eye and noticed that he was sitting stiff and rigid and she looked uncomfortable too. I vowed not to look in their direction again.

I went back to the bar and asked Al for another shot and slung it down. I hadn't eaten dinner and so the two shots already had a buzzed energy spreading through my veins.

You're okay. You're okay.

A burly trucker sitting at the bar who had consumed one too many beers pulled me onto his lap. I gave a fake laugh and struggled to get up, but he pulled me back down. "Hey, come on now," I said, trying to diffuse the situation. "How can I get your beer if you don't let me up?"

"I'd rather take a long drink of you." He laughed loudly and moved his hands up my body.

"Let her go before I rearrange your fucking face." I recognized Kyland's voice immediately. I stopped struggling, and the big guy whipped his head around, releasing his hold on me so I could clamor to my feet.

Kyland was standing behind the guy, his jaw hard and set, his hands fisted at his sides.

"Whoa, man," the guy slurred, turning his hefty body in

his seat. "No harm meant. I was just saying hi to the lady." His eyes ran down my body again.

"Say hi to ladies with your mouth, not your hands."

My head whipped from Kyland to the drunken guy. Now I was a lady? Interesting considering very recently, he'd told me he couldn't live in the same town as me.

"I'd like to do that too." He wiggled his tongue and then let out a sharp bark of laughter.

Kyland's fist was a blur as it flew past me, straight into the guy's face. The guy let out a grunt, his eyes rolled back in his head, and he toppled over, out cold on the bar floor. A loud whoop went up among the bar patrons. This was not an unusual occurrence at Al's. Still, my mouth fell open. I stared at the trucker on the floor for a second and then looked back up at Kyland.

And suddenly I was angry. Maybe it was the liquor flowing through my veins, maybe it was the fact that Kyland thought he could mess with my emotions or that anything that happened to me was any of his damn business. Maybe it was the fact that he'd shown up on my territory twice this week and it'd hurt me deeply both times. Suddenly, I was *furious*.

"How dare you?" I seethed.

"How dare I pull a lecherous pig off you?" he asked. "I'm sorry, I didn't realize you were enjoying being manhandled. Then again, you *are* back here in this goddamned town working at the same goddamned bar." His nostrils flared and I almost wondered if he might paw the ground like an angry bull.

"Maybe I *was* enjoying it. And either way, it's none of *your* business what I like or don't like." I was so angry I was shaking. I grabbed a guy walking by and pulled on his sweater roughly. He stumbled toward me, looking surprised. I planted my lips on his. He tasted like beer and smelled like cheap aftershave. I pushed him away and the guy went stumbling off, muttering, "Wow. I really like this bar."

I looked back at Kyland's face, his expression frozen in something I wasn't sure I could read.

"Tenleigh?" I heard Marlo's voice and saw her in my peripheral vision. I put my hand up, letting her know I was okay, my eyes glued to Kyland.

"I do *what* I want, when I want," I said. What was I even doing? I wasn't totally clear. I just knew I was angry and out of control. And I knew it still hurt down to my soul that Kyland had betrayed me after I'd given him every last piece of myself—the pieces of myself it was becoming very clear I'd never figured out how to reassemble.

"Is that what you did in California?" he asked, moving closer to me.

I lifted my chin, literally turning my nose up at him. "All the time. As often as possible," I lied. "Once you broke the seal, I figured—"

The look of raw pain that crossed his face stunned me and my words died on my lips. But just as quickly my anger flared again. He was upset by the thought of me being with other men? Of all the *hypocritical* bastards! He was here, with *her*, the woman he had cheated on me with—the woman he'd made a baby with.

"That's not you, Tenleigh," he said softly.

I laughed in his face, an ugly, bitter sound. "You don't know me anymore. You know nothing about me. And I don't know anything about you anymore either."

He opened his mouth to speak but then closed it as if

he'd changed his mind. "Christ, I can't do this with you." He turned and started walking away.

Fury flashed through my body.

"Hey, Kyland," I yelled. He turned back around. "Did you ever finish *Wuthering Heights*?"

He blinked, and then furrowed his brows, regarding me with confusion. "I don't have much time for reading these days, *Tenleigh*."

I leaned my hip against the bar and tapped my finger against my chin. "I was just wondering if you found Heathcliff the despicable, cheating bastard that I did."

He started walking back toward me. "We never did agree on much in the literary world, did we?"

"Hmm, true. Still, I would think anyone with half a brain in his head would see what a worthless piece of lying trash Heathcliff was."

"I was more struck by what a dim-witted moron Cathy was…finally getting away from those…*moors* and then fucking coming *back* to experience more misery? Squandering the chance she was given? Doesn't get much more idiotic than that."

My blood boiled under my skin. "So what if Cathy came back for the moors, dark and foggy though they might be? At least she didn't come back for Heathcliff. Clearly Heathcliff was the very *last* thing on her mind. In fact, I found it extremely annoying how…Heathcliff kept showing up everywhere Cathy was."

I barely heard someone behind me at the bar say, "Are they fighting or having a book club?"

And a different person answered, "I'm unclear. Looks like foreplay to me."

We both ignored them.

Kyland looked me up and down. "You so sure about

that? Maybe"—and he looked momentarily unsure rather than just angry—"maybe Heathcliff *had* been on her mind all the time she was away. Maybe Cathy wouldn't have gotten so angry every time Heathcliff showed up if he wasn't still very much on her mind, if her new boyfriend made her feel the same things Heathcliff could." His voice softened. "And maybe she'd been on Heathcliff's mind too. Maybe she was all Heathcliff ever thought of, all he ever dreamed about."

Boyfriend? What boyfriend? "Well, it wouldn't matter. After the way Heathcliff betrayed her, she'd never give him a chance again. He ruined everything. He ruined *her*. He was the most selfish, disgusting character I've ever read about. I'm just sorry any paper was ever used to bring him to life. What a waste of a good tree."

He opened his mouth to say something when he suddenly looked behind him. As he turned, I saw Shelly tapping him on the back. All the fight went out of me and pain squeezed my chest. I had forgotten she was even here for a minute. And whatever battle we had just been engaged in, with that one tap on his shoulder, he'd won. I'd lost. *Again.*

I looked away. In that one moment I realized what I'd always known. I couldn't hate Kyland. He wasn't a bad person. He'd just been bad to me. He wasn't incapable of love. He had just been incapable of loving *me*, unwilling to stay for me. But he'd stayed for Shelly. And that was the most painful part of it all. The grief that battered my heart in that moment almost caused me to fall to my knees.

Not now. Not now—don't fall apart here.

I walked quickly to the ladies' room, where I locked myself in a stall. Marlo followed me in a few minutes later and helped me gather myself together the best I could. When I returned to the bar, Kyland and Shelly were gone.

CHAPTER TWENTY-THREE
Tenleigh

I worked a couple shifts at Al's that weekend, but Kyland didn't come back in. Thankfully. I was still embarrassed about the public argument, but I knew that, at Al's, it wasn't an uncommon occurrence. In fact, Gable Clancy's mail-order bride trying to run him over in the parking lot two hours later upstaged it. No, mostly I was just hurt. The anger I'd held on to felt so much better. It made me feel in control. The hurt just *hurt*. But it was either feel it or turn tail and run out of town. I would see the completion of the school—it was my dream and my legacy to the town I'd been born and raised in, the town that had given me the means to get an education. But after that, I'd consider hiring someone else to ensure the upkeep of the yearly funding and starting fresh somewhere else.

Perhaps this was the closure I needed so I could truly move on from Kyland. Had I been lying to myself? Had part of me desperately wanted to know what would happen if I saw him again? Yes, probably. I hadn't really let go. And that was a problem. But it was better to be honest about it. It had been confirmed—he was really and truly with the woman he'd cheated on me with. He had a son with her. That was *reality*. And it was for the best that I face it.

You've seen it with your own two eyes now, Tenleigh. Can you finally accept it and truly move on? Well, you better, because you have no other choice.

That Monday, Marlo and I had plans to visit Mama. I was ready early and decided to go say hello to Buster. I hadn't seen him since I'd returned. I knocked on his door and when he opened it, he let out a whoop and took me in a bear hug, lifting me off my feet. I laughed out loud. "Hi, Buster! Good to see you too."

"Well, let me look at you, Tenleigh girl." He said after he'd set me down. "Well, damn if you don't look like a city girl. You a city girl now, Miss Tenleigh?" We entered his house, still filled with handmade wood furniture. Just like in the old days, every square inch of surface held a whittled couple engaging in various explicit sexual acts. If I hadn't known Buster all my life, this house would have made me seriously uncomfortable.

"Me a city girl? You know better than that, Buster. I'm hill folk through and through."

He chuckled. "Well okay, just makin' sure. You sure do look fancy."

I sat down on a chair that was the carved, sanded, urethane-d face of an upside-down naked man. Another woman was carved behind him, her mouth full with his private parts. I created the à trois in the ménage. This was the most action I'd gotten in quite some time. *Lucky me.*

"Tell me what you've been doing all this time. How'd you like college?" Buster asked.

I told Buster about the school I'd gone to, about California, a little about what it'd been like to be away, the few friends I'd met and would keep in touch with, and about the school I was building. After I'd finished with a brief summary, I said, "What about you, Buster, how have you been?"

"Good, better than ever. You know about the business us hill folk have, right?"

"No. Business?"

"Sure. We're regular entrepreneurs up here. Some of the folks even take a real pride in it. Got their yards cleaned up."

"Yes," I said. "I noticed that. What exactly is it you're doing?"

"Growing lavender. We have a few products too. We go to the craft fairs in the area. I even sell my figures. They go over real well." He winked.

Lavender. Lavender?

In my mind, a crescent moon hung suspended above me as a beautiful boy worshipped my body, the fragrant scent of lavender in the air. "I bet they do," I said distractedly. "This lavender business...whose idea was that?"

"Oh, Kyland Barrett's. He looked into it. Found out lavender's one of the most profitable cash crops for individual growers—even just a backyard garden. Made an information pamphlet up and everything. Plus, it's the only flower that you can dry and use for other products. We've been making sachets, soaps, oil, the tea you used to give—"

"So you all are making real money from this?" I asked, shocked. I had never even *considered* something like that...

"Sure are," he said with pride. "Unlike other crops, the profits are year-round. Nothing ever goes to waste. It's pretty simple really."

"Well, you sound very knowledgeable, Buster," I said. I sat silently shaking my head for a second. "So why isn't everyone doing it?" I asked, thinking of the homes I'd seen that were just as trashed as ever.

Buster scratched the thin hair at the top of his head. "Ah, well, you know, you can lead a hillbilly to lavender, but you can't make him grow it." He laughed and slapped his knee.

I let out a small, wondering laugh as well. "Well, I'll be," I said. A knock at Buster's door made me startle. It was Marlo come to fetch me. She greeted Buster and we both said a quick goodbye and I told him I'd be back before too long. We hugged and then Marlo and I walked to my car, my mind swimming with what Buster had told me.

"Mar, did you know about the whole lavender thing?" I asked, when we'd started down the mountain.

She glanced at me. "Yeah. It's really pretty cool. I was gonna tell you. You just seemed really torn up about Kyland. I didn't think you necessarily needed to hear about all that your first week back."

I nodded. "It's actually...cool though, right? I mean, those people are making money from something that didn't require any kind of start-up..." I bit my lip. "I wonder why he's not doing it himself."

"Yeah, I don't know."

What's going on with you, Kyland? Although it shouldn't surprise me. He was always entrepreneurial and industrious. Just look at how he had survived on his own for all those years.

We were almost to his house, and this time, I turned my head, taking in the white pickup truck parked out front. I sucked in a quick breath as his door suddenly opened and Kyland stepped out wearing jeans and a flannel shirt, a baseball cap on his head, holding a metal lunch box. I turned my head, leaning forward as we passed by and he halted, our eyes met and tangled, even from the distance of my moving car. I saw his head turn to follow right before I focused back on the road. I'd caught the bumper sticker on his truck, the image of a coal miner wearing a miner's hat, crawling through a dark tunnel with the message "Friends in low places."

I sat back in my seat, upset and troubled. There was so much I didn't understand, so much that still hurt me.

Why are you so very angry with me, Kyland? How could you go from loving me to hating me so fiercely?

"What was that intense stare-fest?" Marlo asked from beside me.

"I have no idea," I answered distractedly. "No idea at all."

A couple hours later, when we pulled up in front of the hospital, I turned the car off and just sat staring out the front window. "Wow," I finally said.

The large brick building was old but beautifully maintained. It was surrounded by lush lawns and landscaped to perfection. Patients strolled, some with nurses and some without, and others sat on benches that were placed on the edges of flower beds. The expanse of green lawn was shaded by ancient buckeye trees.

"I know," Marlo said. "It's a really nice place. And they have the best doctors too—doctors who have made helping people with mental illness their life's work. They don't only rotate through one drug cocktail after another, seeing how long they can get one to help before moving on to another," she said with a sigh. Boy, did we know about that. "They focus on the whole of the patient: body, mind, and spirit too," she finished.

"How does Sam afford this?" I asked as I got out of the car. It looked like a resort.

"He has savings. I've never asked him how much this is setting him back." She glanced at me as we started walking. "I was going to tell him to stop, but then I saw Mama after just a couple weeks here, and I just couldn't do that to her."

I grabbed Marlo's hand and squeezed it.

A few minutes later, we had signed in with the nurse at the front desk and were sitting in the large waiting room.

When our mama walked around the corner, I almost didn't recognize her. Her hair was cut to her shoulders and had obviously been washed and styled, and her expression was bright and excited, but not in that glassy-eyed way I was familiar with. She was wearing jeans and a short-sleeved cream sweater. She stopped, putting her hands up over her mouth, as I stood, incredulous.

"Tenleigh, my baby," she breathed as she came toward me.

"Mama," I said, my voice hitching. "You look incredible."

She squeezed me to her and I breathed in her clean, comforting scent. "Oh, Mama," I said as I pulled away. I ran my hand over her hair and just drank her in. She laughed softly and then looked over to Marlo and grinned.

"My other baby," she said hugging Marlo. "Should we walk?" she asked, gesturing out the window.

We all went outside and started strolling on a sunlit path. A light breeze blew and the scent of freshly mowed grass wafted in the air. Marlo led us toward a bench under a tree, and Mama and I sat down.

"I'm gonna go get us some bottled waters. Do you want anything else?" Marlo asked.

We both said no and she left us where we were sitting. I knew she was giving us some time alone together.

I took my mama's hands and squeezed them. "How are you?" I asked.

"I'm so good, baby. I have my good and bad days, but I think everyone does. I'm learning a new normal. I'm learning how to understand my own emotions and how to deal with them."

"That's good, Mama. That's better than good."

She laughed softly. "Yes, it *is* better than good. The doctors here tried me on a few medications, and the ones they have me on now seem to be the best for me. But what's really helping more than anything is that I'm in several therapy groups too. There are other people here who understand exactly what it's like to have a condition like mine. I think it was the missing piece." Her cheeks flushed slightly. "They understand the guilt of hurting everyone around you, even though it's the last thing you want to do."

I squeezed her hands again and then wiped a tear running down her cheek with my thumb. "You don't have to feel guilty. Not with me, not with Marlo," I said.

She nodded, but her expression was sad. "I do, though. You needed a mama, and all your lives, you and Marlo had to mother *me*. And I embarrassed you so badly..." Another tear ran down her cheek.

"I know you didn't mean to, Mama. I know that. There's nothing to be sorry for."

She took a deep breath and looked up at me. "I have a mental illness, Ten. And that, well, that's not going to change. But there are ways I can cope, things I can do, triggers I can avoid. I know that now. And I feel stronger. For the first time in my whole life, I feel like I have *control* over the monsters in my head. For the first time in my life, I have hope."

I sniffled and smiled at her. "Me too, Mama." I leaned forward and hugged her again.

When I sat back up, I asked, "Are you afraid to come home, Mama?"

"A little. I mean, look at this place." She swept her arm around and laughed softly. "It's kind of been a luxury vacation." She smiled but then sobered. "But I will need to get back to real life eventually, and that's one of the things I work on here with my therapists. When I come back, I'm going to get a job, do something. Sam has offered me a position in his front office and that sounds good." She took a deep breath. "What I do know, though, baby, is that you can be in the most luxurious place on earth or you can be in a trailer on a mountain, and if you're sick, you're sick."

"Our situation didn't make it any easier on you, Mama. I know that. So does Marlo. And now I'm home and I'm going to have a well-paying job. I'm going to rent us a little house somewhere… We might not have a whole lot, but we'll have what we need. We'll live a comfortable life, okay?"

She reached out and cupped my cheek. "My girl, still taking care of me." Her smile turned sad. "You won't have to forever, I promise you. The thing is, Tenleigh, sweetheart, it wasn't always so bad. When your father first brought me to Appalachia, I loved it there, even despite the fact that we lived in a trailer in the woods. I loved the mountains and the streams and the sunsets. And I loved the people—there are characters there unlike any you'll ever meet, with the biggest hearts, and the sweetest souls." She was right about that. "And I was so in love." She looked down. "I know he didn't love me back, at least not in the way I loved him, but I want you to know, my

228

baby, that I loved your father. I loved him with all my heart. When I look at you, you and Marlo, I remember that and sometimes it makes me sad, but mostly it makes me thankful."

Oh, Mama. I felt like my heart was going to burst with all the emotions swelling inside.

I swallowed down the lump in my throat. What Mama was saying reminded me that I'd once vowed to be grateful for the things that broke my heart. And I was breaking that vow by holding so much bitterness toward Kyland. I needed to make a *new* vow, to let him go. To find peace. My mama was fighting for that, and so could I.

"All these years," my mama said, "I had it in my head that the only thing I'd done worth any value at all was winning that stupid pageant." She shook her head sadly. "But I was so wrong. *You*, you and Marlo. You're the most beautiful things I ever did."

"Mama," I croaked out, gathering her in my arms and hugging her.

We strolled the grounds for a while after that, Mama, Marlo, and I, catching up and chatting like girls for the first time in my life. Joy filled me and I found myself wanting to pinch myself every three minutes. Mama asked me all about San Diego, my classes, the school, and I found myself chatting animatedly in a way I'd never done before with her. It was wonderful. And for the first time in years, I remembered how sweet and shy and delicate my mama was when it was really *her*. She was so beautiful.

When we'd kissed Mama goodbye and gotten in the car, I sat there in joyous shock, finally laughing like a loon and looking at Marlo like I knew I had lost it. She laughed too. "I know!" she said, hugging me. "I did the same thing the first time I saw her months ago. I did the same thing."

I knew this hospital had given my mama herself back, first and foremost. But we'd gotten her back too, and we'd also been given a part of ourselves as well, a part of ourselves we'd only experienced rarely: the role of daughter. I'd be forever grateful to Sam for this incredible, life-changing gift.

The construction crew broke ground that week. The school was really and truly underway. I allowed myself a moment of pride. There was still so much work to do, but I was filled with hope when it came to all the hard work I'd done for the town. There was every reason to believe this project would be a success, that I had done something that would make a real difference.

I still had the rest of the small library to pack up—a few more boxes and it'd be done. I'd avoided it—going in there was particularly painful because it reminded me so strongly of the love I'd felt for Kyland—but it needed to get done. The building was set to be torn down in the next few days. *Let go of the bitterness, Tenleigh. Peace.*

I was down on my knees clearing a bottom shelf when I heard the door open behind me. I glanced back and was shocked to see Shelly walking in. My heart thumped more quickly as I stood up.

"Hi, Shelly," I said warily. Why was she here?

"Hey, Tenleigh. I don't think we've ever actually talked." She gave me a small smile.

I released a breath and managed a return smile. "No, I guess you're right. Well, nice to officially meet you." I couldn't help that it came out like a question. She had to be here about the other night. So why was she smiling in a friendly way?

She nodded, her smile disappearing. "You too."

We were both silent for a second before I tilted my head toward the table. "Do you want to sit?"

"Sure." She walked over and scooted herself up on the small table I'd always used as a desk. I leaned back against the bookshelf, taking her in. She was very pretty, with her petite body and thick, blond hair.

"So," she said, "I'm sure you're wondering why I'm here."

I nodded, tensed to hear what she was about to say. Was she going to tell me nicely to get out of Dennville too? To leave her and her little family alone? To stop making scenes with her boyfriend in public bars? Would I actually blame her if that *was* exactly her reason for this visit?

"Have you seen Joey?"

I blinked. "Joey?"

"My son."

"Oh," I breathed. *Kyland's son.* "Only from afar." So she's going to use him to make me realize why me being here isn't productive for anyone.

She nodded. "He looks exactly like his father."

Hurt speared through me as Shelly referred to Kyland as Joey's dad. Yet I also had a sudden feeling of irrational ownership too. I straightened my spine. *Stupid, stupid Tenleigh.* You don't own any part of Kyland—not one single part. If that isn't clear to you in *this* moment, then your ability to reason is seriously defective. It didn't feel reasonable, so why did it still feel so instinctual?

"Which is difficult sometimes since he forced himself on me."

Whoa. *Whoa.* What? Kyland would never *ever*, not in a million... *Oh.* Oh my God. I felt like I was reeling. Her words rocked me to my core. I reached behind myself to brace my hand against the solid bookcase.

"Kyland's not Joey's father?" I breathed. And for some reason, my eyes filled up with tears.

"No. He couldn't be. We didn't sleep together. I mean…" She looked up at me. "We had…in the past." She gave her hand a small wave. "Stupid teenage fumbling. He never loved me. He doesn't love me now—not more than a friend anyway." She was quiet for a minute. "He was the first one I went to—after it happened…after I found out I was pregnant. I don't even know why exactly. Maybe I loved him a little. Maybe I hoped he'd want me in some way—I guess I always had. I realize that now…but I didn't then." She shrugged.

I went and sat down next to her on the table. "He lied to me," I said. I still felt like I was reeling even though I was sitting down.

She turned to me and nodded. "I know."

"Why, Shelly? Why would he do that?"

"I don't know exactly. He said he'd help me. He said he was going to stay in Dennville, that he *had* to stay in Dennville for some reason, and that he'd help me if I needed some money. And then he asked if I'd help him too and back up his lie if you said anything to me. I didn't understand why, but"—she let out a breath—"at the time I was so messed up, I was almost happy to pretend it was his. But"—she shrugged—"you never confronted me anyway so I didn't have to lie."

"No," I said, staring straight ahead. "I left town as quickly as possible after he told me he'd gotten you pregnant." *Had he actually said that? Or had he just told me she was pregnant and I deduced the rest myself? Either way, he'd let me come to the incorrect assumption. He'd wanted me to.*

"I kinda thought that was probably the reason," she said.

"But he's never said. He helps with Joey when he can—my father and my brothers, they"—she took a shuddery breath and it looked like she was going to cry—"said I brought it upon myself by spreading my legs for every guy who came along. For a while, I guess I believed it was true. They refused to help me."

I reached over and put my hand on top of hers and she smiled sadly at me. "How did it happen?" I asked gently.

"I met him at Al's. I went to the hotel on the highway with him," she said. "I went willingly. I even intended on having sex with him. Obviously." She was quiet for a minute. "When we got there, he started getting weird. He wanted to tie me up. I wasn't into it. I started to leave and he threw me down on the bed and started calling me a cock tease. I said no, but I didn't struggle. I never struggled." She shook her head again. "Sometimes I wonder if I had…but, well, what's the use in that, right? He had sex with me and afterward, he said thank you." A tear trickled down her cheek. "He thanked me and I still hear it in my head sometimes. And I don't know why that was the worst part of it, the part that stays with me, you know?"

Because you hadn't given him anything—he had taken. I nodded even though I didn't know how that felt. I could only imagine, but it caused an ache to form in my chest for her.

"Anyway, I found out I was pregnant and you know the rest."

"Did you try to…contact him?" I asked.

"I didn't even get his last name." She laughed a small, quick laugh but looked embarrassed. "He was a trucker. I was barely eighteen, hanging out in a bar, and I picked up a stranger and went back to a cheap hotel room with him. I don't exactly look like the picture of morality."

"You don't have to look like anything to be raped, Shelly. Everyone has the right to say no." I spoke softly.

She nodded, swiping a tear away. I looked around to see if there was anything that could be used as a tissue, but there wasn't. "I know that now," she said. "I mean, intellectually, I know that. And Ian, my boyfriend, he's helped me a lot."

"You have a boyfriend?"

"Yeah. He's great. He wants to marry me, adopt Joey." She smiled, a genuine one.

"That's great, Shelly."

"Yeah." She sighed. After a second she turned to face me again. "The other night at the bar, Kyland actually came with me because Ian was working. They work down in the mine together. Ian, he trusts Kyland. Anyway, I hadn't been back to Al's since...well, since that night. I thought it'd be the last piece of closure I needed, you know, to put it in my past—to focus on the future. And then you and Kyland started fighting and I almost said something, but you were working...and I thought Kyland should be the one to tell you. But I don't know when he'll do that. Maybe he even thinks it's not his story to tell. But I thought, if I were you, I'd want to know. I didn't understand that fully until I saw you two together. I didn't know that you still love him."

My eyes flew to hers. "I don't love him anymore."

She looked at me dubiously. "Well, anyway, it's still good to have all the facts. And I could provide at least a few, so there you go."

"Thank you, Shelly. And if I had known why you were at Al's the other night, I never would have made it worse for you."

She shook her head. "It actually made it better for

me—I was so distracted, I didn't think to feel any anxiety being there."

"Oh. Okay, well good." I smiled. "I really appreciate you coming here. And I'm sorry we never got to know each other before this."

Her returning smile was warm and kind. "It wouldn't have worked before this. I'd have been jealous of you. But now…well, if you realize that you do still have some feelings left for Kyland, I think he'd be real happy about that."

He'd be happy about that? I didn't know what to think. *Because Shelly's pregnant.* The words still haunted me, still wounded me, still echoed in my mind.

This was all such a shock. "I saw you the other day," I said distractedly, "walking on Main Street. Joey was on Kyland's shoulders…" God, that had hurt. I still felt the pain of it, even knowing the truth now. Shelly *had* been pregnant— with another man's baby. And Kyland had known that and had used it.

She nodded. "He's real nice to him, like an uncle. Since he was a baby, he's bought him shoes, diapers, you know— he's helped me out. Especially when my brothers still weren't talking to me. That's just how Kyland is."

Before I could respond, she hopped up. "Listen, I gotta get going. Joey's with my friend and she has to leave for work soon."

I stood up too. "Thank you again, Shelly. Truly. You didn't have to do this and I just… Thanks."

"Sure thing. Good luck, Tenleigh." She walked out of the library, closing the door behind her. I leaned back against the bookshelf again and released a loud whoosh of air.

"Thanks," I said to the empty room. "I need it."

CHAPTER TWENTY-FOUR
Tenleigh

I went back to the trailer later that evening exhausted and dusty. I still hadn't wrapped my mind around what Shelly had told me. Initially, I had been unable to help the low current of joy and relief that had flowed through my body. But now...now I was angry and hurt again. If he hadn't really gotten Shelly pregnant, if he hadn't even slept with her, why would he hurt me like that? It had taken me years to get over what he'd done to me—truth be told, I still wasn't completely over it. And *why*? Just so I'd take the scholarship and leave? Just because I'd suggested I'd give it all up for him? Was that why he'd done that to me?

I got in the small, cracking, plastic shower and attempted to cleanse the day away. Then I put on a nightshirt and settled myself on the couch. I didn't think I'd be able to sleep, but I must have been even more tired than I thought because I was asleep in minutes.

The next thing I knew, I heard yelling outside my trailer. I bolted up, trying to orient myself. Outside the window, something glowed brightly and I smelled smoke. *Oh God! Fire!* I jumped off the couch, flung the door to the trailer open, and looked around wildly. There was a fire blazing in the front part of the trailer across the road, where Ginny Neil lived with her two kids. I ran out the door to join the other people standing in the road in front of the trailer.

"Did someone call the fire department?" I yelled. "Is everyone out?"

"Said they were on their way!" someone answered. Holy shit, this was the worst nightmare for folks like us who lived up in the mountains. The roads were narrow and steep and the nearest fire department was eight miles away. A shack or a small trailer could burn down in a fourth of the time it'd take for them to get here.

"MaryJane! Where's MaryJane?" I heard a woman shriek.

MaryJane? My mind scrambled to place MaryJane, but I couldn't.

I saw Buster standing among the others and ran over to him. "Buster, who's MaryJane?" I called over the ruckus.

"Little two-year-old girl belongs to Ginny Neil and Billy Wilkes," he answered, pointing over to them. "She's out, right?"

I looked around wildly, my eyes landing on Kyland as he ran up to the group, breathing hard. "Is everyone out safe?" he asked over the voices of the crowd, as shouts for MaryJane started to fill the air.

"Kyland, there might be a two-year-old girl in there," I yelled, racing over to him.

Billy Wilkes started back toward the fire, but he was on crutches, Lord knew why. Kyland ran behind him. They conversed briefly as they moved toward the smoky trailer, flames licking out the front.

My heart raced and I brought my hands up to cover my mouth as Kyland flung the door open and smoke poured out. He and Billy both leaned back and Kyland took off his sweatshirt and put it over his mouth while Billy pulled his T-shirt up over his face. Kyland disappeared inside, Billy standing vigil by the door. I could see him shouting inside, but I couldn't hear what he was saying over the loud roar of the flames and the peoples' voices next to me.

Impossibly, my heart started pounding even harder. I moved back with my distressed neighbors as the smoke in the air became thicker. Time seemed to stand still as I imagined what was going on in that trailer. The flames seemed only to be in the front, where the kitchen was, but the smoke was so thick in the rest of it. Could anyone survive in that? And for how long? *Ky*.

I gripped my fists tightly down by my sides, helpless to do anything other than pray.

Suddenly, a figure came bursting through the smoke, holding something covered in a blanket. I gasped and moved forward as Kyland emerged. Billy Wilkes hurried beside him as fast as he could move on crutches, and when they were a safe distance away, Kyland handed the blanketed item over to Billy and bent over, heaving in big gulps of air and coughing. The blanket in Billy's arms fell back to expose a small blond head.

Billy laid his daughter down on the grass and went down on his knees beside her as we all rushed forward.

"Is she breathing?" her mother sobbed, kneeling down on the grass beside her.

"Someone go get some water!" I yelled, and Buster answered, "Be right back!"

"She has a heartbeat," someone else said. "I think she's breathing."

The next few minutes were a frenzy of her parents crying, Buster returning with water and washing her face of the soot, and people yelling.

Finally, finally, we heard sirens coming up the mountain. A few minutes later when the emergency vehicles got there, the paramedics loaded MaryJane into an ambulance. She was breathing and crying, which had to be a good sign. Apparently, from what I could gather of the conversations, she'd been sleeping in the back of the trailer and each parent thought the other had gotten her. In the fear and mayhem of Billy trying to put the fire out in the kitchen and both of them getting the other two children up and out, little MaryJane had been left behind. I hadn't even known Ginny was living with Billy Wilkes or that they had a little girl between them. Ginny's husband had been one of the men who died at the mine eight years before. I was glad to know she'd found some happiness. *And now this.* Suddenly, I felt badly for not getting more updates on what was happening on the mountain from Marlo while I'd been away. But it had been less painful not to talk about home at all.

Firemen were able to put the fire out with a large extinguisher. It was mostly contained to the front of the trailer, but with the smoke damage, the trailer was ruined. Every possession that family had was gone—and I knew better than anyone that they hadn't had much to start with. Now they had nothing. Despair filled me, for them, for all of us.

I stuck around while everyone discussed what they had to offer the family when they came back from the hospital. Cora Levin was going to take the two older children in and Cheryl Skaggs had room for the parents and little MaryJane.

Standing there listening to everyone band together made my heart fill with pride. These people, as destitute as they were, had always attempted to help their own if they knew they needed assistance of some kind. They were good people—good people who barely had a pot to piss in. And yet they were offering up anything they had to give.

"I have a little money in the bank," I said. "I'll go into town in the morning and buy the kids some clothes."

There was a bevy of nods. "Thanks, Tenleigh."

I looked over at Kyland and he was focused on me, only me. I couldn't think about him right now. I couldn't think about the lie he'd told me anymore. I didn't have the strength.

I turned around and walked back to my trailer. When I was a few hundred yards away, the emotion came full force and I wanted to fall to my knees. I stumbled. The overwhelming sadness came for all the pain and hardship these people had to endure, some their entire lives. It came for the family who had just lost every single possession they owned—the ones who would struggle to replace even a few of those items. It came for the way it hurt to be back here… and the way it felt so right at the same time. I was weary, so very weary. And yet a release felt just out of reach. I'd held it back for so long, I didn't know how to access it now.

I sat down on my front steps and put my head in my hands. No one could see me from here.

"Hey."

My head snapped up and there was Kyland standing several feet in front of me with his hands stuffed in his pockets.

"Hey," I said quietly. I was sure I looked like a complete and utter mess. But Kyland looked pretty bad too—soot on his face, his shirt torn and dirty. He looked kinda like a man who had just run into a burning trailer to save a little girl.

I scooted over on the step and tilted my head toward the space I'd just made. He looked briefly surprised by my gesture but then moved immediately toward me and sat down, our bodies close. I could feel his warmth. I remembered his warmth so well, the way it'd felt at my back in the middle of the night, the way it'd surrounded me.

I turned toward him and leaned back against the rickety handrail. "That was brave, what you did."

"Nah. Those people, they would have done it for me too."

"Yes," I said. "They would have."

He nodded, not taking his eyes from me. "All those years ago, sometimes, you know, a basket of rhubarb or a couple tins of beans or something would show up on my front porch. I still don't know exactly who it was, but…I think, I think they probably knew I was lying about my mama still living with me. I think they were doing for me what they could. It kept me alive some months."

I was silent for a second, absorbing his words. "The rhubarb, that was Buster," I said quietly.

He nodded, sawing his teeth along his bottom lip in a way that left it plumped and reddened when he finally let it go. I blinked, tearing my eyes away, back up to his.

Who are you now, Kyland? I don't know you anymore and why does that hurt me so much?

"Is that why you gave them the idea of the lavender?" I asked.

His eyes widened. "Who told you about that?"

"Buster."

He rubbed the back of his neck. "I, yeah. I read about it and thought maybe I could give back. You know, to those who were interested in the idea. Really, it's nothing."

"Sounds like it's working out pretty well for several families."

Despite the nonchalant way he'd spoken of his idea, a glint of pride came into his eyes. "It is."

241

"Ky?"

"Yeah?"

"It's something. It's a whole lot of something."

He let out an exhale. We were quiet for a second before Kyland finally met my eyes again and said very softly, "I'm so sorry, Tenleigh."

I stilled. "For what?"

He ran his hand through his hair and looked up at the sky. "For treating you the way I did the other day and then at Al's." He shook his head. "You didn't deserve it. I just... God, Tenleigh, when you got out of here, I thought...I thought you'd finally escaped this place. To see you come back...and to see that you... Well, it made me crazy. It made me"—he let out a laugh that sounded anything but amused—"crazy." He paused. "Crazy and mean. I'm sorry."

I studied him for a minute. "I know you wanted to get out of here, Kyland. I know better than anyone. I guess I can understand you being upset to see me do something you wouldn't have done if you had won that scholarship. But you lost the right to pass judgment on my choices." *Are you going to tell me the truth now? Tell me why you lied to me? Explain to me why you broke my heart? Why you were able to send me away?*

"I know. God, Tenleigh, I know." He released a large, shaky breath.

I looked up to the star-studded sky. "I'm sorry too," I said. "About the other night. I acted immature. I had taken a couple shots and...I've always been an angry drinker." I laughed softly but then went serious, fidgeting with the hem of my shirt. "I shouldn't have made a scene. My mama used to do that when she was sick, and the last thing I'd want to do is make people talk about her. Those Falyn women..."

"Oh, shit, Tenleigh." His voice hitched. "No. No one

said that. It was just a run-of-the-mill fight. I was wrong. When I saw you there, working at Al's again after... I lost it."

I nodded sadly, running my hands along my thighs.

"Anyway," he said, "no one's talking about us. Everyone's talking about Gable Clancy and his—"

"Mail-order bride," I said along with him. "Yeah, I was in the back cleaning up when all that happened, but I heard about it."

His lip quirked up in a small smile and my eyes lingered on his mouth before I looked away.

A small silence ensued and Kyland filled it. "Of course, Gable isn't sure if she was really trying to kill him or if the car got out of her control on account of her prosthetic leg."

A laugh bubbled up my throat. "Wait, what?"

"Yeah, I work with him. I know more about mail-order brides with prosthetic legs than I ever wanted to know."

I looked over at his amused expression and intended to smile back, but instead, I felt a wave of nostalgia wash over me. A tear escaped my eye and I swiped at it, looking down at my finger in surprise. I hadn't shed a tear in so long.

Kyland's expression was suddenly raw and pained. I shook my head as if I could deny the emotion that was practically drowning me in that moment: *grief*. Grief for the loss of him, although he was sitting right next to me. All these years, I had been so focused on the anger, in just surviving, moving forward, that I hadn't allowed myself to remember the sweetness. But, oh God, how I'd missed him. Despite my heartbreak, despite my anger, I'd missed him so desperately. Besides Marlo, he had been my everything.

He scooted closer, keeping eye contact, asking silently if I was okay with him moving toward me. I was. And I shouldn't be. This was hardly going to bring me *peace*. I should tell him

243

to move away. I should tell him I didn't even want to breathe the same air as him. But I didn't. I looked him in the eye and I didn't move away. Very, very slowly, he put his arms around me as if I were a skittish animal who might run at any moment. He pulled me into his broad chest and I sucked back a sob and clutched at his smoky T-shirt. He held me as I finally cried the tears I'd held at bay for so very, very long, and I let him.

We sat there for what seemed like forever, his strong arms around me, his heart beating steadily under my ear. Finally, my tears dried and I tilted my head up and our eyes met.

"Tenleigh," he whispered, his voice as smoky as the rest of him, filled with need.

There were so many things we needed to say to each other, so many things I wanted him to explain to me. So many emotions were swirling in the air around us, so many unanswered questions. But in that moment, it seemed like all that could wait. And so when his lips touched mine, I let out a sound of encouragement and pressed myself into him. Maybe it was foolish. Maybe...*probably*. His tongue entered my mouth tentatively and he let out a groan that sounded half-tortured and half-blissful. I met his tongue with my own and reached up around his neck to weave my fingers into his short hair. He put his hands gently on either side of my face and tilted my head. The kiss went deeper. Just like the fire we had watched earlier, my whole body felt alight with flames, my flesh burning with need. But fire destroyed. Fire left you devastated and singed beyond recognition. Fire was anything but peaceful.

I pulled away, Kyland letting out a small sound of loss. I stared at him, his lips red and wet. He was gazing at me like a starving man looking at a buffet of delicacies. I tried desperately to control my ragged breathing. I wanted him. Hadn't

I always wanted him? Why did everything about us seem so simple and yet so complicated at the same time?

"Kyland, I…" I said softly.

"I know," he answered. And I believed that he did even if I didn't entirely.

"You should go home and shower. And I should…I have a big day tomorrow."

He was silent for a second and then he nodded. "What you're doing with the school, it's really…well, it's amazing."

"You know what I'm doing?"

"Yeah. I asked about it in town."

"Oh."

"I better get going, let you go to sleep."

"Okay."

He paused. "Okay." He stood up. "Do you need anything before I go?"

I shook my head, remembering the time he'd come here unable to ask me to go back to his house to sleep in his bed. Was Kyland still lonely? Something told me he was. But I couldn't offer him anything now. I felt both too empty and too filled with a lingering ache. I had once wanted to give him everything, lay my life and my heart at his feet, but right now, after his lies had crushed me, I just couldn't.

"Okay, then, good night."

"Good night." He walked away from me and I watched him retreat. After a minute I went back inside. I tossed and turned for the rest of the night. Sleep was elusive, visions of Kyland and me as we once had been skating through my mind, snippets of conversations filling my head, the memory of the feel of his rough hand moving across my skin, invading my senses. I finally fell into fitful dreams, just as the first light of dawn appeared in the trailer windows.

CHAPTER TWENTY-FIVE
Kyland

The sun streamed through my window way too early. I hadn't been able to fall back to sleep after I'd gotten home, showered, and gone to bed—despite the fact that I was exhausted. The truth was I had barely slept a wink since Tenleigh had returned to town.

Tenleigh.

My heart thudded in my chest. I needed to tell her the truth. I'd been about to last night, but the timing had just seemed wrong. How were we going to be able to talk about anything sitting in front of her trailer in the dark? Or maybe I'd just been a coward. But I hoped, I *had* to hope, that if I apologized, if she knew the truth, she'd find it in herself to forgive me.

Then again, how did you apologize for a lie when the lie itself was almost as cruel as if it had been the truth? I'd gutted her. On purpose. I brought my hand up to my head and raked my fingers through my hair.

Christ.

And there was the small matter of *him*—Jamie Kearney.

Jealousy flashed through my body, propelling me up and out of bed. I walked into the kitchen and leaned against the counter. All the time she was away, I'd tortured myself with the knowledge that she was probably dating other men, maybe even falling in love with someone else. It made me feel insane with jealousy. I knew she had loved me, but I'd hurt her so deeply. Her love for me wouldn't be enough to stop her from moving on. And it shouldn't have been—I had set her free. It was the choice I'd made—I had to live with it. And so I had, for almost four long years. I just had never expected her to return with Jamie Fucking Kearney of all people.

I knew he'd rescued her that day on the road between here and Al's and I was grateful to him for that. But his father was a disgusting pig, and I had no idea what kind of character Jamie had. He could be a nice guy for all I knew. Still, when I'd seen him standing in the lot where Tenleigh's school would be, holding her in his arms, the only thing racing through my mind was all the remote places up in the mountains where a buried body would never ever be found.

Stop overreacting. Maybe they're just friends. Yeah, maybe. She'd let me kiss her after all. But I still couldn't stop picturing them together and it was making me ill.

I turned on the stove and started to boil water so I could make some coffee. As I waited for the water to heat, my mind returned to the night before.

I had fucked up so badly since she'd come home. I hadn't been ready to face her, never in a million years imagined it'd be under these circumstances…*here*. I'd reacted like a crazy person—or like a complete asshole. She had no way to know that she'd upheaved all my plans. I needed to make this right.

When Tenleigh had let me hold her, comfort her, it'd felt so damn good. If she never forgave me, how would I handle it? The last four years had gone by in dismal misery. But seeing her looking the way she did, classy and sure of herself, it filled me with pride. She'd done exactly what I knew she could do. That same familiar grief and loneliness welled in my chest when I thought about who she used to be, who *I* used to be. Because as much as I was happy about the ways she'd changed and as much as I accepted who I was now, back then, she'd been mine. Back then, she'd looked at me with trust and love in her eyes. Back then, she'd wanted me, despite all the ways I was lacking. Back then, she'd been willing to fight tooth and nail for me. Back then...

Stop it, Kyland. Now is now, and you have to deal with that.

This was going to be a long day. I had to be at the mine at ten. Even now, I had to work to prepare myself mentally to go underground. It'd gotten better over the years—tolerable—but it would never be easy for me. That ball of dread would always start forming as I descended into the depths of the earth. The difference was, I had more coping mechanisms now and I practiced every one of them.

I planned to leave a little early because I wanted to stop by the library one last time before they tore it down. I figured the demolition would happen any day now.

That damn library...

After Tenleigh had left, I had gone and sat in it day after day just to feel close to her. I had sat at the small table in the back and I'd suffered. And it was no less than I deserved.

———

I stepped into the small building, empty now save for the shelves that were still bolted to the wall. I stood there simply looking for several quiet minutes. Was this even wise, or was I just torturing myself? I inhaled the air, closing my eyes briefly as all the memories, both happy and sad, went through my mind. I heard a small click behind me and whirled around. Tenleigh was standing there, a surprised expression on her face.

"Hi," she breathed, coming in and shutting the door behind her.

"Hi," I said, my heart suddenly galloping. She was wearing a pair of jeans and an SDSU T-shirt. Her hair was in a ponytail, a few pieces falling loose. She was the most beautiful woman in the world. To me, she always had been. She always would be.

As I stood looking at her, I realized that something had shifted between us since last night. She still looked wary, but the look in her eyes was softer too, and it gave me hope. Despite everything between us. Despite Jamie Kearney.

"I'm sorry," I said, taking a step toward her. "If I shouldn't be here, I'll—"

"No, it's fine. The crew isn't coming for an hour or so. I just." She bit her lip, glancing away from me for a quick moment. "I just wanted to spend a little time here before they tear it down."

Oh. "I kind of had the same idea."

Our eyes held for several beats, the air thick with that energy Tenleigh and I always seemed to create whenever we were in the same room. She walked toward me.

"You got contacts," I said softly.

She looked surprised. "I did. How'd you know?"

"You used to squint. It's how I knew when you were looking at me from across a room."

She laughed softly. "Hmm, I didn't know anyone ever noticed that."

When it came to you, I noticed everything. I fell halfway in love with you before we ever spoke a word.

249

"And your voice, I mean, your accent—it's back."

"My sister said the same thing. It didn't take long for my body to remember I'm a Kentucky girl."

My Kentucky girl.

She took a deep breath and looked away, running her hand along the bookshelf. "This place saved me from a lot of loneliness." Her expression was wistful.

"Same here. After you left, I...came here a lot."

She tilted her head. "Really?"

"Yeah."

"Why?"

"Because I missed you so much, I thought I'd die," I admitted.

Her eyes widened and she swallowed. "You did?"

"Yeah, I did." I paused. "Yeah I did," I repeated, allowing the memory of that anguish to assault me for a brief second.

She bit her lip, her brow creased in a small frown as she watched her finger trail along the shelf.

"Joey isn't mine, Tenleigh. I never even thought he was," I blurted out.

Her finger stilled. "I know."

I froze for a second and then I let out a long breath. "Shelly?"

"Yeah. She came by yesterday."

I brought my arms up and laced my hands behind my head. I couldn't say I was surprised. She'd demanded I tell Tenleigh. And I was going to... "I wanted to be the one to tell you myself. I just...I was trying to come up with the right time."

"When is there a right time to tell someone you shattered their heart with a cruel lie?" she asked.

"You wouldn't leave, Tenleigh. You were going to give up that scholarship and stay. I couldn't let you do that. I *couldn't.*"

"There were other ways."

"Maybe. I couldn't think of any at the time. I couldn't think of any way to guarantee you'd leave and never look back."

She huffed out a breath. "Well, you accomplished that, that's for sure." She looked away momentarily. "Why couldn't you have come with me? Did you even want to? I mean, at the time…did you want me at all?" She looked like she was close to crying.

I moved closer to her. "I just couldn't. I wanted to, God I wanted to, but I couldn't."

"Why?" Her voice was breathy and filled with sadness.

I moved closer to her, right into her space, just as I had done the very first time I'd kissed her, the very first time I'd tasted her mouth. "Because I wanted more for you," I said, hoping she wouldn't ask me any further questions. I wouldn't give her more than that. The rest was mine. And it only ever would be.

Her shoulders drooped, but she didn't look away. For several beats, there was only silence between us.

I glanced up at the shelf that used to house all the books we'd read together, leaving small love notes in them for each other to find. That's what they'd been, in my mind at least. "Right here is where I fell in love with you." I paused and she blinked in surprise. "I tried to figure it out after you left. Where was it that I lost my heart? As if the moment…the *place* would matter somehow, would make it easier for me to get hold of, to understand. And I did figure it out—it was here. Right here." Love mixed with pain rose in my throat and my voice lowered to a raspy whisper. "I fell so damn hard, Tenleigh. Standing right at this bookshelf. I gave you my heart and you weren't even in the room." I threaded my fingers into the hair at the base of her skull. She closed her eyes for a second, letting out a breathy sigh. "I've messed up so badly, hurt you so much, but...I never did take my heart back. And, God." I shook my head slowly, moving even closer, pressing my body to hers. She blinked up at me, her lips parting. "Someday I hope you might want it again."

Her eyes moved over my face, large and full of some emotion I couldn't name.

"Tell me what you're thinking, please," I begged her.

Her lips parted, but no words came out. She cleared her throat, but when she spoke, her voice still came out in a whisper. "I was thinking the same thing as the first time we stood here just like this. I was thinking, 'God, I hope this boy kisses me right now.'"

My heart skipped a beat and my stomach tightened, my body blazing to life with the immeasurable heat and passion I felt for her. I leaned in and took her mouth, parting her lips with my tongue. When I slid inside the warm wetness of her mouth, a primal groan came up my throat and I pressed her back harder into the bookshelf. She tasted like coffee and chocolate and Tenleigh. A small, breathy moan came up her throat and it enflamed me, my erection throbbing.

I took my mouth from hers and trailed my lips down her throat as she leaned her head back. I licked the fluttering pulse at the base of her neck and then just rested my lips there.

"'You pierce my soul. I am half agony, half hope. Tell me not that I am too late, that such precious feelings are gone forever...I have loved none but you,'" I whispered against her skin, quoting the words I knew she'd remember.

Her body stilled, but her pulse quickened and I breathed in her scent.

Christ.

I took a second to try to reel myself in. Except for the kiss the night before, it'd been almost four years since I'd touched a woman, since I'd touched Tenleigh. My body was bound to react this way each time I was near her. I murmured her name against her skin.

She threaded her fingers through my hair and pulled my head back until she was looking into my eyes again. "What are we doing, Ky? What am *I* doing?" she asked almost as if to herself.

"I don't know. I hope…I hope we're working toward something? There's so much… I'll take whatever you have to give me, Tenleigh. Anything."

Her eyes moved over my face. "I…I just, I don't know. I don't know if I can."

I rested my forehead against hers and we just breathed for a minute. "Is it because of Jamie?" I had to know. I had to know if he was even part of the reason she was unsure about giving us another shot.

"What *about* Jamie?"

I blew out a breath. "I saw you two together. I thought you might be seeing him."

Her brow furrowed for a second and then she laughed. "No. Jamie's gay, Ky."

"He is? Oh." Well, okay then. This was promising news. "So I guess you're not seeing him."

"Um, no. Last time I checked, I was a woman."

I chuckled softly. "Yes, you're definitely a woman."

Her smile was filled with genuine amusement. My heart flipped. I loved that smile. I'd missed that smile. I'd *yearned* for that smile.

"And you're so beautiful," I whispered.

"Ky," she whispered, and I heard the longing in her voice.

If she'd let me go, it hadn't been completely. My heart rejoiced as she leaned forward and I met her halfway. This time, our kisses went wild, and the noise in my head became static.

Tenleigh leaned back against the shelf behind her and brought one leg up and around my hip, fitting my erection between her legs. I let out a deep groan, pressing myself into her softness. God, she felt so good. Blood was pounding furiously through my veins.

Suddenly, we were all hands and gasping breaths and grinding bodies, frenzied, needy, out of control.

I palmed her breast over her shirt and used my thumb to circle her nipple and she cried out, reaching down and unzipping my jeans. When she wrapped her hand around my bare shaft, I sucked in a breath and pressed into her hand. "Tenleigh, fuck, oh God," I groaned out.

Her eyes were wide, filled with lust, her lips parted. I paused to suck in a quick breath at the beauty of her face in that moment.

She kicked off her shoes and unzipped her jeans, urgently pushing them and her underwear down her hips so she could step out of them quickly. She wrapped her arms around me, bringing her leg up again. We kissed deeply, desperately. My mouth moved up her neck, her jaw, sucking and nipping at her lips right before I lined myself up and surged inside her. Our mouths broke apart, our eyes meeting as she gasped loudly. I clenched mine closed at the tight, blissful grip of her surrounding me.

I was inside Tenleigh. Happiness expanded in my chest as I started moving. She moaned again and leaned her head back against the shelves behind her and sighed, "Yes, yes, yes." I tried to go slow. It'd been so long. I reached between her legs and stroked her, my mouth against her throat as she moaned.

"Jesus, Ten, you feel so good." I couldn't help the ragged

groan that followed my words as I felt the orgasm swirling in my abdomen. I moved my fingers on her faster. She was so wet. I lifted my head and gazed into her eyes as her moans became louder.

"Kyland, I…I…" she choked out.

"I know, Ten, I know." And then she was clenching all around me as her head fell back again and she cried out.

"I'm coming, Tenleigh," I gasped as I jerked into her one final time. My orgasm hit me with so much force, I fell forward on her, unintelligible words flowing out of my mouth as the pleasure moved in waves to my stomach, my legs, all the way down to my toes.

We both stayed like that for several minutes, our breaths raspy as reality flowed back in. I felt like I was home— complete. And yet, at the same time, I was suddenly so unsure. I stepped back and Tenleigh pulled her jeans up and slipped her shoes on while I tucked myself back inside my zipper. Her cheeks were flushed and when she brought her head up, she looked slightly shell-shocked. I could relate. I leaned in and kissed her, smoothing the pieces of hair away from her face that had fallen out of her ponytail.

"I guess…I guess we both needed that release," she said quietly, glancing to the side.

I shook my head. "That's not what that was for me. It was more than that. Tell me that was more for you too."

Her eyes met mine again and she let out a breath. She nodded. "It was more than that for me," she said quietly.

Hope surged in my chest even though she looked conflicted by her own statement.

We both startled when we heard a car pull up outside. "Shit. That's probably Jamie," she said, straightening her clothes. "He was going to stop by before work."

I nodded, feeling relief in the fact that I knew Jamie was

only a friend. "I better go anyway. I have to be at work. But maybe I can stop by tomorrow?" I asked hopefully. "You tell me, Tenleigh. Just tell me what to do and I'll do it."

"Why are you working at the mine?" she blurted out.

Damn. "Why? Because I need a job and those are the only ones available." *Liar.*

"I don't understand. You were going to leave. You were never going to look back. If Joey really isn't yours, if you lied about that to make me leave, then why stay?"

I glanced at the door. I could barely remember my name right then and I needed to form cognitive answers. "It was just for the best. I realized Dennville is my home. I decided to stay. That's all." She looked unconvinced but remained quiet. "I better go. I'll be late," I said.

"Okay. I'll see you later then."

"Yeah," I said, feeling hopeful for the first time in nearly four years.

"Have a good day... at the mine."

"You have a good day too, Tenleigh." I didn't kiss her again. She looked so conflicted. But I wasn't quite ready to take my eyes off her either. I didn't want to leave. Like before, I never wanted to leave. I started backing out. When I got to the door, I pushed it open with my back, my smile increasing. She shook her head, but smiled back as the door shut between us. Outside, Jamie was sitting in his car talking on his cell phone. I gave him a brief wave as I got in my truck and pulled away.

As I drove, I felt the euphoria expand in my chest of having just touched Tenleigh, of having been inside her. God, I could still smell her sweet, musky scent on my fingers. I hoped I'd said enough to convince her that I still loved her, that I'd never stopped. Things were still up in the air, but I finally had *hope*—something I hadn't had an ounce of for four years.

CHAPTER TWENTY-SIX
Tenleigh

I stood staring at the closed door after Kyland left. I wasn't sure what to think, what to *feel*. What was I doing? What were *we* doing? Was I really even entertaining the possibility of starting something with Kyland again? Was I really willing to put myself in a position to start loving him again? Had I ever really stopped?

Had I really just stripped my pants off and had intense sex with him up against the library wall?

I groaned and brought one hand to my forehead. I didn't know what to do.

The door to the library opened and Jamie walked in. "Hey, you okay? You look sick."

"I think I am. Unfortunately, there's no medication for my ailment."

"I hear heroin shuts out the pain."

"Simmer down, pillbilly. I'm not on the road to illegal self-medicating just yet. However, the operative word is *yet*."

"Well, you let me know. I hang on the corner of Gutter and Skinsores and I could hook you up."

"Oh, I bet."

He came over to where I was standing and leaned against the shelf. "Kyland? I saw him leaving."

"Yeah," I breathed, staring straight ahead. After a minute I turned to him. "I just can't go through what I went through after he broke my heart," I said. "And I don't know if I trust him not to pull away from me again. Things are." I frowned, searching for the right explanation. "I don't even know exactly. I feel like he's not telling me something." There had been a shadow over his expression, a shortness to his answers when I'd questioned him about the mine... "And if that's the case, should I really resume any kind of relationship with him again?" *You sorta just did, Ten. Yeah, but perhaps that needed to be a one-time thing. A brief physical encounter. Nothing more.*

"If you don't try, you'll never know," Jamie said.

"Maybe that's for the best."

"Maybe." He shrugged. "You're the only one who can make that call."

"I was kinda hoping you'd just tell me what to do."

Jamie chuckled. "I'm the last one you should ask for advice. Unless it involves how to cope with parents who believe you were born with an embarrassing, inoperable 'condition.' Then I'm a font of wisdom."

My heart hurt for him. I put my hand on his shoulder. "Is your mama still giving you the silent treatment?"

"Yeah." He looked crushed. "I expected it from my dad. We never saw eye to eye on anything—never had much of a relationship. It's not like I *ever* had his approval. I certainly didn't expect him to embrace this. But my mama, I thought she'd at least ignore it. And I... I hoped..." His words died.

"I know, Jamie. I'm sorry."

"My dad is such a fucking asshole, in so many ways, you

only have some idea." His lips formed a thin line. "The way he treated your mama, that's how he treats his workers, his family, everyone—a means to an end."

"I never thought about that before I knew you," I said. "I guess I kind of always thought he treated us like trash because that's what he thought of us, that we were in some separate category for him."

"No. I was worried about how he acted when he came to give you that scholarship. I was worried about how you must have felt to have him in your home...again." His eyes darted to me and away, finally resting on the wall in front of him. *He* felt the shame his father never had. *Jamie.*

"It's okay. He didn't come to me personally. The whole school was there."

He looked confused for a second. "Oh. He usually went in person to the recipient's home and gave it to him or her before making the announcement in school." He looked thoughtful for a second. "Maybe he actually does have a tiny smidge of decorum, deciding not to come to your trailer in person."

"Huh. Maybe. Anyway, that's all ancient history." I tilted my head. "Can I ask you a question?"

"Yeah, of course."

I chewed on my bottom lip for a second. "Have you seen Kyland at the mine? I mean, does he seem okay, like he's okay going belowground? He was so evasive about it."

"I don't spend too much time with the underground miners to be honest. But I've heard word around the company that he's pretty impressive. Apparently, he's been successful in putting some new safety measures in place, not that he'd ever get the credit. But the guys talk. He's well liked among the other miners."

"Have you been down there before?"

"God no." He shivered. "I couldn't do it."

I nodded, still frowning. *How do you do it, Kyland? How do you go down there into your own personal hell day after day after day?*

I do, every day. For you.

For me...

My thoughts were interrupted by the sound of trucks arriving outside.

"The crew is here," Jamie said, standing up. "I'm off. Give me a call later or come by and see me."

"Corner of Gutter and Skinsores?"

"Can't miss it." He winked.

I laughed. "Thanks for stopping by."

After Jamie left, I took another minute to look around the small space, closing my eyes and breathing in the dusty smell for the final time. When I was ready, I walked outside, closing that door behind me.

———

I sat down at the bar next to Marlo and she looked forlornly over at me. "Whoa. What's up with you?"

"Sam, that's what's up with me."

"What'd he do?"

"Asked me to marry him—again."

"Wow, what a bastard."

"What'll it be, girlie?" Al asked, shouting over to me from the end of the mostly empty bar.

"Diet Coke with lime," I said loudly. Marlo had called me an hour before and asked me to meet her at Al's to "drown her sorrows" after her day shift. I hadn't known exactly what that meant at the time, but now I did.

"So Sam, the evil bastard, has asked you to commit to

letting him shower you with love for a lifetime. How quickly do you think we can gather a posse with pitchforks to hunt him down? No mercy should be spared."

She heaved out a breath and sat down next to me. "Har har. Make fun. But I told him I was never going to marry him. I *told* him, and he won't give it up. He's making my life a living hell."

Go to hell. I do. Every day. For you.

I turned toward her on the stool. "You're not in love with him, Mar?"

She sat there just looking straight ahead. "I mean, I guess I love him. A little."

"Wow. The romance is overwhelming." I rolled my eyes. "Don't bowl me over with too much of that love talk, Shakespeare."

Marlo rolled her eyes. "Seriously, Tenleigh, listen. I just don't want to get let down. I finally feel comfortable, safe, and marriage *changes* things. I'm just not sure I can trust him. I don't want to love him and then have him walk away," she said, looking at me sadly. "And once they know you love them, that's when they all walk away. You know I'm right," she finished quietly.

I took a sip of the Coke Al put in front of me. "Marlo, I think…" I bit my lip picturing Sam's face, the way he gazed at Marlo as if she hung the moon. "What more does Sam have to do? I mean, he's been trying for more than *four* years, and he's never given up. Frankly, you're lucky he hasn't. You must be a real pain in the ass to be in a relationship with."

"We're not in a relationship," she muttered.

"Give it *up*, Marlo. You and Sam are in a relationship. You can't act one way and say something else. It isn't honest, and it isn't fair. Frankly, *you're* the jerk in this relationship."

She huffed. "Fine, you're right. I'm acting like a wishy-washy ass. It's just…you don't remember because you were just a baby, but I remember when Dad left. I loved him, Tenleigh. He was the first man I *ever* loved, and he just walked out of here and never even said goodbye to me. All these years, he never checked on us once. Not once. That's what I know of *love*." She fiddled with a napkin on the bar. "And even after that, I still held out hope there would be someone who would love me the right way. And well, we all know how that worked out."

"Yeah! You ended up with a good, decent guy who begs you to marry him. It *did* work out. If you'd let it!" I sighed. "I don't think you can judge every man by one or two who let you down. And Dad, well, that wasn't your fault. But that Ronald, maybe there were a few clues there that he was mostly untrustworthy or maybe you just didn't take long enough to find out. And listen, you're right. I *get* it. You know I do. Kyland…for so long I just couldn't under-stand what he'd done. Even now, the lying part still hurts. Everything I knew of him told me he spent his life doing things for other people in this selfless way. And then…" I shook my head. "But *Sam*, Sam who moved to Appalachia to fix people's teeth out of the *goodness* of his heart. What has Sam ever done except treat you like gold and pay for our mama's hospital care? Good grief, what more can the guy do to prove to you that you can trust him, that he's a good guy, that he loves you?"

She studied her fingernails. "Well, actually, that's another thing we were fighting about." She looked up at me. "Apparently, he isn't paying for mama's care. The truth is, he doesn't have that kind of money. He used all his savings to move here and open his practice, and well, you know what he gets paid. He gets paid in cornbread and trapped muskrat half the time."

"What?" I breathed. "Then who…who's paying for it?" It felt like the barstool beneath me was about to tip over. What in the world?

"He wouldn't say. He just said he had worked it out with someone who wanted to remain anonymous. He lied. So see, he *is* capable of lying—even if it's for something that was mostly for us. What else is he capable of lying about? And then right on the heels of that confession, he has the gall to ask me to marry him?"

One part of her sentence stuck out in my head. *An anonymous donor.* An anonymous donor? Who…Why? An idea began forming in my mind, taking shape. Clarifying. *Oh my God.* It couldn't be. My heart dropped into my feet. Yes it could.

"I have to go," I said, standing up suddenly. "Oh my God, Mar. I have to go."

"Wait. What? Where are you going? I wasn't done drowning my sorrows! Sam's not picking me up for an hour. Sam, remember? Lying, nagging Sam who I'm definitely not in a relationship with and shouldn't marry?"

"Sam can help you wallow," I said shakily, taking a couple dollars out of my wallet and throwing it on the bar. I knew if she was letting Sam pick her up, she couldn't really be all that mad at him. She'd just needed reassurance. And a swift kick in the ass.

"Your money's no good here," Al said, swiping up my money and putting it in his tip jar anyway.

I turned toward Marlo, taking her shoulders in my hands and shaking her slightly.

"What are you doing?" she asked, her voice shaking along with her body.

"I'm shaking some sense into you," I said.

"Wait, you're the one with the motto—"

"Screw my motto. Screw *your* motto. Talk to him, Mar. Let him explain why he lied about Mama's care. Listen to him and stop being so damn hardheaded. He might hurt you. But he might not. He might not. I'm placing my bets on Sam. And I love you more than anyone in this world. I would only ever bet in your favor. Stop letting the past control you—look at what's right in front of you." I let go of her shoulders, squeezed her tightly, and kissed her on her cheek as she gaped at me. "Look at what's right in front of you." I ran out to my car, tore out of the parking lot, and pulled onto the highway. I forced myself to take several deep breaths. My hands clenched the wheel as I tried to get my thoughts straight.

Oh, Kyland.

Tears sprung to my eyes as what I knew was the truth slammed into me, making me feel weak and breathless. Oh my God. *Oh my God.*

Kyland, you stupid, prideful, beautiful, selfless man.

A small sob came up my throat, but I swallowed it down and again, forced myself to relax.

I was right. I knew I was right. It all suddenly clicked into place. All—

My car sputtered and lurched before it died at the base of the hill. I let out a frustrated cry, barely maneuvering it to the side of the road. I turned the key in the ignition, but the engine wouldn't turn over. I let my head fall to the wheel, banging it lightly several times. Well, there went my car luck. My heart was pounding in my chest as I jumped out and started running.

This was just like *that* day, the day I'd run up this very

hill, my heart beating triple time, my love for Kyland a living, breathing thing.

I looked at the rock I'd sat on to make that stupid, stupid list, letting out a small sob as I raced past it.

Kyland, Kyland, Kyland.

What did you do?

God, what did you do?

Go to hell.

I do. Every day. For you.

CHAPTER TWENTY-SEVEN
Kyland

A loud banging sounded from my front door. Geez, simmer down. I assumed it was one of the hill folk, but why they were pounding like that, I didn't know.

I put my paperwork aside and started for my bedroom to get a shirt. I had only put on jeans after my shower. But when the banging grew more insistent, I swore under my breath and turned toward the door. When I pulled it open, surprise caught in my chest. It was Tenleigh and she was standing there, obviously out of breath, her eyes filled with tears.

My heart dropped and I opened my mouth to ask what was wrong. But she held up her hand and took a big, shuddery breath. "You won that scholarship. I didn't win it, you did."

I froze, and my breath hitched. We simply stared at each other for what felt like a long time. Finally, I managed, "How'd you know?"

She sagged against the doorframe, her face contorting as if she was going to sob. "You just told me."

I stared at her, not knowing what to say. Denying it now seemed pointless.

Goddamn it. She was never *ever* supposed to know that. Ever.

I stuffed my hands in my pockets and stood looking at her as she gathered herself together. When she finally spoke, she said simply, "Why?"

I shrugged as if it was simple because when you got right down to it, maybe it was. "Because I loved you so desperately. Because I couldn't leave you here."

Four Years Earlier

"Kyland Barrett?"

"Yes," I said way too quickly. I rubbed my sweaty palms over my jean-clad thighs and stood up.

The secretary, a young woman with long blond hair, smiled at me as her eyes slid down my body. I was dressed terribly for this classy, impeccably designed office. I had been afraid to sit down on the light gray couch, worried I'd get some kind of smudge on it. It's not like I could do anything about that, though. The only clothes I had were old and worn and had been used not only to attend school in but to collect metal, trap badgers, collect wild grapes...

"Mr. Kearney will see you now," she said as I offered her a small, tight smile.

"Thank you."

She walked ahead of me down a long hallway, her hips swaying. Our footsteps were soundless on the plush gray carpeting. On the clean, white walls were old-fashioned black-and-white pictures of what must have been the very early days of the coal mines—men in overalls with coal-dust-blackened faces, standing unsmiling at the entrance, having obviously just emerged from the dark earth. I swallowed. Their faces reminded me of the way my father and my brother had looked when they'd returned home each night. And strangely, looking at the photos gave me strength. They'd done what they had to do, every day, out of love and responsibility for the people who waited at home for them to return. They'd sacrificed, and I would too. I pulled in a deep breath and straightened my shoulders. *You can do this.*

The secretary stopped at a door at the end of the hall and opened it, gesturing me inside. I nodded and walked past her into Edward Kearney's office. The door closed with a soft click behind me.

"Did you forget to ask me something about the scholarship last night?" Edward Kearney said before he used the golf club in his hand to hit the ball on the floor at his feet. I watched the golf ball travel down the green portion of carpet and clunk softly into the hole at the far end.

I cleared my throat. "I did, sir." He turned to me, leaning on his golf club. "I, uh, I'm sorry. It was a surprise and I wasn't prepared. I didn't know you'd come to my home to tell me about the scholarship, and I wasn't thinking clearly."

He furrowed his thick black brows. "Weren't thinking clearly about what?"

"About the fact that I can't take it. I want to transfer it to someone else."

He laughed, a sharp, surprised sound. "Why would you want to do that?"

"I have my own reasons for that, sir, but I figured if I won it, it's mine to give to someone else if I choose to."

When Edward Kearney had shown up at my house the

night before, I'd been shocked, almost rendered speechless. I had no idea he came to inform the recipient of his or her win in person. I hadn't been ready. But as soon as he'd left, as soon as that fancy black car had pulled away from my house, I'd gotten myself together and prepared the words I needed to say. And so here I was.

Edward Kearney chuckled and turned to walk back to his desk. He leaned against it, crossing his arms over his broad, barrel chest. He was silent, both of us staring at each other. His black hair, sprinkled liberally with gray, had a straight, severe part down the side. His suit was obviously expensive and tailor-made, his shoes polished to a high mirror shine. I straightened my spine and didn't look away. His eyes narrowed, but there was some kind of recognition in his expression as he took me in.

"You can't transfer the scholarship. You were admitted to Columbia University—and you accepted. The scholarship you won is being processed to pay that school."

I closed my eyes briefly. *Columbia University.* For a second, a fierce longing twisted my gut. But then I pictured Tenleigh with her black eye, the defeated expression in her eyes. I thought about Shelly and how her lip had trembled when she'd told me she was pregnant by some nameless trucker who wouldn't take no for an answer. This town was tough on men, but it was even tougher on the women, and that was the simple truth. There was no way I could take Tenleigh with me. I didn't have the money for a plane ticket, an apartment for her, hell, even for more than a few meals. And if I left for four years, earned a degree, what would happen to Tenleigh in that time? Would the defeat become part of her like it did to so many in these coal mine towns? Would the poverty slowly chip away at that bright, beautiful spirit? The spirit of the woman I loved with my whole heart? How could I leave her here when I couldn't protect her? I couldn't. It would kill me.

"Please, there must be something that can be done? Some paperwork that could just be transferred? No one knows I won yet. The person I want to transfer it to is on the list of finalists, Tenleigh Falyn."

He cocked his head to the side, rolling his bottom lip between his teeth. "I saw where you live. I saw the life you lead. I came from circumstances just like yours. That picture over there"—he pointed to a photo on the wall of a small, crumbling shack—"that's a picture of where I grew up. I had to claw and fight for every inch I received in life. I know it's the same for you. I'd never give up what I had to fight for…for anyone. You shouldn't either. Especially not some damn woman."

We're not the same, you and I. We're nothing alike.

"She's not just some woman, sir. She's more than that. To me, she's everything."

He laughed, but it sounded cold. "Clearly." He considered me for another minute before he continued. "Unlike you, I'm not a man who does something for nothing. That's why I'm standing behind this desk." He walked around the large mahogany piece of furniture and placed his fingertips on the inlaid leather top. "And you're standing on the other side of it begging me for my help in a pair of shoes that wore out two years ago. That's not how I got to be where I am today. I never give anything away for free. Am I clear? If I do this, I'll expect to be compensated."

"You're part of giving out a very generous scholarship every year. That's—"

"PR, son. Tyton Coal took a hit when the Dennville

mine cave-in happened. Things like this encourage people to forget. People forget, stock goes back up. I become a very rich man."

Bastard. How had anyone ever wanted this man?

I took a deep breath, forcing the rage back down my throat. "Please, sir. I'll do anything. If you'll help me, I'll do anything. I'll pay you back. I'll set up some kind of payment plan. Anything."

He considered me for so long, I began to think he wouldn't answer at all. "You'll work for me. I'm short on belowground miners. I'm always short on belowground miners. You sign a contract to work for me for the four years Tenleigh's in school and I'll have the scholarship transferred to her, the housing, everything."

A wave of fear made me dizzy and I almost stumbled back. *Belowground miner.* I couldn't do that. It was the one thing I couldn't do. The *only* thing I couldn't do. And then how would I eventually make my way to where she was? If I was here...*stuck*...again.

Tenleigh.

Tenleigh.

"I'll do it," I croaked out. "You have a deal."

His face spread into a slow smile. "Figure you at least have the blow job of your life coming for this one. If she's anything like her batshit crazy mother, it might even be worth it." He laughed as if we were friends. He laughed as if there were anything remotely funny about that.

My jaw tightened and I fisted my hands down by my sides. I shook my head. "I'm not telling her. She can't know. She'll never let me do this if she knows. She won't take it. Tenleigh, she—" I stopped talking. *She's fierce. She's loyal. She's a fighter. She smells like wildflowers and mixes mountain*

271

talk with SAT words. *And she's so unbelievably beautiful.* But I wasn't going to give this pig anything of Tenleigh. "She can't know," I finished.

"Relax. It was a joke, son."

I stood there, unsmiling, letting him know I hadn't found it funny.

"I'd prefer her not know anyway," he continued. "Or anyone for that matter. I don't want it getting out that the scholarship is transferrable, under any circumstances. So let's keep this between you and me. You keep it quiet, you sign a contract to work for me, and the scholarship goes to her. You quit, you die, the scholarship is rescinded. Are we clear, son?"

Stop calling me "son," you piece of shit. I'm the son of a man who worked himself to the bone, day in and day out, for the piddly salary you paid him. He went deep into the dark earth every day for his family, for pride, because he'd do anything to put food on the table and clothes on the backs of those he loved. That's the blood I have coursing through my veins. I am not your son. I'm Daniel Barrett's son. And I've never been more proud of that.

"We have a deal. I'll work for you. I won't tell her."

"What are you going to do? How are you going to keep it from her?" he asked with interest.

"I'm going to break both our hearts." My voice sounded dead even to my own ears.

He stood looking at me for another second as if I was some form of alien that had come down from a distant planet. Finally, he held out his hand. I walked forward and grasped it. We shook. It was done. I felt as if I'd just made a deal with the devil. And now I was going to hell.

Tenleigh stood in my doorway, moving her head from side to side. She opened her mouth once to speak, but then snapped it closed. "Can I come in?" she finally asked.

I hesitated. "Tenleigh, my house, it doesn't look so nice."

"None of our houses look nice."

"I know, but what I mean—"

"Let me in, Ky." Her voice was weak.

Shit. As I drew in a much-needed breath, I felt ashamed she would see what my place had become—or rather, what it had not. But it was time to own up to what I'd done. I moved aside and she passed in front of me. I shut the door and turned to her as she looked around. I never bought new furniture or a stove. The pipe still hung from the ceiling like a daily reminder of the life I never got to live. I never unpacked most of the boxes I'd packed almost four years ago. I still didn't even have a bed. I slept on the floor in a pile of blankets, a couple space heaters nearby to keep me alive in the winter. There were containers sitting everywhere to catch the water that leaked from the roof.

But for all that I didn't have, I had plenty of books—piled everywhere, all with little white slips of paper sticking out of them.

Tenleigh brought her hands up over her mouth as she looked around. "Why?" she started and then stopped, looking around some more. "Why are you living like this?" A tear slipped down her cheek.

"Don't cry, Tenleigh." I reached up and swiped the tear with my thumb, brushing it aside. "This is nothing to cry about. It's my choice. And it wasn't going to be forever... just until..."

"Just until what?" she whispered.

I ran my eyes over her features, her expression filled with

sadness. "Just until I could come find you. Just until I left here to find you and beg you to forgive me. Wherever you were, that's where I was going to go."

She sucked in a big breath. "Oh my God. But I came back." She started to cry. "I came back."

I moved forward and wrapped my arms around her. I felt the wetness of her tears against my bare skin. "Shh, you came back to help kids who grew up just like us. It's a good thing, Ten. It's a heroic thing."

She tipped her head back and looked up at me. "Why didn't you come find me sooner, Ky. Why?"

I shook my head and looked out the window behind her. "Because I made a deal and I couldn't break it. In order to transfer that scholarship to you, I signed a deal. If I broke the deal, you lost your scholarship. Truthfully, I don't know if Edward really would have rescinded it if I quit. But I couldn't risk it."

"What? No," she choked out. "You made a deal to work at the mine?"

I nodded. "I had to. It was the only way Edward Kearney would agree to transfer the scholarship. But it was my choice. I wanted to do it."

Her eyes flared and she pulled her shoulders back. "I wouldn't have let you if I knew." Her face was a study in intensity. Fierce Tenleigh. Always right beneath the surface. "I would never have let you go down in that mine for me if I had known. Not in a million years. *Never.*"

"I know, Ten," I said softly. "Don't you think I knew that? But I also knew if you hated me, you'd leave here and wouldn't look back. You wouldn't even have to know."

Her beautiful, expressive eyes were brimming with tears. This girl. "That's why you lied. So I wouldn't stop you. So

I wouldn't give up the scholarship to keep you from doing what you planned to do."

I released a hiss of breath. "Maybe it was wrong. I've tried to consider a million different ways I could have done something different, achieved the same result without you getting hurt, but...I did the best I could under pressure, without very much time to consider all the possibilities. I couldn't figure out a way to fight for *us*, and so that was my way of fighting for *you*. And in the end, you got out of here and earned your degree. And so I can't dwell on it anymore. I can't lie here night after night and torture myself. I made the choice I made and I just hope...I hope someday you can forgive me. I'll do anything if you'll just forgive me, Tenleigh. Anything."

"Oh, Kyland." She shook her head back and forth. She was crying outright now and my heart was beating triple time in my chest. She still hadn't told me she forgave me or that she still loved me.

But I was willing to wait. I pulled her to me again and I kissed the top of her head, smiling and repeating her name.

We stood there holding each other for a long time. I breathed in her scent and let my heart rejoice at the feel of her in my arms, willingly and completely. I never dared to dream she'd be in my arms this way again.

"Those slips of paper," she said after a few silent moments, "are those for me?"

I looked at a pile of books sitting on the coffee table. "Yes."

"Why?" she asked. "Why did you write them?"

"Because I missed you. Because I didn't have anyone else to talk to, and so I kept talking to you, even though you never answered." I tipped her chin so she was looking into my eyes. "You, Tenleigh, you are the voice in my head when I feel unsure. I still talk to you a hundred times a day. I tell you about things I think you'd like. I…" I laughed self-consciously. "Do I sound crazy?"

She laughed and sniffled. "No," she whispered. "Not at all." She nodded her head to a pile of books with notes sticking out of them. "Can I read them?"

I kissed her forehead. "Yes. Whenever you want."

She nodded, but then she studied me for a minute. "Kyland, you're making a decent salary now. Don't you think you could have at least fixed your roof?"

"Uh…" I hedged, glancing around at the pots and pans sitting on the floor everywhere. I had needed a new roof five years ago. The thing was probably about to cave-in for all I knew. "Tenleigh." I stepped back from her and rubbed my hand over the back of my neck. "The thing is, I'm kind of spending most of my paycheck on something. I hope—"

"My mama," she said, her shoulders sagging. "I knew it. You're paying for my mama's hospitalization."

"How'd you know?"

"You just told me."

I grimaced. "Hell, I'm pretty forthcoming today."

Tenleigh smiled a small, weak smile. "Why did you ask Sam to tell Marlo he was paying for it?"

"I hope Marlo's not mad at Sam. He would have paid for it if he could. He tries to offer me money whenever he can, but I won't take it. He really—"

"Marlo will get over it, trust me."

"Okay. I only asked him to take credit because I knew neither one of you would have accepted if you knew it was me. And because I figured you would have an easier time moving your mama and your sister to California if your mama was doing well. And because I knew you might come back if your mama *wasn't* doing well. And because I had the means to do it. What else was I gonna do with my money, Tenleigh?"

"Save it so you could get a college education once you quit the mine? Save it so you could start somewhere new?" She raised her hands in the air and let them fall by her sides.

"I did. I was saving. I was saving every penny I earned. Other than my used truck, I didn't spend any of it. But then your mama...I don't make enough monthly to pay for her stay there and so I had to supplement with some of what I'd saved. What little I have left, I wanted to keep in the bank so I could come to you as soon as possible, move where you were. There was no point in fixing up this house when I knew I'd be leaving soon."

"You put your own happiness aside for me, and then for my mama."

I paused, feeling uncomfortable. I had never wanted her to know any of this. "You make me sound selfless, Tenleigh. But you should know that I was plotting ways to get you back. Some of them involved bribery... I'm not above guilt trips."

She laughed and then shook her head. "You're so above guilt trips."

I put my hands in my pockets and looked down.

She was quiet for a moment. "You were so angry the first time you saw me back in town," she said sadly.

I flinched, looking up. "I know. I'm sorry. I wasn't prepared to see you back here. I was planning to come for you, to finally get out of here. And then you were back, and again, I was stuck here. And I thought you'd not only come back but you'd come back because of Jamie. I thought you'd come back here so you could be with him and that I'd have to see that, every day. I'd just lived through hell, and it seemed like a new form of it was beginning again."

"Kyland," she said sadly. "You could have left anyway. Me being back here, even *now*, doesn't mean you have to stay." Her eyes flitted away and then back to me.

"Yes, it does. If you were inside my heart, you'd know that it does."

She looked at me with a sweet, confused smile and I couldn't help wanting to pull her into my arms and beg her never to leave. "Tenleigh, when I say it was my choice to do what I did, to sacrifice getting out of here so you could, I meant that I did it happily. I mean that. I suffered, yes, but I realized I would happily suffer for you because that's what loving someone is. Willing to do anything for them, willing to make any sacrifice, suffer so they don't have to. I loved you then, and I still love you now."

"Kyland." She shook her head. "I don't know what to say. This is so much…" She walked to my couch and sunk down in it, the springs groaning. She looked up at me. "I bombed my finals," she said. "I did horribly on them so *you* would get that scholarship."

"It worked," I said, going to sit next to her. "Only we both had the same idea."

"I don't know whether to laugh or cry."

"Me neither."

She paused for a moment. "Kyland, I know I'm back, but it's by choice. I can leave if I want to, get a job somewhere else—anywhere I want. You gave me that freedom, that opportunity. You gifted me that. And now, let me gift the same to you. The school will be built in six months and I'll be making good money. I don't need to move into a house. I'll live in my trailer and I'll sacrifice for you like you did for me. I might not be able to pay for a real fancy college, and you'll have to work for your living expenses, but—"

"Ten," I said, bringing my fingers up to her lips. "If there's any chance of us working things out, if"—I ran my hand through my hair, feeling exposed and vulnerable—"if there's any chance you can start to forgive me, that we can rebuild what we had, then we can decide together what that looks like. I'll work in the mine or somewhere else maybe. If you—"

Her fingers were suddenly at my lips the same way mine had been at hers a minute earlier. "I already do forgive you. And I never stopped loving you." She shook her head. "I tried. I tried so hard, but it didn't work. I love you, Kyland. I always have."

I sucked in a breath. Gratitude, relief, love, rolling through me all at once. She forgave me. She'd never really left. My fighter. *This girl. My beautiful girl.*

I stood up so fast she squeaked. I scooped her up into my arms as she let out a short, surprised laugh.

"I'm taking you into my room now. And pitifully enough, I don't even have a bed. There's a quilt on the floor and a pile of blankets on top of that. And I feel ashamed and sick that I'm about to bring you in there, but God help me, I can't wait one second longer to get you naked."

She laughed. "Kyland, walk," she ordered. "Walk fast."

She didn't have to ask me twice.

CHAPTER TWENTY-EIGHT
Tenleigh

I was in Kyland's arms. He was taking me to his bed—his bed on the floor. And I didn't care a single whit. Although the state of his house was sad and pathetic and it made me want to cry for how he'd lived all this time, I would happily be with him anywhere. And he had done this for me. *Kyland.*

He set me down when we got into his room. It looked the same as I remembered it, except in the place where his twin bed had once been, just like he'd said, there was a quilt laid out with a folded pile of blankets on top of that.

For a moment, he simply gazed at me. I saw the love in his eyes and it filled me with wild wonder. All this time… so much sacrifice… I leaned forward and kissed him, slowly, deeply, and then we began undressing, the air filled with a delicious anticipation. Unlike earlier that day, we were going to take our time, enjoy every moment. I pulled my shirt off over my head and dropped it to the floor. Kyland's naked chest was already on display—hard muscle covered in smooth male skin—and I took a minute to let my eyes roam over it. I licked my lips, my eyes focusing on one dark brown nipple. God, he was even more beautiful than I remembered, every part of him. His body and his heart.

"Tenleigh, if you keep looking at me that way, this isn't going to last very long."

I laughed shortly. "Have you"—I cleared my throat— "been with anyone else? It's okay if you have," I rushed on. "I wouldn't blame you of course, I just...for me, yesterday was the first time since I was last with you and I want you to know that, even if—"

"Tenleigh, I haven't been with anyone else."

Oh, thank God. "You haven't?"

"No. If I was, how was I going to get you to forgive me for leading you to believe I had slept with someone else if all the time you were gone, I really *was* sleeping with other people? Because I have a perfectly functioning right hand *and* because I haven't *wanted* anyone since you."

Tenderness filled my heart first and following that, I couldn't help the image that came into my head of Kyland lying right here, his thick erection in his hand as he brought himself to orgasm. It definitely wasn't an unwelcome vision.

"I haven't wanted anyone else either," I said.

He released a long breath and I moved closer to him, my fingertips lightly moving over his skin, up to his shoulders and down his arms. He was utterly still and when I glanced up at his face, his expression was tense, almost pained.

I couldn't believe this. I couldn't believe I was here, with Kyland. He had given everything up for me. He loved me. He'd never betrayed me—he'd only ever sought to make my life better. And I still loved him. I'd always loved him. Somewhere, *somewhere* inside, the hurt had seemed so unbelievable because it didn't make sense. I knew this man.

I knew his heart, his soul. And he was only good. I sucked in the emotion that threatened to overwhelm me. Kyland brought his hand to my cheek and stroked his thumb over my cheekbone, and I leaned in to his touch. *Home.*

I needed to be as close as possible to him. I needed to touch him everywhere. I needed to convince myself this was real.

My jeans slid down my legs after I'd unbuttoned them, and I kicked them and my underwear aside. Kyland did the same and we stood before each other naked.

I glanced down at his straining erection, and like the day before, I couldn't help reaching down to caress it several times from base to tip. Kyland let out a guttural groan.

When he leaned toward me, I expected his kiss to be hard—filled with the trembling lust I was feeling—but instead it was soft…sweet and slow. He tilted his head and nibbled tenderly at my lips, finally sliding his tongue against mine in a hypnotic dance.

Our bare bodies pressed against each other, igniting me, and when I pulled back to lie down on the blankets, he came with me, taking my mouth in another slow, sliding kiss once we were both lying down.

"I've always loved the way we fit together," Kyland murmured, pressing his body closer to mine. I felt his hardness nestled between my legs and moaned longingly. "Spread your legs a little, Ten," he said against my mouth. Lust shot through my body and I did as he said, widening my legs so he could guide himself to my opening.

He eased in just a little, inch by slow inch, the expression on his face one of focused bliss. God, he was beautiful, his high cheekbones tinged with pink, his lips parted, and a slight sheen on his brow. "I love you," I said.

"I love you too. Always have. Always will." And then with one thrust, he was completely inside me.

I gasped at the intense feeling of fullness, my body relaxing around his invasion as I wrapped my legs around his hips.

For just a second, I recalled the way he'd felt the first time he'd thrust into me, tearing my flesh and filling me in a way I'd never been filled before. It had hurt so much I'd almost told him to stop, but I hadn't. And after a few minutes, the worst of the pain had begun to ease and I'd been able to focus on the awe of Kyland above me, moving inside me. I'd been so desperately in love with him.

I still was.

He brought his mouth to my nipple and flicked it with his tongue as he began to move, and I was suddenly very much back in the present. I groaned and wove my fingers into his short hair, my fingernails scratching his scalp. A groan escaped his mouth as he came up off one breast and moved to the other, still thrusting leisurely into me. "Kyland, oh God," I moaned. I brought my hands down to his shoulders. The steady drumbeat of arousal between my legs was increasing and I raised my hips to meet his thrusts.

"You feel so good, Ten."

I tried to speak, but my words dissolved on my tongue as the most intense orgasm I'd ever had detonated and sent shock waves all the way down to my toes. I leaned my head back with a whimper as I clenched and spasmed around Kyland.

His movements became jerky and uneven and then he thrust into me one final time, spilling into me as he moaned his orgasm into my neck.

We lay there for several minutes, our breathing labored, our skin dewy with exertion. Finally, Kyland brought his head up and smiled down at me. "God, I missed you so damn much. I wondered if yesterday would be the last time." His smile was so incredibly tender, but there was sadness in his eyes.

I put my hand up on his cheek and ran my thumb over his cheekbone. "We have a lot to make up for. But all the time in the world." I smiled, my heart filled with hope and joy.

Kyland pulled out of me and I winced slightly. He rolled to the side and sat up to pull a blanket over us. Then he gathered me in his arms and I rested my head on his chest.

"I'm really sorry about this bed situation."

I snuggled closer and turned my nose in, to his skin, inhaled, and then kissed his nipple. "What bed situation?" I asked, smiling against his chest.

He chuckled. "I don't know. I forgot what I was talking about."

I propped my hands on his chest, and rested my chin on them so I could look at him. "What are we gonna do, Ky?"

"I guess we'll buy a bed."

I laughed. "Not about that. About everything. About us."

His hand halted. "What do you want to do?"

"I want to figure out where we're going to live—"

He released a breath. "Oh. We'll figure all that out. Once I find the willpower to get out from under these blankets with you. Which could be three months from now."

I laughed. But I got up and sat on my knees facing him and looked at him very seriously. "I have to stay here and finish this school. I made a commitment and it's important to me. And I know you're still working to pay for my mama's care." I paused to revel in that knowledge again. It was still unbelievable. "But after that, Kyland, I can hire someone else to run the funding for the school and I can work anywhere. Like I said, I get to give that gift back to you now. And so it's your turn to go to college." I was speaking quickly, the ideas coming fast and furious into my brain. "Rather than staying here, I could come with you, wherever you want to go—anywhere. And I'll get a teaching job there and we'll get a really small, inexpensive apartment and we might have to take out a small loan, but—"

Kyland laughed, a joyful sound. I halted talking, realizing that, like that day we'd gone sledding so long ago, his expression was filled only with joy. "That's all very sweet," he said. "And we can talk about all that, but Ten, you're topless right now and I haven't had any sex for four years, so I'm finding it hard to concentrate here."

I laughed and leaned in and kissed him. He smiled against my mouth, kissing me back. I squealed when he flipped me over and gazed down at me, grinning his beautiful grin. "We have options now, beautiful girl. I have a couple more months at the mine and your mama is going to be in the hospital for a few more months too, but after that, the world is our oyster. Or at least it feels like it." Peace. I finally felt it, and I could see he did too. That smile spoke peace— peace and *hope*.

The breeze blew through the open window next to Kyland's makeshift bed, ruffling the curtains, and I smelled the unmistakable smell of lavender. I gasped and turned my head. "There's lavender out there."

"Yeah. That's why I used the computer at the Evansly library to look up how to plant it initially. The smell of it reminded me of you. It helped me remember why the suffering was worth it. It helped me focus on what I was doing and why. It helped me remember the moment at the edge of our lavender field after we'd made love, when I realized I'd do anything to get you out of here, even if it meant breaking your heart." Sadness filled his expression, but only for a moment. "I brought some inside in the winter. Christmas was the hardest time for me."

"Oh, Kyland." My breath hitched. "For me too," I whispered, squeezing my eyes shut as I recalled those desolate holidays—the ones I'd spent with our old principal's niece who had taken me in when I'd first moved to San Diego.

He shook his head. "Let's not be sad. You're here now. It was worth it. And also, that's how I found out about lavender being a good cash crop. It's helped a few people. Some good came from it."

"Yes," I whispered. I leaned up and kissed his lips softly.

He made love to me again, this time soft and slow, our initial desperation quenched. Afterward, as we lay together in the dwindling daylight, the sun slanting through his window, and as I gazed at the man I loved—finally beside me—the world seemed only full of light and hope.

CHAPTER TWENTY-NINE
Kyland

That weekend was the most joyful weekend of my life. We spent half of it on the floor of my room, the breeze blowing the scent of lavender through the open window, making love until our limbs were sore and I didn't remember where she ended and I began. My Tenleigh, the one woman who soothed my soul and excited my body at the same time. Nothing had changed in that regard.

When our backs were achy from lying down too long, we took a hike in our mountains. Once I had only seen desperation and poverty here—and there was no lack of pain and struggle in Appalachia. But now, walking hand in hand with Tenleigh, what I saw was the wild beauty of the forests just coming to life after a long winter. The wildflowers were blooming everywhere, the meadows awash in color, the streams were sparkling in the sunlight, and the air was warm and tasted of the sweetness of spring. These were the hills of my blood, the land my father and all his fathers before him had worked and loved in, toiling in the coal mines, working the soil of their land, and falling in love with women who would give them proud Kentucky sons and daughters. For the first time since I'd been a little boy, I felt fierce with the love of home, of these mountains, of the people who lived here, trying, failing, trying again, hanging on by their fingernails to their God-given pride and their enduring love of Appalachia.

There were some ornery backwoods mountain folk in these parts. And none of them would tell you any different. But they were strong, and they were brave. And mostly, they were good-hearted people who did the best they could and worried about each other. How had I forgotten about that when it was right in front of me all this time? And maybe I was one of them too. Maybe I'd helped a few along the way as well for no other reason than they were my people. My kinfolk. Part of my soul.

Tenleigh and I brought a picnic lunch and ate on the edge of the meadow where I'd first made love to her and where I'd realized I would sacrifice everything I had for her: my dreams, my heart. It was the place that had forever changed me. And now we'd come full circle.

We sat in the grass at the edge of a small stream, the water rolling and splashing by, as we made plans for the future. I'd spend the small amount of money I had put away to fix the roof on my house and buy some furniture. We'd live there until I was done working at the mine and Tenleigh's school was built and running. We'd set up a nice room for her mama and I'd go through the process of applying to colleges for the second time in my life. When the time came, and when I knew what schools I'd gotten into, we'd all decide what we wanted to do. I knew I couldn't work underground for the rest of my life. I did it now and I had gotten somewhat used to it, but it was still a challenge for me. Every day I went down into that dark mountain, but I still had to force myself to do it.

"How did it feel the first time?" Tenleigh whispered, her head on my lap, those gentle green eyes staring up at me. With the light shining down on her, I could see the blue and gold around the outer rim, her eyelashes a dark frame.

"What?" I asked, my mind calm as I appreciated the texture of my girl's skin under my fingertips, the glossiness of her hair spread out on my thighs as she gazed up at me.

"The mine," she said, as if she'd been reading my thoughts from a few moments before. "How did you do it, Ky? How did you go down there?" She reached up and cupped my cheek in her palm. I turned to it and kissed the warm skin of her hand.

I closed my eyes briefly, moving my mind from all things open and filled with happiness back to the small, dark spaces I moved through every day. "It was truly like taking a trip down to hell the first time," I said. "I put a few sprigs of lavender in my pocket and when I thought I couldn't do it, when I felt like I'd lose my mind, I took them out and smelled them. I closed my eyes and felt you with me; I pictured those lavender fields blowing in the breeze. It got me through those moments." I shrugged. "I did it because I had to. I did it because me going down there meant your freedom. And eventually, like most things, even terrible things, you learn to live with it."

Her eyes were filled with love, but also a touch of sadness. "What's it like?" she asked with a small hitch in her voice.

"It's dark. So pitch-dark, there should be a different word to describe that kind of dark. And it's hot—at first I could hardly catch my breath."

She turned slightly toward me and wrapped her arms around me in comfort. I leaned down and kissed her temple.

"And you'd think it'd be quiet, you know, so far beneath the earth, but it's not. You hear it shift and groan, like it's unhappy

289

with our invasion. Like humans have no place down there and it's reminding us that it wants to fill the spaces we've carved out. Those noises sound like some kind of warning most days."

"But you've managed it," she said, almost in disbelief.

I paused. "Yeah…mostly. I hate the dark and I hate the hot, thick air. I hate working hunched over all day. I hate feeling enclosed and at the mercy of something that's a million times more powerful than me. But…there are the guys— the other miners who go down there every day to do a job most people have no clue about. They do it with pride and with honor. They come out with blackened faces and dust in their lungs, and they do it because they have families and because their fathers before them did it. They do it because it's an honest day's work. They do it despite the fact that most people have no idea that coal is how they get their electricity."

"Each time you flip a switch, thank a coal miner." She smiled. "I'm so proud of you."

I smiled back down at her. "I do the same thing thousands of other men do too. But being down there, it's brought me a pride in my father and my brother that I didn't have before. It's given me some peace about the way they died. In some ways, it's a hell for me, but in others, it's been a gift."

"I love you," she whispered. It was in her expression. She understood me. She understood the anguish I had felt. She understood the sacrifice, and she understood the pride too. I hadn't thought it was possible to love her more, but I did.

This girl.

My girl.

"I love you too."

On Sunday, we went to breakfast at a small diner up the highway. She told me all about San Diego, about the ocean, about classes, about applying for the grants, about the coffee

290

shop she'd hung out in almost every day. I soaked her in, her enthusiasm, her beauty, her pride, her intelligence. And I was so proud she was mine.

"I worried all the time," I said, not making eye contact.

She grabbed my hand and I focused my eyes on our linked fingers. "About my safety?" she asked.

"That, a little bit, but more so I worried...I worried that you'd meet someone else. Fall in love." I raised my eyes to hers and I could feel the vulnerability that must have been in them.

But she shook her head. "It's always been you. No one else. I didn't want to admit to myself that building the school... well, as much as it's for the kids here, a way to give back to my hometown"—she looked down and then back up into my eyes—"I wanted to be close to you again. Even though I knew it'd hurt. I couldn't let go of you. I never did—all that time, I never did. Even when I thought you'd betrayed me. Or maybe somewhere inside, I knew you couldn't have."

I leaned across the table and kissed her.

We drove to a craft fair a couple of hours away, across a covered bridge, where Tenleigh took out her cell phone and snapped pictures of me, laughing when I offered up a tense, unnatural smile, finally making me laugh a genuine laugh with some ridiculous, goofy faces. She seemed pleased with the picture of me looking to the side, my teeth flashing in a grin, the bridge a quaint backdrop. She made it her screen saver. "You really want to look at that every time you turn on your phone?" I asked, even though it made me happy and I hoped she'd keep it there.

"Yup," she said. "I like to look at my handsome boyfriend, especially when he's not around."

I pulled her into me and kissed the top of her fragrant

hair. *Boyfriend*. The word didn't seem big enough to describe the extent to which I belonged to her.

I bought her homemade ice cream churned by an old woman with rosy cheeks, who wore a brightly colored calico skirt. She looked at us and smiled a warm, knowing smile as if she understood something we hadn't told her in words.

We walked hand in hand as Tenleigh looked at the arts and crafts made by local artisans, listening to their lyrical mountain speak—a language mixed with simplicity and poetry. I knew some of the local people on our mountain growing lavender had gone to one of these a few weeks before. Just seeing the many Appalachian entrepreneurs filled my heart with pride.

We sat under a giant buckeye tree and listened to a bluegrass band, the music filling the air, every note singing *home*.

I leaned in to Tenleigh and whispered in her ear, "I'm going to marry you."

She leaned her head back and gazed at me. "You better," she said. "I want babies. Lots and lots of them."

I laughed. "As many as you want. I'm going to make all your dreams come true. All my life."

Her eyes filled with tenderness. "And I'm going to make all *your* dreams come true. All my life."

I leaned in to kiss her. *You already have. You are my dream.*

When the sun was setting over the mountains, we drove back to my house, hand in hand in the cab of my truck.

We ended the day making love under my open window, the floor familiar now, the fit of our bodies bringing the joy I'd lived without for too long. I drifted off to sleep happy, content, and filled with peace.

EPILOGUE
Kyland

Six Years Later

My wife stood at the big picture window, gazing out at the golden, sunlit mountains—the view that would never cease to take my breath away. It was early, just past sunrise, but the air inside the house was already still and humid, the distant noise of the cicadas filling the trees outside. It was going to be another hot one. Tenleigh lifted her hair off the back of her neck and rolled it forward, as if she was working out the kinks.

I walked to her, wrapping my arms around her swollen middle, putting my palms against her belly where I could feel our baby moving inside. "Hey, beautiful," I said, my voice raspy with sleep. She gripped my hands at her waist as I laid my chin on her shoulder, breathing in her scent. "Baby keeping you awake?" I asked.

"Hmm," she hummed. "He's a strong little sucker." She massaged a spot on the lower side of her belly as if she'd been kicked. "I've been telling him to go to sleep since four a.m. He's as stubborn as they come."

I smiled against her skin, running my nose along it and letting my lips linger there. She shivered and pulled me closer. "He?" I asked. "Sounds like a *she*."

She turned her head, laughing softly, nuzzling her cheek against mine.

"I didn't want to wake you…or Silas."

"Silas will be asleep for a while. That kid played for hours at the creek yesterday." I had taken him fishing with me for his first lesson. *My boy.* I kissed Tenleigh's neck again. "Plumb tuckered himself out."

"Careful with that kind of talk now. That's how this baby got in here." She rubbed her belly again.

I made a soft growling sound. "Come to bed. I'm fixin' to give you a back rub."

She hummed a sound of contentment. After turning, she took my hand and I led her back to the queen-size bed in our room.

Four years ago, we had moved into this old, drafty farmhouse on the outskirts of Dennville. When we'd first walked into it, we could clearly see it was a fixer-upper, but when we'd entered the family room with the high, cedar-beamed ceilings and the huge window with the breathtaking view of our mountains beyond, we'd known it was exactly where we wanted to be. It was simple, but it was beautiful, and it was ours.

It was the place we worked tirelessly to make our own. It was the place where we began our life together. It was the place where I touched Tenleigh often and with love, never taking for granted that she was in my arms. It was the place where I brought my wife small grocery store cakes with perfect pink flowers on the edges, instead of bouquets, because I knew what brought her joy.

This was the home where I'd carried my bride over the threshold after she'd taken my name in a small but beautiful wedding ceremony on the edge of our lavender field, our closest friends and family in attendance. It was where we'd brought our now three-year-old son, Silas, home and where she'd told me she was expecting again. It was the home where Jamie visited, knowing he was welcomed with friendship and love, where Shelly dropped Joey off regularly for Friday night pizza so she and Ian could have a date night, where Marlo and Sam, along with their little boy, Elijah, and Tenleigh's mama came to dinner every week, where we all sat at the impressive hand-carved table Buster had given us as a wedding gift—the one that needed to be covered with a tablecloth when children were present.

We had talked about me going away to college, maybe even just commuting somewhere while Tenleigh worked, but in the end, I'd decided that my life, my heart, was here. And so I'd completed my civil engineering degree online at the University of Kentucky. I had worked my way up—literally—at the mine, moving to an aboveground management position shortly after Tenleigh's mama came home, and then being promoted to engineer after I earned my degree.

I hadn't been able to save my father and my brother then, but now, I was in charge of the safety of all the men who hung up a metal tag and bravely went beneath the ground day after day, risking their lives to bring power to America. No one took it more seriously than I did. And when we were in Evansly and saw those coal-filled trains roll out of town, I would grip my wife's hand tightly and stand tall.

As for Edward Kearney, he passed away from a heart

attack a short time before Tenleigh and I were married. He never reconciled with his son, and his wife had left him a few months before. I couldn't say I was too sorry to hear the news of Mr. Kearney's passing—he'd never shown himself to be anything other than a cold, self-serving man, and it helped me make my decision to stay at the mine. Edward Kearney died with every material possession money could buy, and yet, to my mind, he died with nothing at all.

Tenleigh and I had left Dennville a few times—once, to go to New York City for a two-week honeymoon, once to attend my graduation in Lexington, and once for a weekend trip to Louisville. I'd wanted to leave Kentucky once upon a time. I'd planned on never looking back, but now I felt the pull of home when we were away, the pull that told me I'd had a fun vacation, but I was ready to get back to where I belonged. I was a Kentucky boy at heart, and I always would be. Someday, our sons and daughters would know and love the wild beauty of these hills just like we did.

The hill folk, and a few others in town, were still growing lavender and had made quite a business out of it. A year after Tenleigh and I got married, they organized a large lavender festival and a Kentucky paper wrote an article about how a small, impoverished coal town with a tragic past had started growing flowers that brought hope. The national news picked it up and people came from all over to learn about Appalachian culture, purchase wares from local craftsmen, and enjoy the beauty of the area. It brought business to the town and now we looked forward to it every summer. Poverty is never a simple problem, but for a few, those flowers *had* provided hope, and for that, I was proud.

Tenleigh's mama lived in Evansly with Marlo and Sam. She worked part-time at Sam's practice and helped out with

Elijah. She was doing great and was better at recognizing the signs when she felt overwhelmed and knew when to reach out to those there to help her. She stayed with us in the summers, when Tenleigh wasn't teaching at the Dennville school, and they took long walks in the hills, finally getting to know each other as mother and daughter.

"Comfortable?" I asked as Tenleigh lay down on our bed, putting her pillow between her legs. The fan at the end of our bed made a soothing whirring sound as it blew cool air in our direction. Someday we'd save up and wire this old house for AC.

"As comfortable as I'm going to get with this big belly," she said. I could hear the smile in her voice. I moved my hands over the skin at the base of her spine. She sighed, her body relaxing.

"I love you," I said simply.

"I love you too," she whispered back.

As I massaged my wife's back, my mind wandered, my heart full. I had thought once, that I had lost myself because of love. But the opposite was true. I'd found myself when I'd given my heart to Tenleigh, found what was important to me, what really mattered. And now, running my hands over her smooth skin, there was nowhere on earth I'd rather be than here in this bed, living the life I led. The truth was, we didn't live a complicated life nor a fancy one. But we knew the simple joy of a warm night at home watching TV, the deep thankfulness of a refrigerator filled with food, the love of family and friends, and the quiet grace of white mist rising over the mountains outside our window on a cool, fall morning.

And suddenly, lying right there, I knew something. No, I didn't know it. I *felt* it—felt it in my gut and felt it coursing through my blood.

"Ten," I said, laying my hand on her belly, "you know that something?"

"What something?" she asked sleepily.

"That something I felt like I was meant to do."

She turned her head and her eyes met mine. My heart skipped a beat. "Yes," she said softly.

"I'm doing it."

Tenderness filled her expression and she brought her hand up to my cheek as I leaned in to her caress and she ran her thumb over my cheekbone. "Is it enough?" she asked on a whisper.

I leaned forward and kissed her, never in my life feeling more sure about anything. I whispered against her lips, "It's more than enough. It's so much more than I ever dreamed."

We had everything we needed. None of it was big. Most of it was simple. But what I knew in that moment was that the size of your home, your car, your wallet doesn't have one single thing to do with the size of your *life*. And my life…my life felt *big*, filled with love and with meaning.

Want more of Mia Sheridan's addictive, emotional love stories? Get lost in the romance of Wine Country in GRAYSON'S VOW

Kira

"Never fret, my love, the universe always balances the scales. Her ways may be mysterious, but they are always just."
—Isabelle Dallaire, "Gram"

In a long history of bad days, this one was at the top of the list. And it was only nine a.m. I stepped from my car and took a deep breath of the balmy, late-summer air before walking toward Napa Valley Savings Bank. The sultry morning shimmered around me, the sweet scent of jasmine teasing my nose. The peaceful beauty seemed wrong somehow—the bleakness of my mood in direct contrast to the warm, sunshiny day. An arrogant idea, I supposed. As if the weather should express itself according to my mood. I sighed as I pulled open the glass front door of the bank.

"May I help you?" a cheery brunette asked as I approached her teller window.

"Yes," I said, withdrawing my ID and an old savings book from my purse. "I want to close this account." I slid both toward the teller. A corner of the savings book was folded back, revealing numbers my gram had entered when showing me how to keep track of our deposits. The memory tore at my heart, but I forced what I hoped was a cheerful-looking smile as the girl took the book, opened it, and began entering the account number.

I thought back to the day we'd opened the account. I'd been ten. My gram had walked me here, and I'd proudly deposited the fifty dollars she'd given me for helping with yard work throughout the summer. We'd made trips to this bank over the years when I'd stayed at her house in Napa. She'd taught me the true value of money—it was meant to be shared, used to help others, but also represented a type of freedom. The fact that I currently had little money, few options, and every material possession I owned was stuffed in the trunk of my car, was proof of how right she'd been. I was anything but free.

"Two thousand, forty-seven dollars and sixteen cents," the teller stated, glancing up at me. I nodded. It was even a little more than I had hoped. Good. That was good. I needed every cent. I joined my hands together on the counter and exhaled slowly as I waited for her to count out the cash.

Once the money was safely tucked into my purse and the account closed, I wished the teller a good day and then headed toward the door. When I spotted a drinking fountain, I turned to make a brief stop. I'd only been using the air conditioning in my car sparingly so as to save on gas and had been consistently hot and thirsty.

As the cold water hit my lips, I heard faintly from the office around the corner, "Grayson Hawthorn, nice to meet you." I froze and stood slowly, using my thumb to distract-edly wipe the water off my bottom lip. Grayson Hawthorn...

Grayson Hawthorn? I knew that name, remembered the strong sound of it, the way I had repeated it to myself on a whisper to hear it on my lips that day in my father's office. I thought back to the quick glance at the file my dad had slid closed as I'd placed a tray of coffee on his desk. Could it be the *same* Grayson Hawthorn?

I took a few steps and peeked around the corner but saw nothing more than a closed office door, the shade on the window pulled down. My curiosity still piqued, I walked to the restroom on the other side of the corridor from the office Grayson Hawthorn occupied. *Snoopy much, Kira?*

Once inside the restroom, I locked the door and leaned against the wall. I hadn't even known Grayson Hawthorn lived in Napa. His trial had taken place in San Francisco, so that must have been where the crime was committed—not that I knew what that crime might have been, only that my father had taken a brief interest in it. I bit my lip, moving to the sink and staring at myself in the mirror as I washed and dried my hands.

As I was leaving the restroom, a man in a suit, most likely a bank executive, entered the office across the hall. He closed the door behind him, but it didn't click into place and stood very slightly ajar, allowing me to hear a few words of introductions. I paused, pulling the restroom door most of the way closed, and then stood there trying to listen.

Really, Kira? This is shamefully nosy. An invasion of privacy. And worse, somewhat pointless. *Seriously, what is wrong with you?* Ignoring my own reprimand, I leaned closer to the crack in the door.

I'd leave this less-than-stellar moment out of my memoirs. No one needed to know about it but me.

A few words drifted my way. "Sorry…felon…can't

give…this bank…unfortunately…" Felon? Yes then, it *had* to be the Grayson Hawthorn I thought it was. What a strange, random coincidence. I barely knew anything about him. All I really knew was his name, the fact that he'd been accused of a crime, and that my father had participated in using him as a pawn. Grayson Hawthorn and I had that in common. Not that it was likely my father remembered the name of one man, when he ruined lives so regularly and with so little afterthought. In any case, why was I eavesdropping from inside a bathroom, trying to listen in on his private conversation? I wasn't sure. However, an abundance of curiosity was one of my confirmed faults. I took a deep breath and started to exit when I heard the scraping of chair legs and paused yet again. The words from across the hall were clearer now that they had probably moved closer to the door. "I'm sorry I can't approve a loan for you, Mr. Hawthorn." The male voice that spoke sounded regretful. "If you were worth more—"

"I understand. Thank you for your time, Mr. Gellar," came another male voice. Grayson's I assumed.

I caught the brief glimpse of a tall male figure with dark hair in a heather-gray suit leaving the office and leaned back inside the restroom, clicking the door closed again. I washed my hands once more to stall, and then left the small room. I glanced at the office Grayson Hawthorn had been in as I passed and saw a man sitting behind the desk in a suit and tie, his attention focused on something he was writing.

Outside, the day had grown brighter and warmer. I let myself into my car, which I had parked up the street. I sat there for a minute, staring out the front window at the quaint downtown area: crisp, clean awnings adorned the fronts of the businesses, and large containers of brightly colored flowers decorated the sidewalk. I loved Napa, from downtown, to the riverfront, to the outlying vineyards, ripe with fruit in the summer and colorful with the vivid yellow wild-mustard flowers in the winter. It had been where my gram retired to after my grandfather passed, where I'd spent summers at her cottage-style house with the covered front porch. Everywhere I looked I saw her, heard her voice, felt her warm, vibrant spirit. My gram had been fond of saying, *Today may be a very bad day, but tomorrow may be the best day of your life. You just have to hang on until you get there.*

I drew in a deep inhale of air, doing my best to shake off the loneliness. *Oh, Gram, if only you were here. You would take me into your arms and tell me everything was going to be okay. And because it was you saying it, I would believe it to be true.*

I leaned back against the headrest and closed my eyes. "Help me, Gram," I whispered. "I'm lost. I need you. Give me a sign. Tell me what to do. Please." The tears I'd been holding at bay for so long burned behind my lids, threatening to fall.

I sighed as I opened my eyes, movement in the passenger-side mirror immediately catching my attention. As I turned my head, I spotted a tall, well-built man in that same heather-gray suit I'd seen inside the bank...Grayson Hawthorn. My breath faltered. He was standing against the building next to my car, to the right of my bumper, the *perfect* location for me to see him clearly in my mirror without moving. I slunk down in my seat just a bit, leaned back, and turned my head to watch him.

He had his head leaned back against the building behind him, and his eyes were closed, his expression pained. And my God, he was...breathtaking. He had the beautifully carved features of a knight in shining armor, with almost-black hair a tad too long, making it curl over his collar. It was his lips that were truly devastating, though—full and sensual in a way that made my eyes want to wander to them again and again. I squinted, trying to take in every detail of his face before my gaze traveled down his tall form. His body matched his beautifully dark masculinity—muscular and graceful, his shoulders broad and his waist narrow.

Oh, Kira. You hardly have time to be ogling beautiful felons on the sidewalk. Your concerns are slightly more pressing. You're homeless and well, frankly, desperate. If you want to focus on something, focus on that. Okay, except…I was unable to drag my eyes away. What had his crime been anyway? I tried to look away, but something about him pulled at me. And it wasn't just his striking good looks that made my eyes linger on him. Something about the expression on his face felt *familiar*, speaking to what *I* was feeling right that very minute.

If you were worth more…

"Are you desperate, too, Grayson Hawthorn?" I murmured. *Why?*

As I watched him, he brought his head straight and massaged his temple, looking around. A woman walked by and turned as she passed him, her head moving up and down to take in his body. He didn't seem to notice her, and fortunately for her, she turned, looking ahead just in time to narrowly miss colliding with a light pole. I breathed out a laugh. Grayson stood staring off into the distance again. As I watched him, an obviously homeless man moved toward where he stood, holding his hat out to people walking by. They all moved quickly past him, looking away uncomfortably. When the man began to approach Grayson, I pressed my lips together. *Sorry, old man. It seems to me the person you're about to approach is in pretty dire straits himself.* But to my surprise, when the man approached Grayson tentatively, Grayson reached into his pocket, hesitated only briefly, and then grabbed the bills inside. I couldn't be sure from where I sat, but when the dark interior of his wallet flashed my way, it looked like he'd emptied it for the old man. He nodded his head once at the man in rags, who was thanking him profusely, and then stood for a moment watching the homeless man walk away. Then Grayson strode in the other direction, turning the corner out of sight.

Watch what people do when they think no one's watching, love. That's how you'll know who they really are.

Gram's words floated through my mind as if she had spoken from somewhere just outside my car. The shrill ringing of my phone startled me, and I let out a small gasp, grabbing my purse from the passenger seat to rifle inside for my phone.

Kimberly.

"Hey," I whispered.

A beat of silence. "Kira? Why are you whispering?" She was whispering, too.

I cleared my throat and leaned back. "Sorry, the phone just startled me. I'm sitting in my car in Napa."

"Were you able to close the account?"

"Yeah. It had a couple thousand dollars in it."

"Hey, well that's great. That's something at least, right?"

I sighed. "Yeah. It'll help me get by for a little bit."

I heard Kimberly's boys laughing in the background, and she shushed them, holding her hand over the phone and speaking to them in Spanish, before coming back to me and saying, "My couch is always yours if you want it."

"I know. Thank you, Kimmy." I couldn't do that to my best friend, though. She and her husband, Andy, were squeezed into a tiny apartment in San Francisco with her four-year-old sons. Kimberly had gotten pregnant when she was eighteen and then learned the shocking news she was carrying twins. She and Andy had beaten the odds so far, but they hadn't had an easy time of it. The last thing they needed was their down-and-out friend sleeping on their couch and putting a strain on their family. *Down and out? Homeless. You're homeless.*

I took a deep breath. "I'm going to come up with a plan, though," I said, a feeling of determination replacing the hopelessness I'd felt all morning. Grayson Hawthorn's face flashed quickly in my mind's eye. "Kimmy, do you ever feel like…a path is laid out in front of you? Like, clear as day?"

Kimberly paused for a beat. "Oh no. No. I know that tone in your voice. It means you're scheming something I'm going to try—probably unsuccessfully—to talk you out of. You're not considering that plan to advertise for a husband online are you, because—"

"No." I cleared my throat. "Not exactly, anyway."

Kimberly groaned. "You've gotten another one of your spur-of-the-moment, Very Bad Ideas, haven't you? Something completely ludicrous and most likely dangerous."

I smiled despite myself. "Oh stop. Those ideas you always call 'Very Bad,' are rarely ludicrous and seldom dangerous."

"The time you were going to market your own all-natural face mask from the herbs in your garden?"

I smiled, knowing her game. "Oh that? My formula was almost there. Right within reach, actually. If my test subject hadn't been—"

"You turned my face green. It didn't go away for a week. *Picture-day* week."

I laughed softly. "Okay, so fine, that one didn't work out very well, but we were ten."

"Sneaking out to Carter Scott's party when we were sixteen—"

"Totally would have worked if—"

"The fire department had to come get me off your roof."

"You always were such a wuss," I said, grinning.

"The time you were home from college on summer break and hosted that Japanese-themed dinner party where we all had to wear kimonos, and then you almost killed everyone there."

"An ingredient error. How was I to know you needed to be licensed to cook that particular fish? Anyway, that was forever ago."

"That was two years ago." She tried to deadpan, but I could hear the smile in her voice.

I was laughing now. "Okay, you've made your point, smartass. And despite all that, you love me anyway."

"I do." She sighed. "I can't help it. You're completely lovable."

"Well, that's debatable, I guess."

"No," she said firmly, "it's not. Your father's an ass, but you already know how I feel on that subject. And honey, you need to talk about what happened. It's been a year. I know you just got back, but you need—"

"Not yet," I said softly, shaking my head even though she couldn't see the movement from the other end of the phone. "And thank you for making me laugh for a minute there. But seriously, Kim, I'm in a very bad predicament right now. Maybe a Very Bad Idea is what I need." I couldn't help the small hitch in my voice at the end of my sentence. Kimberly never failed to lift my spirits, but truly, I was scared.

"I know, Kira," Kimberly said, understanding in her voice. "And unfortunately, if you're determined not to use any of your father's business contacts, you might have to get a waitressing job until you figure out what you're going to do."

I sighed. "Maybe, but would you really want me anywhere near food preparation?"

"You do make a valid point." I heard another smile in her voice. "Whatever you decide, it'll always be the Kira and Kimmy Kats, okay? Forever. We're a team," she said, referring to the band name I'd come up with when we were twelve, and I'd devised the plan to sing on the street corner for cash. I'd seen a commercial on TV about kids who didn't have enough to eat in Somalia, and my dad wouldn't give me the money to sponsor one of them. In the end, we'd been caught sneaking out of the house in the very inappropriate "costumes" I'd made from construction paper and tape. My dad grounded me for a month. Kimberly's mom, who worked as the live-in head of our housekeeping staff, gave me the twenty-two dollars I'd needed to help feed and educate Khotso that month, and then every month I couldn't come up with the money on my own after that.

"Always," I said. "I love you, Kimmy Kat."

"I love you, Kira Kat. And I gotta go, these boys are getting out of control." I heard Levi and Micah's squeals of laughter and loud shouts ringing in the background over the sound of small running feet. "Stop running, boys! And stop *yelling!*" Kimberly yelled, holding the phone away from her mouth for a second. "You gonna be okay tonight?"

"Yeah, I'm fine. I think I might even splurge and rent a cheap hotel room here in Napa and then walk along the riverfront. It makes me feel close to Gram." I didn't mention that earlier that morning, I'd hurriedly packed my stuff and climbed down the fire escape of the apartment my dad had paid for, as he'd yelled and banged on the front door. And that now, said *stuff* was jammed into my car's trunk. Kimberly would just worry, and for now, I had some cash and a partial, but arguably Very Bad Idea, roaming around in my head.

And in my illustrious history of Very Bad Ideas, this one might just take the cake.

Of course, I'd be thorough in my research before making a final decision. And I'd make a list of pros and cons—it always helped me see things in a clearer light. This one required some due diligence.

Kimberly sighed. "God rest her soul. Your gram was an amazing lady."

"Yes, she was," I agreed. "Kiss the boys for me. I'll call you tomorrow."

"Okay. Talk to you then. And Kira, I'm so glad you're back. I've missed you so much."

"I've missed you, too. Bye, Kimberly."

I hung up and sat in my car a few minutes longer. Then I picked my phone back up to do a little Internet sleuthing and to find a hotel room I could afford.

Acknowledgments

Special thanks to my storyline editors: Angela Smith and Larissa Kahle, for the hours and hours of time you put into this book. You both are like sisters to me, and your guidance is invaluable. Thank you for loving me and loving my characters, and for wanting to make us all look our very best.

Thank you to my developmental and line editor, Marion Archer. Not only do you make my work better—so much better—but it is such a joy to work with you. (And I hate that you didn't edit *this* page because I know, left to my own devices, it is surely riddled with grammatical errors.)

Thank you to Karen Lawson, who polished my book even further. Your down-to-the-wire editing was so appreciated and helped make *Kyland* that much better.

Gratitude to my beta readers who put up with my tight timeline on this book and read as I wrote: Cat Bracht, Natasha Gentile, and Elena Eckmeyer (who selflessly read through my manuscript twice). To Karin Hoffpauir Klein, my friend and mental health expert, and Nikki Larazo, my forever cheerleader. And once again to my author beta reader, A.L. Jackson—your willingness to read my story when it was still eighty thousand rambling, non-spell-checked words is so very, very appreciated.

Thank you, once again, to Elle Chardou for her quick formatting. I can't thank you enough.

To Bloom for helping me update and spruce *Kyland* up. It's been an honor to work with you.

Huge thanks to my agent, Kimberly Brower. I'm so lucky to have you in my corner; you make everything fun with your enthusiasm and love for your job. I can never get too many calls where the first words out of your mouth are, "Are you sitting down?"

And to all the readers and all the blogs who review, recommend, and support my books: unending love and thanks.

My husband…I can't begin to express my love and gratitude for all the work you put into *Kyland*. We were a true team on this one, and your love for this story filled my heart to overflowing. If I know anything of love stories, it's because of you.

About the Author

Mia Sheridan is a *New York Times*, *USA Today*, and *Wall Street Journal* bestselling author. Her passion is weaving true love stories about people destined to be together. Mia lives in Cincinnati, Ohio, with her husband. They have four children here on earth and one in heaven.

Mia can be found online at MiaSheridan.com, @MSheridanAuthor on Twitter, @MiaSheridanAuthor on Instagram, and at facebook.com/MiaSheridanAuthor